ASTRAPHOBIA

Table of Contents

CHAPTER ONE

A frail young man in his early twenties sat under a Ramada in the park overlooking the Golden Gate Bridge. It was a stormy day, and according to the last weather report he heard in his new ford, it was going to get worse overnight. He was feeling overwhelmed with anxiety about everything in his life. Yesterday he had gone back to his comfortable apartment and checked his mail. There was the usual junk in his mail box, setting in the middle of the cluster of other mail boxes, for the apartment building: there was also a letter from the draft board in San Francisco. He kept the notice, and threw the envelope along with other junk mail in the trash can in his small kitchen.

His slender frame was bent over a concrete table under the pitched concrete roof of the Ramada, shaking with fear and apprehension. The thunder storms made his perverse soul start to take him over; while the rain increased, his physical sickness from thinking about his unwanted induction into the army made him retch until his body was torn in spasms.

As the afternoon moved into the gray shadowed curtain of evening, he let his perverse persona take over. There was no stopping it. He fought against it, until his body and mind could not compete with it anymore. The frail young man stood up slowly, watching the cool sheets of rain move over the bridge below. He walked in the rain to his car. By the time he opened the driver's side door he was drenched. With the car started, and lights on, he switched the windshield wipers to full speed. Even with the wipers whipping across the windshield; they couldn't keep up with the torrential amounts of rain falling. He turned his car lights to bright and drove out of the park. The frail young man drove through the streets going over his plan, one last time. He had what he needed to complete his task laying on the front seat next to him; a sharp double-edged kitchen knife, a pair of gloves, and a bump key.

The way to the mansion took him down Chain of Lakes Drive to Lincoln Way and headed for Ashbury Heights. The perverse persona grew in strength and anticipation as it neared Lincoln Way and turned onto Fredrick street. The frail young man could feel the strength exploding in him. It felt like a gigantic storm wave pounding against Pacific Ocean barrier cliffs.

The old mansion sat with Buena Vista park behind it. It was getting dark early with the heavy overcast and the flooding rain. He drove around the mansion, and parked on a vacant hill behind the mansion on Buena Vista Avenue. He watched for any activity around the mansion, and used the time by putting on the rubber gloves. He picked up the double-edged kitchen knife in his left hand. It excited him even more as he thought about what he was going to do with the kitchen knife. He planned on changing into the clothes in the back seat, after he completed his task.

A brilliant flash of lightning and a booming clap of thunder drove his demented soul from the car. He had intended to wait for some movement at the mansion, or some light to indicate where his quarry was located. He darted from tree to tree and reached the gate to the backyard, as another lightning bolt struck the television tower at the top of the highest hill behind the mansion. A clap of thunder raised the hair on the back of his neck, and made him even more determined to accomplish his goal.

The hasp with the lock on the gate was an old one. The bump key was of no use on the old lock, he quickly used the kitchen knife as a lever to break the hasp. The old, rusted lock fell to the ground at the base of the weathered wood gate. He crossed the backyard in a rush. He was deathly afraid he would be struck by the next bolt of lightning. A light was showing at the back of the house where his prey's quarters were.

The devil in him went up to the back patio where the main back door was located. He tried the door handle, it was locked. He didn't want to stay in the rain and get struck by lightning. He was getting more frustrated until he saw a second door for use of the maid.

He moved swiftly to that door, and tried the door handle. It was unlocked. He turned the door knob carefully until he heard the bolt pull back into the sill of the door. He opened the door quietly, peering around the edge. The hall was dark, except for a dim light midway down the hall.

He looked forward to the relief from his torment, and the terror caused by lightning and thunder. He slipped into the shadowed hallway, walking silently to the closed door of the maid's quarters. He tried the knob, it turned easily. The door swung open quietly, and allowed him to see the entire living area in one quick glance. The adjoining rooms were empty. Music was playing in the bathroom. He walked toward the bathroom door. The demon in him could hear water running, either into the bath or from the shower head.

His prey was sitting in the tub as it filled with warm water. The shower curtain was drawn half-way closed. His torment increased as he walked to the shower curtain at the end of the tub. He was now filled with anger and hate. His frail demeanor was now one of blind rage. He drew in a deep breath. There was a smile on his face; as he grabbed the woman's hair jerking her head back to expose her neck. It was the face of a young woman, not much older than he.

His rage had to be satisfied! Relief from the anguish and torment he was suffering had to come to an end, no matter who had to be sacrificed. He cut her throat with a savage thrust of the knife. It cut deeply enough that the only thing holding her head on her shoulders was her cervical spine. The young woman's head lulled to the back, forced that direction by erupting red blood coming from both the right and the left carotid arteries. He stood back trying to stay out of the way, and watched as the young woman's body bled out. There was a look of utter fear and surprise in the eyes of the body, while it died.

The enraged young man felt a total relief of fear and anxiety from the lightning and thunder outside. His anguished soul thought back to the times he had killed to get escape from the terror of the awful storms. They were all animals of one kind or another. He had discovered; when some blood from a neighbor's cat got on his hand, that enjoying some of the victim's blood made his relief that much more euphoric in its nature. His twisted soul reached into the slowing flow of blood from the maid's arteries, and cupped a handful of her blood in his hand. He sipped it at first, not sure what it would taste like. It was more salty than other animals he had killed; and had the taste of a metal, maybe copper, in the background. He decided that it was rather pleasing to him, and what a bang he got from it. He felt like he could walk through a storm, and never bat an eye.

He was overwhelmed in his success. He reached down into the tub and pulled up the bodies left hand; with his sharp double-edged kitchen knife he cut the first joint of its left index finger off, taking it with him as he hurried out of the house and back up to his car. He didn't notice the severe thunder storm raging around him. He changed his blood covered clothes in the torrential rain, dropped his gloves and the kitchen knife in a plastic bag with the now bloody, wet clothes.

CHAPTER TWO

Kat McNally locked the front door to the Taekwondo studio where she worked as an instructor, and walked across the parking lot to an all-night gas station for a cup of coffee. There was a car at one of the pumps with the hose pumping gas but no one attending it.

A bell rang when she opened the door to the convenience store, and again, when it closed on its own. The inside of the store was lighted by florescent bulbs; the long thin type, that cast a strange yellow light over the inside of the store.

A clerk was standing at the counter taking cash for the gasoline that was being pumped into the car out front. Kat went down a short isle between the candy shelf and the food shelf, as she had done many times before, to the coffee maker. She heard the doorbell ring, as she filled her coffee cup. She looked out the store window thinking she would see the man that had been paying for his gas, walking to his car to put the pump hose back where it belonged and leave the station.

She noticed a car backed into a parking space at the front of the store with the driver's side door open, and its car lights shining on the pumps in front of the store. The driver of the car left it running with the door open. Leaving the door open, and the engine running was asking to have it stolen, she thought, as she placed a plastic lid on her coffee cup.

Kat walked down the candy isle toward the checkout area when she heard a male voice yell, "THIS IS A STICKUP. PUT YOUR FUCKING HANDS IN THE AIR AND DON'T MOVE!"

She stood still for moment; and looked quickly toward the front door, and the car that had been left running. There was a tall skinny man standing at the car door with a pistol of some sort in his hand.

"I want the money from the cash register. Now! You by the counter, give me your wallet and the cash in your pockets. Do it now!"

Kat left her coffee on a shelf at the corner of the candy isle, and quickly went back to the coffee area. She peered around the edge of the candy isle. There was a man standing in front of the cash register with a gun in his hand. The gun moved back and forth between the clerk, and the bystander finishing paying for his gas.

The clerk was taking the cash from the register drawer, and having a hard time of it: his hands were shaking badly. The customer at the counter was taking his wallet from his pants pocket with one hand in the air. Kat touched the pistol under her blouse at the small of her back, but decided against using it. There were too many people in a small space. An innocent was bound to get shot if a gun fight started.

The clerk wasn't getting the money from the cash drawer fast enough to please the stickup man.

"Put the fucking drawer on the counter!" The stickup man told him.

The clerk did as he was told. The customer had placed his wallet on the counter, and was digging into his pocket for the money clip he kept there. The robber had his full attention drawn to the drawer that was on the counter. Kat ran the short distance to the stickup man, and turned on her left foot at full speed. Her right foot came up with all the force of a quick whirling turn, and kicked the gun that was in the robber's right hand across the store to the restroom hallway. She followed the kick with a closed hand punch to the robber's throat. He fell against the counter, and then to the floor with his hands on his neck, choking and coughing from the blow. She pulled her short-barrel Smith and Wesson .357 magnum from the small of her back, and pointed it at the robber, while he was gasping for breath.

She grabbed a can of motor oil from a shelf to her left. She threw the can at the door guard, and followed right behind it. The stickup man at the door tried to dodge the oil can, forgetting all about the gun in his hand. Kat kicked him in the crotch as hard as she could. He started to bend over in pain, but her sledge hammer like knee blasted into the robber's chin as he doubled over. His gun went flying. He hit the cement floor of the gas station in a heap.

A bullet crashed through the glass door above her head. "CALL THE POLICE," she yelled at the clerk. "STAND AWAY FROM ME," she told the customer. "I don't want you to get hurt waiting for the police to arrive."

She left the holdup man's gun where it had fallen underneath the edge of the potato chips isle. She threw herself through the shattered door like a bull coming out of a china shop. A bullet hit the door at her side, glancing off in a high-pitched whine.

Kat put three shots into the car as it started to move away from the building. Two in the door, and one through the open window. The shots were so close together, they sounded like only one. The car engine started to roared. The car swerved toward one of the gasoline pumps and hit it head on. There was a loud crashing sound. The engine kept roaring with the accelerator apparently jammed to the floor of the car. The rear tires stopped turning and engine stopped running.

KOORUMPH! The explosion knocked Kat off her feet. A huge red, yellow and black burst of flame and smoke shot into the sky. Kat picked herself up, and ran into the store shouting for the clerk to turn on the emergency shut off switch to the gasoline pumps.

Both of the stickup men in the store were still down and out! The gasoline fire was still going when Kat looked back at the pump area. She wasn't concerned about the guy in the car. He would be a crispy critter!

It was only a minute or so until Kat heard the police siren coming down the street; and saw the police car screech to a stop in front of the car with the door open, with its lights on, and the engine running. An officer came running through the door, and saw Kat standing in front of the counter with her gun pointing down at the floor, where the stickup man she had hit in the throat was still having trouble breathing.

The young officer drew his pistol and said, "drop your gun, turn away from me, and hold your hands in the air!"

Kat placed her gun on the counter and faced the clerk. He was white as a sheet.

A second officer came into the store, and asked the clerk to tell them what had happened. The first officer kept his service revolver pointed in Kat's direction. When the clerk had finished telling his story the second officer turned on Kat, and asked her if she had permit to carry the gun. She told him she did.

"Let me see it and your identification."

Kat handed the officer three laminated cards that she had in a small leather credential wallet from her back pocket.

"What's your name?" The officer asked after he had looked at all three cards.

"My name is Kathleen NMI McNally, officer."

"What does NMI mean?"

"No middle name."

The officer looked at the second card carefully and asked if she was a P.I.

"Yes, I'm a P.I." she answered testily. Men always asked that question, because she was a woman, a woman that was five feet six inches tall and one hundred-twenty-five pounds. On top of that she was always told she was, "cute."

"Okay, who else was involved in the attempted stickup, and the take down of the three perps?" The second officer, that seem to be in charge asked the clerk.

"The young woman kicked and punched the man at the counter, and without firing a shot, took out the second guy at the door. I was so surprised from the first stickup man going down that I didn't notice how she took the second man down. I do know that she is one tough woman. She didn't pull her gun until she was shot at by the getaway driver," the clerk told him.

A fire trunk with its siren's blaring, with an ambulance right behind it, came to a screeching halt near the burning car and gas pump. The fire truck started pumping foam on the fire. The ambulance pulled closer to the store.

The young police officer said to the clerk, "yah tryin' to tell us that this little girl took out three stickup men; all of the them armed to the teeth? There ain't no way that happened. Did someone leave the scene of the crime? You ain't tellin' us the truth dumb ass! Now tell us how it really went down, and where the other men are that stopped the stickup!"

"The clerk is telling you the truth. I was the only one involved in stopping the robbery. If you don't like it, tough shit. Stick it in your ass and smoke it," she told the rooky cop.

The rooky started toward Kat, but was stopped by his partner. He asked Kat, "do you have any special training that would make us believe that you're the only one that stopped this robbery?"

"I am a veteran of the United States Army. I served in the military police and then in CID. I am a sixth-degree black belt in Taekwondo, and teach it at the shop in the strip center behind the gas station. I fired expert in the army with pistol and rifle. Is that enough for your fucking cave man partner?"

"That's enough for me. What the cave man believes doesn't matter to me," the senior officer told her.

He then asked, "Yah say your name is McNally. Yah any kin to Shay McNally?"

"He's my father," she answered.

The officer smiled and told her, "tell him hello for me, my name's Chuck Thompson. He broke me in when I was a rookie."

"You'll be needed when these two go to trial, along with the two men. You'll be notified when the court date is confirmed."

"I can write the robbery notes from what you've told me," he said to the clerk, and the customer that was buying gas. "Please write your contact information down, and give it to the other officer. You men should be thankful that the young woman happened to be in the store, and put the stickup men down."

The police car left the gas station in no particular hurry with only the senior cop in it. The firemen were still working on the smoking gasoline fire, the ambulance had the two injured stickup men on stretchers in the back with the fucking cave man guarding them.

Kat left the store with a free cup of coffee, and the promise of a gas fill up the next time she needed it. She was glad she was able to stop the robbery at the gas station. She always carried with her a sense of inadequacy about being qualified for her chosen profession. She figured it came from being an only child. Her mother had left her father for another woman. Every sense that happened; when she was only a young girl, she had been trying to make up for her mother leaving them, and for that matter, for being a girl, and not the boy that she thought her father wanted or needed.

The traffic was light, and she made her trip to her apartment in good time. It was a small apartment, but cozy. She picked up her daily newspaper at her front door and flicked on the lights in the living room, tiny dining area, and the kitchenette. She looked across the room to her apartment sized desk where the message recorder was located. She always looked at the recorder first. It wasn't blinking.

Her desk was covered with books from two classes she was taking on Tuesday and Thursday nights at U.C. Berkeley. Both were requirements for her psych major. The Korean War G.I. bill was paying her way. The apartment was tidy, but in a lived-in way.

She called her dad in the morning, and told him she had run into a sergeant Chuck Thompson. He asked her how she had met Thompson. She passed over the convenience store holdup. She knew he would fill in the blank spaces. He asked her whether she had any new cases to work.

She told him, "the message light hasn't blinked since I received the call about finding a man's lost dog."

"That was only a week ago, and if I remember right a patrol office referred that to you. The new yellow pages book came out last week. You should see an uptick in cases from that shortly."

When they hung up, Kat changed into more comfortable clothes, and sat down to read that day's San Francisco paper. Its headline was about a gruesome murder that took place near the Haight-Asbury area in the old part of the city, overlooking Golden State Park. The piece didn't have any specifics, just innuendo and hearsay from this neighbor or that police officer who asked to remain anonymous. Generally, that meant to McNally there was no police officer, probably a secretary at one of the local police offices. The bold black ink headline did mention a mansion as the site of the apparent nightmarish crime, but gave no further information about the location of it.

Kat McNally still had some contacts in the murder squad through her dad. She dialed the number that she knew by heart.

The phone rang twice; a female voice answered with a hurried tone to her voice, and asked who was calling.

"It's Kat, Chris!"

The voice softened a bit, and sounded less bothered by the call. "Kat, I know you aren't calling about having lunch today. What can I do for you?" Chris asked.

"Anything you can tell me about the mansion murder that is on the front page of the paper today?"

"The body was just found last night, by the handyman-gardener, at the mansion. He had noticed the maid's quarters door was slightly ajar after the thunder and lightning storm from that night, and decided he should check on the maid to make sure she wanted it slightly open for some reason. He's the one that called it in. I don't know how the paper got wind of it so fast! The murder squad is keeping everything mum for now," she told Kat.

"Let me know if anything pops." Kat said, and then she told Chris she knew how busy she was, and that they would have lunch sometime soon. They hung up.

Kat sat back in her chair at the tiny desk, and thought about the murder squad, and what they might be doing in the early stages of the murder investigation. She remembered her time in the CID, commonly called the Criminal Investigation Command, while she was in the Women's Army Corps. She sat in her chair wondering what the murder squad was discovering at the murder scene, and then remembered her last investigation had been finding a man's lost dog.

It helped pay the bills, and it did make her day when she brought his dog back to him.

There was a call that came in while she sat at her desk. She let it go to the recorder. The message light started blinking at her from the corner of her desk where the phone was located. She hit the play button: she had a hate-love relationship with the message recorder. It was someone wanting to sell her life insurance. She erased it!

CHAPTER THREE

T he frail young man drove his car to a long-term storage facility in Modesto and locked it up. He parked it in a dark corner on the third floor. He used the parking garage last summer when he took his trip to Spain.

There was a bus terminal not far from the storage building, and he bought a ticket to Oakland, California where the Army induction center was located. The bus was late arriving at the terminal in Modesto. He took the time to re-read the draft notice, and make sure he knew the address for the Induction center. The bus finally came an hour late. It was twelve fifteen a.m. when the bus left the Modesto terminal for Oakland. The bus ride took an hour and a half to get to Oakland.

From the bus terminal in downtown Oakland, he walked to Clay street and turned right. It was after two o'clock in the morning when he reached the induction center. To his surprise, there was a long line of young men standing on the low steps of the building. The line went down the block and around the corner. Some of the young men were standing near or leaning on the exterior walls of the building, and still others were asleep on the cement walk that ran next to the street. He walked past the entrance and around the corner, to find the end of the line and took his place. It was going to be a long wait: he didn't care. He had relieved his anguish and torment, and the thunder storm had moved east, away from the coast of California.

The line began to move around the corner of the building at precisely seven a.m. A man with stripes on his sleeves and dressed in fatigues, moved from one young man to the next, checking their induction notices. The not quite six feet tall; frail, almost skinny, young man watched as the soldier with the stripes pulled several men out of line and sent them walking down the street. When the soldier came to him, he gave his notice to him. After the soldier checked his notice, he was told to move forward and fill in the line. He asked the soldier why the men in front were told to leave the line. The soldier shook his head and said, "the damn civilians came to the wrong induction center. It happens all the time. They have their heads up their asses so far they can't see daylight."

The frail young man, soon to be a soldier, followed along in the line until he was allowed to enter the building. His heart was racing, and he had a hard knot in his stomach. On one side were stations for drawing blood. There were six stations that were busy all the time. When he had his blood drawn he hoped no one saw his hands shaking. Another soldier with stripes on his uniform told him to

23

stand in another line, and wait at two large doors that swung in and out. They reminded him of the doors into the gym at his high school. He wanted to run out of the building and never stop, but there were so many soldiers, and other young men getting examined he was afraid to try it.

His group of twenty young men were told to go through the swinging doors; a soldier on the other side pointed one young man to the far side of what would pass as a gymnasium, and the next young man was pointed to the near side, there ended up being two lines of ten young men facing each other across the gym.

A soldier with strips, both up and down, on his sleeves, and a swagger stick in one hand told them, "take off your clothes, and stand next to them. The doctor; he pointed with the swagger stick at a young doctor with a stethoscope around his neck, will examine you carefully. You must do everything he or I ask you to do. We are very busy, and have no time for bashfulness. Do you understand me?"

The two lines of men were silent.

"When I ask a question, you will answer in a loud voice, yes sergeant. Now let's try that again."

The sergeant said in a loud voice, "UNDERSTOOD?"

"YES, SERGEANT!"

The doctor walked passed the far line of men, shining a light into their mouths, and then listening to their hearts. He came down the line that he was in, and stopped in front of him. He flashed the light in his mouth, and then listened and then listened again, to his heart. He stepped back and looked him over.

He knew his heart was racing, and then hope sprang into his thoughts. Maybe the doctor was going to send him home because his heart was bad. The doctor turned from him without saying a word to him, and checked the last two men in his line.

The sergeant shouted out; "the doc will be checking you next for hernias."

His doctor had done that check before, but this doctor was different. He waited without looking around, afraid someone would say something about him looking at the other men. The sergeant stood to his side, and told him to turn his head and cough. He felt the cold end of the swagger stick push his short arm to one side and a finger stabbed into his scrotum.

"Cough!"

He coughed!

He felt a finger jab hard again and he coughed. He was told to milk his penis several times. He had never been asked to do that before.

He figured they were looking for gonorrhea or syphilis. The two men moved to the next in line.

This went on until both lines were completed, then the far line was told to tune around,
 and pull their butt cheeks apart. The doctor followed the sergeant down the line. He shined a light on each man's anis, and then the sergeant slapped the man on his butt with his swagger stick to let him know he was finished.

When the other men were dismissed to dress, the sergeant told him to take a seat on a bench, and wait for the doctor to check him again. Another twenty young men were ushered in, and the same checks were done on them. When they were leaving the gym, the doctor came over to check his heart rate again. He turned to the sergeant and said, "his heart rate is down now. You can send him on to boot camp with the others. He was just scared shitless."

CHAPTER FOUR

K at McNally had finished her morning run on the trail overlooking Treasure island, and on a clear day, Alcatraz Island. She drove back to her apartment, with the window down to cool off. She took a shower and dressed for the day. She was in no rush. Her phone hadn't rung for days; and when it did, it was a wrong number, or someone wanting her to find his lost dog.

She dressed in her usual pair of 501, button up fly, Levi jeans, and just for a change, she put on a bright flowered short sleeve blouse, thinking it might brighten someone's day. She wore a pair of Lucchese western boots, and her San Francisco Giants ball cap, with her hair in a pony tail.

She walked from her bedroom into the front room thinking about making some coffee. Like she always did, she looked toward her desk, and saw the red light on her answering machine blinking red, like a warning light on a train hurtling at high speed down the rails toward a busy traffic crossing. She opened the shades on her living room window, and settled down behind her desk. Her pistol was poking her in the back. She reached to her back, and adjusted it to make sitting in the desk chair more comfortable.

Kat reached across her desk, and started to hit the delete button on the recorder, but stopped short, with her hand hovering over the button. She fought with herself for a moment about being such a pessimistic schmuck. Even if it was a call from someone wanting to find their lost car keys it would be something for her to do; someone helped, no matter how little, it would help her pay the bills. Kat had learned from her contact with every sort of unlawful people while she was in the army, to not have any faith in people. She didn't trust them as far as she could throw them. She didn't think about the good in people; that way she was never disappointed in them when they tried to turn on her. She had not a bit of kindness in her. Kat slipped up from time to time, and did some little kindness for someone. Then when it was thrown back in her face she became even more bitter.

She punched the button next to the blinking red light, and waited for the message to start.

It was a woman's voice.

"PLEASE CALL ME BACK, IT'S IMPORTANT! I NEED YOUR HELP FINDING A MURDERER!" The disconcerted voice left her call back number in a rush.

McNally had to play the call back number a few times to get the phone number down right. Her hands were shaking slightly with excitement. Maybe this was her break. She recognized the area code, it was the same as the area code she had. She called the phone number back.

A woman's voice answered. "Yes?"

"My name is Kat McNally. I'm returning your call."

"Yes. I need your help. The police haven't been able to move forward with their investigation for some reason. I want this finished, so I can get back to my life!"

"What's your name?"

"I'll tell you all those things when we talk. You can come to my home. I won't be seen coming to your office. There are always people that follow me."

"You must tell me why you are calling me, or I will have to assume this is a prank call," McNally told the woman.

There was a noticeable sigh. "It's concerning the murder that happened at the mansion in San Francisco a few weeks ago. It was in all the papers."

"When do you want me to make contact with you?"

"Today! I'm tired of the police fooling around!" The woman said in a shrill, irritating voice.

"I'm available at one o'clock today. Give me your address, and your name," Kat McNally told the voice on the phone.

The woman gave her an address in the Haight-Ashbury area of San Francisco, but refused to give Kat her name.

Kat hung her phone up, and sat back in her chair. She wondered what she might be getting into. The woman sounded straight enough, but something was wrong. It was the itch at the back of her neck that warned her when she getting into something dangerous. 'What the hell,' she thought, 'all I'm going to do is talk with the woman. It doesn't mean I'll take the case.' It sounded to Kat like the woman might have been panicking.

The woman caller put her phone down and smiled to herself. She had picked the private detective with the smallest yellow pages ad, and a female to boot. She figured she would be the least likely to discover things that didn't need to be exposed and give her a clean bill of health. She didn't want a man poking his nose where it didn't belong. The silly little girl thought she would be able do a better job than the murder squad who were all men. She would probably turn tail and run the first time she ran into trouble. Any kind of trouble!

That would be perfect for her. After all, she was much smarter than a little winch playing at being a private investigator.

Kat McNally drove across the bay bridge, and went east to the Haight-Asbury area. She located a mansion with the right address and drove up the curved driveway. She parked in a paved area marked for visitors. She sat in her car trying to figure out why she had received the call from the unknown caller? The police should be handling the investigation. Why all the secrecy over the phone? Something was fishy about the entire thing. She reached to her back and made sure her .357 short barrel Smith and Wesson was there.

She rang the doorbell and waited. No one answered. She rang the doorbell again. The door lock was thrown; the door moved open a crack, only wide enough for her to see an eye looking at her: it was badly bloodshot. There was a hand holding the edge of the door, ready to slam it closed if necessary.

A woman's voice asked, "what do you want?"

McNally could tell by the woman's voice she was the one that called her. "My name is Kat McNally. I'm the private investigator you talked with earlier today," she flashed her P.I. license in its folder at the bloodshot eye.

"Oh, yes, of course. You're here about that nasty business that happened while I was away?"

"I have an appointment with you for one o'clock this afternoon. It is now one o'clock in the afternoon," she told the eye in the crack of the door.

"Officer, I am unavailable at the moment. Will you come back when I have time for you?"

"My time is valuable as well! I'm not an officer! If you don't want to keep your earlier appointed time, I will have to make a different appointment with you. It will have to be at least a week away," she put a little aggravation in her voice.

"I understand, but you are intruding at a time when I am very busy," said the woman with the bloodshot eye.

"I'm here at your request. If it isn't important for you to talk with me about a possible murder, then you're right, I'm very busy, as well," she turned to walk back to her car.

"Miss McNally!" The woman called out. "I'm afraid I got up on the wrong side of bed this morning."

"It's one o'clock in the afternoon and she just now got up!" Kat yelled to herself.

The door was pulled open, and the woman stood to the side to allow Kat to enter the entry hall. McNally noticed she was in a nightgown with a robe over it. A lighted cigarette was in her right hand, her hair was disheveled. She was a tall woman with blond hair and blue eyes, and was in her middle forties, if McNally was any judge of a woman's age. She led the way into the rather large living area, but walked through it to an equally large kitchen area. She offered her a stool at a granite covered breakfast bar where there was an ashtray; a half empty bottle of Vodka, and what looked like a partially finished Bloody Mary, sitting near a rather large ashtray, filled with cigarette butts.

"Would you care for a cup of coffee or a Bloody Mary, Miss McNally? I must have my Bloody Mary to function during the day. You know how it is," the woman said.

Kat said, "No mam, I've had coffee today. I would like to ask why you called me, and what murder you're concerned about."

"Ask away," the woman in her nightgown said in an impertinent way.

"Is this the mansion that was in the San Francisco newspaper a while back? If it is, is that the murderer you are concern about finding?"

"That's why I called you, Miss McNally. I was able to keep my address out of the paper, to keep lines of rubberneckers from forming in front of my home," she told McNally.

33

"That's interesting mam. How was it possible for you to keep a newspaper from publishing the address where a homicide was committed?"

"I happen to own the majority interest in the Globe newspaper!"

"You do? That would make sense then. So, your name is Robinson?"

"That's right Miss McNally."

"That's cleared up. Let's get down to some facts," Kat said with a bit of authority.

"The murder happened while I was visiting the Greek Islands with my boyfriend. I have no first-hand knowledge of the homicide, as you call it."

"Why do you want me to investigate a homicide when the police department is doing its best to find the murderer?"

"I want to know what happened, when it happened, and why it happened? The longer the police take the more it hurts my reputation, and my public esteem. I want the person responsible caught, and caught quickly. The police won't tell me a thing. All they do is keep asking me questions that I don't have any answers for."

"If you want me on the case, I'll be asking a lot of the same question that the police have asked. Are you prepared for that Mrs. Robinson?"

"Yes, but I want to be the only person in your information loop. Is that acceptable to you, Miss McNally?"

"You're the one retaining me. You'll be the one I report to when I have something of value from my investigation," she said, "I'd like to know when exactly you left the country before the homicide took place, and if you left because you had been threatened by someone?"

Mrs. Robinson looked at her in disgust. "What do you mean by asking a question like that? No one has ever threatened me. Why would someone want to do that?"

"I have to establish your alibi for when you left the states and the reason for your leaving. You'll also need to show me your passport to prove when you re-entered the United States. The first thing I must do is make sure you weren't involved in any way with the death of the person found in you mansion."

Mrs. Robinson got a fawn like look on her face, like she had been caught in the high beams of a car's lights. "Well, if you're going to be like that! I'll go to my bedroom, and get my passport from my safe. I'll be right back, Miss McNally."

She reappeared in a few minutes with her passport. Kat checked the dates for her most recent travel out of the country. The date for leaving was before the murder occurred, and the date of return was shortly after.

She gave the passport back to Robinson and told her, "I need a bit more information from you before beginning my investigation."

"And what would that be?"

"How long had the murder victim be employed by you?"

"Only a year."

"Did you have a maid before you employed her?"

"Prior to hiring her, I employed the same maid for just over twenty years."

"What happened to that maid to make you suddenly hire a new one?"

"She was diagnosed with dementia, and her family had to put her in a long-term care home."

"Do you have a contact for the dead maid's family. I'll need to speak with them, as well."

"No. I don't have that. Maybe the police have it and will give that information to you. I had one of my staff at the newspaper check her background before I hired her. I didn't see any reason to ask her for her family's contact information. She was a student at San Francisco University. She needed cheap housing that was close to the university. I let her stay in the maid's quarters for free, as payment for keeping the mansion in order for me, while she attended school.

"Are you divorced."

"What's that have to do with the murder of my maid?"

"I need your personal information, Mrs. Robinson, to help rule out your immediate family as a perpetrator of the homicide."

"My husband is deceased. He committed suicide over twenty years ago."

"How did he commit suicide?

"What the hell does that have to do with what has happened now?"

"There are people that hold grudges for years over something like that, Mrs. Robinson."

"He shot himself in the head." Mrs. Robinson said, taking a long drink of her Bloody Mary.

"Any other family?"

"No!"

"Do you know of anyone one that would want to kill your new maid?"

"No, I don't have a clue. I wish it had never happened. Now I'm swarmed by the media, and the police, and I don't want that notoriety."

Kat noticed that Mrs. Robinson didn't express any sorrowfulness about the murder of her young maid, but complained about being in public scrutiny.

"Is it possible that she was killed by accident?" McNally asked.

"What do you mean by that?"

"Could the killer have wanted to kill the old maid, but killed the new maid by mistake?"

"That's a pretty wild assumption on your part, Miss McNally. My new maid killed by a crazed killer by mistake. That's really out of this world thinking," she told Kat.

"By the way, who found your maid's body?"

"The handyman-gardener that I employee to fix things around the property and take care of the grounds."

"How did he happened to find her?"

"He told me that he had noticed the maid's private entrance at the back of the mansion was ajar for several days running. There was a severe lightning and thunder storm the night before he noticed the door was ajar. He told me he thought the storm had somehow blown the door open, the latch wasn't very substantial, he went to check it. The maid's car was parked in the employee lot; he wondered if there was a problem with her. He told me he figured she would have closed the door, if she was coming and going to the university each day, like she normally did. He checked the door, then entered the hallway that leads to her quarters. He found her in the bathtub with the water still running and the floor flooded."

"I'll need to contact him also. Do you have his contact information?"

"He is here three times a week, Monday, Wednesday, and Saturday, unless there is an emergency that I report. I have his phone number, and will give that to you before you leave."

"Can you add anything that will give me a string to follow, Mrs. Robinson."

"Nothing was taken from the mansion as far as I know. It doesn't look to me like a robbery gone bad. Does that help?"

"Please tell me where the maid's quarters are located. I will need to see the scene of the murder. You will not need to be in the quarters with me," she told Mrs. Robison.

The cleanup squad had been in the maid's quarters ahead of McNally. She figured they would have been there as soon as the murder squad was finished getting evidence, and taking photos of everything as it was, immediately after the murder took place. The maid's quarters were spotless. On the living room wall, there were two banners, one was for San Francisco University, and the other was for a sorority called Delta Zeta. She wrote that down in her notepad, and continued her search of the murder scene. She then walked down the hall to the entrance door and checked it out. Nothing had been forced or it may have been repaired. She returned to the main living quarters and asked Mrs. Robinson, who was sitting in the kitchen drinking coffee, and looking out on the huge veranda that was accessible from the kitchen, "was the lock on the exterior door to the maid's quarters repaired after the murder?"

"Not that I know of. Did you find anything important?" Asked Mrs. Robinson.

"No, I didn't. It looks like the police did a thorough job. I'll be leaving now. This is my card. Call if you think of anything that might help in finding the killer. I would appreciate the contact information you have for all the individuals we have covered today, and I'll need my retainer fee, and money to conduct my investigation. I will give you an itemized list of expenses each time I report to you while I'm on the job," offered Kat.

Mrs. Robinson handed her ten one hundred-dollar bills, plus two other orange bank wrappers of one hundred-dollar bills that covered their agreed upon retainer fee, and for beginning operational expenses. Kat McNally took the cash, and waited to count it until she was back in her car: she had learned not to trust anyone.

Mrs. Robinson gave her the list of contacts that she had, as well. She had made it up after getting the cash from her safe, while McNally was in the maid's quarters. The contact information was written on a sheet of typing paper.

"I'll be in touch when I have something worthwhile," said Kat.

After Kat left the mansion, Mrs. Robinson went back to the kitchen for a cigarette, and another cup of coffee. 'That silly girl won't discover anything I don't want her to find out. That's all well and good,' she thought, as a cloud of smoke curled up into her bloodshot eyes and irritated them even more.

CHAPTER FIVE

K at counted the cash before she started her car. It was the right amount. It was more than she had made for any investigation since she had received her P.I. license. She started her car, and sat for a moment with the engine running, wondering why she had paid her in cash. Was it because she didn't want a paper trail, or was there some other reason? She put the cash next to her on her car's bench seat, and drove down the mansion's driveway. She had the cash wrapped in the sheet of paper that had the information she needed written on it.

She felt there was something that Mrs. Robinson didn't want her to know. Kat noticed each time Mrs. Robinson didn't want to answer a provocative question there was gaze aversion or excessive blinking when she answered. Something didn't ring true about the agreement she had supposedly made with the maid. The maid lived in a large private apartment in Mrs. Robinson' mansion, and the only thing the maid had to do was to keep the mansion clean. There was only one person living in the mansion, other than the maid. That seemed like a really good deal for her. There was something curious about the whole arrangement. Her feeling of having no faith or trust in people raised its head, and warned her to look behind the smoke screen that was hiding something Mrs. Robinson didn't want Kat to know. Maybe she could figure it out after she talked with the old maid or her family. Was she being too critical about being paid in cash? Kat didn't like most people: Mrs. Robinson was a perfect example why.

She drove to her bank to deposit her windfall, and put her concerns to the back of her mind. She was on a murder case: she was going to find the killer. No matter what!

She didn't want to use her contacts with the murder squad in San Francisco until she felt she had exhausted all possible leads concerning the maid's murder. It was mid-afternoon and San Francisco University had classes, she knew, from early morning until late at night, for all the working students that needed options for classes. She was heading there to cross her first lead off her mental list.

The afternoon traffic in San Francisco slowed her drive to the university that was just a short distance from the branch bank that she used. The distance was short between the mansion and the university, as well. She was beginning to understand why the young woman had taken the job as a maid. It would have been hard to pass up living quarters for maids work that could be done at almost any time of the day or night, and have the short drive to the campus. She wondered where the young woman's home was located.

She pulled her car into the visitors parking area, and walked into the Administration office. She asked a young man who was at one of the desks behind the counter that separated the clerks and visitors.

"How do I get to the office of student records?"

The clerk walked over to her, and took a small floor map from under the counter.

"You're here," he said, and made a circle with a ball point pen around a portion of the floor map. "This is the Academic Records office. Walk down this hallway to the T intersection and turn left. It's about half-way down the hall on the right side."

Kat followed the map to the Academic Records office. There was another university student there.

The young woman asked, from behind the counter, near the front door to the office, "how can I help you?"

"I need to check a student's entrance record. Is this the right office?" She asked the clerk.

"Yes, it is. However, all student records are considered confidential," the clerk told her.

"This is a police matter," Kat pulled her leather credential I.D. holder from the hip pocket of her jeans and flashed her P.I. card at her. The P.I. badge that was by the card was usually enough to get her where she wanted to go.

"I'm sorry, Miss. We get all kinds in here wanting information on our students for all kinds of weird reasons. Give me your students name, and I'll pull the file for you."

"Her name is Gayle Pauline Windsor," she told her.

"This will take a few minutes. Take a seat at the table in the corner. You can use it to check the files contents, also."

She took the clerks advise, and took a seat at the small corner table to wait for her return with the student file of the murdered maid. It took five minutes for the clerk to return to the counter and wave her over. The clerk handed her the student file for Gayle Pauline Windsor, and told her to ring the little bell when she was finished. Someone would take the file.

She took the file to the small table, and pulled out her notepad and pen. The maid's personal information was on the inside of the cover page of the file. What she was looking for was there. Her parents' names and address were listed as emergency contacts. Kat McNally rang the bell on the counter after she had copied down the address for the maid's parents. She gave the file back to the young woman when she came from an area of tall shelving.

Kat drove back to her apartment and packed an overnight bag. The file at the university didn't list her parents phone number. It was possible that they didn't have a phone, but then, it could have been left off on purpose. She was going to drive up to Eureka, a large ocean fishing port north of San Francisco. It would take her five hours to drive there depending on how heavy the traffic on the northbound one-o-one coast highway was at the time.

She went to check her recorder for any calls that might be waiting for her. Now that she was on a major case, she needed to be more conscientious about her work.

She figured she would reach Eureka in the evening. If the maid's parents were listed in the Eureka phone book, she could make a call and set an appointment for the next day.

The drive along the California coast was one she always enjoyed. It was a constant breathtaking panorama of rugged rocky coast line, and beautiful sand beaches that were begging for someone to come and play on them.

Five hours later she pulled into a parking space in front of the office of the Thunderbird Lodge motel on the outskirts of Eureka. It was early in the evening. The sun had just set in the west and was casting red, yellow and orange arrows on the sparse ocean breeze clouds high in the evening sky.

After she had received the key to her room she asked the clerk if there were Eureka phone books in the rooms.

"No Miss," answered the clerk. "If you need a number you can call the office, and the clerk on duty will look it up for you."

"How 'bout you letting me see the office copy now, and I won't have to bother you later tonight?"

She found the number she wanted and wrote it down in her note pad. She left the office to drive her car around the pool that was on the side of the office building, and into the parking lot between the office, and a two-story building where the rooms were located. She found her room on the ground floor in the middle of the long building.

McNally unlocked her room, hitting the light switch at the door. The room was clean, and had a modern look to it. She went to the phone that was on a night stand by the bed, and dialed the number from her notepad. It was answered on the second ring by a feminine voice.

"Hello."

"Is this Mrs. Windsor?" Asked McNally.

"Yes. Who's calling?"

"Mrs. Windsor, my name is Kat McNally. I am a private investigator hired by Mrs. Robinson to investigate you daughters murder."

The phone banged on something at the woman's end, like it hit something solid with a hard blow. The phone was silent.

"Mrs. Windsor! Are you there Mrs. Windsor?"

The phone remained dead.

McNally held the phone next to her ear, hoping that Mrs. Windsor was going to come back on the phone.

After a few moments, a gruff masculine voice asked, "who the hell is this?"

"My name is Kat McNally. I didn't mean to upset Mrs. Windsor. Is she okay?"

"My wife, McNally, is still grieving over the loss of our daughter. Please don't call here again."

"Mr. Windsor, I understand why you wife is upset, however I have been employed by Mrs. Robinson to find the murderer of your daughter. I need a few minutes of you time to get a better background about your daughter."

"Miss McNally, my wife won't be able, for the foreseeable future, to discuss our daughter's murder with you. The police have already upset her enough. Why is Mrs. Robinson butting into this, when the police are trying to find the killer?" Mr. Windsor asked.

"I'm not sure of that, Mr. Windsor. It might be that she has a sense of quilt, or it could be a sense of loss. I can't explain why she hired me to find the murderer of you daughter; but I need to speak with you, if only for a few minutes, to give me some background about your daughter."

"I'm the captain of an offshore fishing vessel, Miss McNally, and I am leaving early in the morning for a week-long tuna fishing trip. I will talk with you at the dock, before I leave in the morning. Under no circumstance are you to contact my wife again."

"Give me your trawler's docking address, and I'll meet you there in the morning. What time will you be free?"

"My boat will leave the dock at exactly five o'clock in the morning. I suggest you come aboard at four-thirty."

Mr. Windsor gave McNally the trawler's docking information and hung up.

Kat McNally, hadn't experienced talking with a family of a murder victim. She could tell it wasn't going to be easy for her to get past her not trusting anyone or to show kindness to the family. Getting to know what the young maid was like had to be done, and what they tell her might solve the case quickly. It was her job to find the killer, and hopefully give the grieving family members a chance of getting over the terrible anger that the grieving process leaves behind.

There was early morning sea fog covering the coast around Eureka when McNally drove up to the pier number that the maid's father had given her over the phone the evening before. She parked in a small lot at the foot of the pier, and proceeded down the pier to the trawler moored at its end. There was a small bell mounted on the boat's rail at the end of the gangplank. A small copper plate below the bell told her to ring it before boarding.

The sound of the small bell rang through the fog around the boat. It traveled on until the ringing sound faded away, like a soft whisper in the early morning fog.

She heard a door of some type open, and a voice from higher up in the fog asked, "Miss McNally?"

"Yes," replied McNally.

"Walk forward a few steps, you'll find a set of stairs. Come up those. I'll leave the door open for you."

McNally touched her back, making sure her .357 magnum was secured: She didn't know why. A small shiver ran through her body, as if there was something eerie about this entire meeting on a ship in a dense fog at four-thirty in the morning. She shook it off and climbed the stairs.

There was a soft yellow luminescence to the fog along the outside of the boat's cabin. It seemed to move as the fog crept over it in small waves.

"Miss McNally, come in." Mr. Windsor closed the door behind her. "It'll keep the fog out of the deckhouse, so we can see each other while we chat." Mr. Windsor asked. "Would you like a cup of coffee? It's black and strong enough to float a boat."

"I could use a cup."

The captain of the fishing trawler, Mr. Windsor, was a tall, lanky man. McNally put his age in the fifties. There was a slight tinge of gray at his temples, and he had deep, English, blue eyes.

When McNally had her cup of coffee and had tasted it, she told the Windsor that she would make the questions short and to the point.

Windsor nodded his thanks, and asked what McNally wanted to know about his daughter.

"Do you recall your daughter ever having someone aggressively confront her, or threaten her in any way?"

"She never dated much when she was in high school, and the boys she did date seemed to end up as friends. Is that what you're getting at?"

"I am more concerned about recently."

Windsor was quiet for a minute and then told her, "since she moved to San Francisco and started college, her mother and I have heard little from her, Miss McNally. That's one of the reasons my wife is having a hard time with her murder."

"What do you mean, when you say you heard little from her?"

"My daughter was always a happy person. She was very involved in social and school activities. She was a cheerleader for the teams at high school. That sort of thing. Then when she went off to college things started changing. She stopped calling her mother to talk, and we hadn't seen her since she moved down there."

"Kids get caught up in being away from home, and involved in school and social things it offers. Is that what you mean?"

"I mean, when her mother would call her, Gayle would be sharp with her. She didn't share any happenings about school, or her new job at the mansion. We wanted to know that she was alright, living there in that big old place with only the owner around. To be honest, she changed, her whole personality changed. It was like we were a bother to her. Her mother couldn't understand. They were very close while she was growing up. Then it was like a curtain had been pulled down between them."

"This change happened quickly?"

"At first no. It was sort of gradual. Then a few months before her death she stopped answering our calls."

"Did you contact her school or her employer?"

"We didn't think the school would be able to tell us much. She was in a sorority, but they are closed mouth about their members. We did try to call the owner of the mansion. I think her name is Mrs. Robinson. We left several messages on her machine, but never heard back from her."

That struck McNally! Mrs. Robinson had told her she had no contact information for the maid's family, yet her father just told her they had left messages for her to call them about their daughter. Since Mrs. Robinson didn't return those calls, she must have not paid any attention to them, or she didn't want to tell McNally about the messages. Why would she not think that was important? Was it possible that Mrs. Robinson forgot about the messages left by the Windsor's?

"Any reason for you not driving down to San Francisco and checking on her?" Responded McNally.

"We are kicking ourselves for not doing that very thing. Maybe we could have stopped this terrible thing from happening to her and to us. We didn't want it to seem like we were interfering in her new life. We now know that was ridiculous of us. We should have gone!"

"Have you given the coroner's office the funeral information?"

"I did that yesterday," Windsor told her. "It's taken some time for him to complete his examination, I guess it was because she was murdered."

McNally asked him if she could contact him, if she thought of anything else she needed to know that might help her find the killer of their daughter. Windsor told her to please contact him, but not to bother his wife. He gave her a phone number at the company office for her to call. McNally noticed when she left the deckhouse that the fog had lifted somewhat, and that someone on the boat had turned on their working and running lights in preparation for leaving the pier. She walked along the pier headed back to her car, but stopped to look back at the big trawler fishing vessel. Her eyes caught the name of the trawler in the lights that had been turned on. The name of the boat was, "Gayle Pauline," and there was a black wreath hanging from the bow.

Kat figured the family wasn't very high on her list of potential killers of their daughter. She started back to San Francisco. She was going to the morgue and to check the body. The autopsy at the coroner's office had been completed according to what the father had told her. Windsor had given the coroner's office the families funeral arrangements the day before. It usually took several days for the paperwork to be completed before the body was moved to the funeral home. Kat had requested a note of permission to view the body of Windsor's daughter. It took a few minutes for Windsor to write it; his hand was shaking badly while he tried to write it.

An assistant to the coroner checked McNally's credentials, and placed the note from Windsor on a stack of papers in a metal file container on his desk with the title, 'TO BE FILED'.

The clerk walked McNally down a short hallway to a closed door. The room on the other side of the door had several surgical tables aligned in a row from the front of the room to the back. On three sides of the room were large drawers, rising from floor to the ceiling. This wasn't the first time McNally had visited a coroner's autopsy room. It was quiet now, but she had been there when the coroner was actively working with a cadaver to determine the cause of death. After the first time she was prepared for the smell, and the low voice of the coroner recording what he was seeing during each phase of the autopsy. That afternoon there was no on-going autopsy. The large vent fans were turned off: the room was eerily quiet. McNally thought of a pin dropping in the room.

The clerk went to a drawer at the back of the surgical room, and pulled out the drawer that held the body of the murdered maid, Gayle Pauline Windsor was on her toe tag.

The clerk told McNally, "I have to stay in the room while you are examining the corpse, and you'll need to wear surgical gloves. He held a pair out to McNally.

"That's fine." McNally told him. She pulled on the tight surgical gloves with some help from the clerk.

McNally started by checking the corpse carefully from head to toe. All the normal incisions made by the coroner had been sutured closed, including the scalp and chest. Her neck wound had not been sutured close. It remained the way it was when the police found the body, for legal reasons. She checked her arms carefully for old needle marks, in case she had been a drug user. She found no needle marks, and was about to turn to the corpse's stomach area, when she saw something that seemed odd to her. She was looking at the right wrist area. There was a very light discoloration that encompassed the wrist at the joint of her hand. She walked around the open drawer to check the corpse's left wrist area. The mark around her left wrist was even lighter than the one on her right wrist; she leaned in over the edge of the drawer to get a closer look. Once she was closer to the hand and wrist area the circle was there, but something else jumped out at her. The maid's left hand was missing the tip of its index finger. It had been severed at the same time she was murdered. She took out her notepad and scribbled some notes. She continued her inspection of the corpse.

Everything looked normal to her as she worked her way from the stomach and pelvic area toward the lower extremities. There were no track marks from drug abuse anywhere on the body's lower torso. She checked the bottoms of her feet and under her nails. She turned to her ankle area on her right leg. There was the same vague outline around her ankle. She checked the left leg and found another faint ring around that ankle.

She reached into her pocket, and withdrew a Zeiss 35mm Viewfinder camera. It was small, but produced very clear black and white photos. She took photos of the front showing the faint circles. Then a special one of the missing first joint phalange of the maid's left hand. Next, she gently lifted the foot to take a photo of the back of the ankle on each foot. She did the same with both wrists. She took a photo of the neck wound.

When she was finished, the clerk pushed the drawer closed, and put Kat's surgical gloves in a human waste container.

CHAPTER SIX

K at drove to a camera shop that she had used previously, and told the man behind the counter that she needed two copies of each photo on the 35mm film. She was told they would be ready for her in two days.

She went across the bridge to her apartment, and changed into running shorts and a T-shirt with U.C. Berkeley on it. On the way to the trail overlooking the bay she thought about calling Windsor, and asking whether his daughter ever wore leather, or metal bracelets on her wrist or ankles. She remembered Mr. Windsor had left for a week on his trawler; she would have to wait.

At the beginning of the trail, she did her normal stretching, and then hit the trail. Her runs cleared her mind, and more often than not, the run would help her decide what to do next. That day was no different. She dropped the idea of calling Windsor about his daughter. She didn't want to ask pertinent questions of anyone over the phone. It was always better to hear their reactions in person, and to see their body language.

Windsor would be out for a few days trawling for fish. The time depended on how the catch was going. The photos would be ready in that time frame as well.

She made the half-way turn on her run. There were a number of things that she should be doing until Windsor returned. She figured the next thing on the list in her head was to talk with the family of the old maid, and, if possible, talk with the old maid herself. The last half of her run was all up hill. She left all the plan making behind, and concentrated on the run. She finished her daily run, exhilarated as always. It always left her with a clear mind, and this time a desire to question the old maid or her family.

She drove back to her apartment and took a shower. Dressed in clean Levi jeans and a sport shirt she stepped into her boots, and put her .357 magnum at the small of her back. She sat at her desk, and dialed the number for the old maid's family.

A man answered the phone. After Kat told him Mrs. Robinson had retained her, and that she needed to speak with the them, the man agreed to an evening meeting for that evening.

She tried studying, but her thoughts kept going back to the mansion and the murdered maid. There was one thing she hadn't done during her meeting with Mrs. Robinson. She should have spent some time walking the grounds. She called her number to ask permission to do that, but her call went to the answering machine. She didn't leave a message.

She rolled the windows down on her car, and drove over to the Haight-Ashbury part of San Francisco. She drove around the mansion that took up a half city block. She noticed a parking area that was on the side of an undeveloped hill. There was a sign at the edge of the parking area that indicated the property past the sign was private. About half way to the back of the mansion there was an old fence that encompassed the back yard, like there was a dog at the mansion. A swimming pool and covered patio with a large bath house took up a good part of the backyard.

She walked to the gate in the fence, checking the ground along the narrow path she was using. The latch and lock for the gate had been broken, and forced from the wood of the gate and its post. The gate swung open easily, and she wondered why the lock and latch were still on the ground, as she walked to the door that was obviously the maid's entrance. The door lock didn't show any scratches that weren't normal. She tried the door knob, figuring it was locked. She turned it first one way and then the other. The latch clicked open. She couldn't believe it! Some idiot had left the door unlocked leaving the mansion and the murder room with easy access.

The hallway that led to the maid's quarters was empty. She slipped past the door leaving it ajar, and walked down the hall with her right hand on the grip of her pistol. She moved up to the entry door of the maid's quarters and opened it slowly, standing against the corridor wall, until she could see around the doorsill. The living room was clear. The corridor continued without turns until it ended at a door some distance away. She moved toward the door at the end of the hall. It had to be the entrance into the main part of the mansion that was for the maid's use.

Kat was midway down the hall when she saw a faint circular change in the texture of the adjacent wall. She stopped for a moment, and concentrated on the spot. It was so faint that she started to dismiss it as a blemish on the wall, but something told her to go closer and check it carefully. She put her fingers on the blemish, and moved them around until she found a thin disk that slid to the side. Under it was a key lock. A hidden key lock in the hallway wall didn't make sense to her. There didn't seem to be a door that went with the lock. She drew closer to the lock, and saw that a perfectly fitted metal door had been textured exactly like the rest of the hallway. She could barely feel the edge of the hidden door with the tips of her fingers. It was so well hidden that most people walking down the hallway wouldn't notice it: the key lock matched the wall perfectly.

She stood next to the hidden door, and tried to figure out what it was doing in the hallway to the maid's quarters, and what purpose did it serve? It piqued her curiosity. What was behind the hidden door?

Why was it in the hallway near the maid's quarters? Did it have anything to do with the young maid that was murdered? The killer had come in from the outside through the exterior unlocked door. Someone had a key to the hidden lock. It was in her to figure out why it had been placed where it was. She had to make sure it didn't have anything to do with the maid's death. Her lock pick was in a small cabinet in her apartment. She took out her note pad and put it in the list of things she needed.

She continued down the hall to the door that she figured led into the main part of the mansion. The door moved slightly when she turned the knob, enough for her to see the connection devise on the edge of the doorsill. She cautiously closed the door, and waited for a second to see if an alarm went off. Luckily, she hadn't broken the contact totally. She thought it was interesting for the mansion to have an alarm system, but the exterior door to the maid's quarters didn't have one. It dawned on her that the maid needed to come and go when the mansion alarm was on. That made sense. But why wasn't there a separate alarm for the maid to use? That was a question that Mrs. Robinson would have to answer.

She closed the entry door to the maid's quarters behind her. She started her car and left the mansion behind. She felt like the trip to the mansion had been good and bad. She was able to get a feel for how the killer had entered the maid's quarters; the ease of entry, with no alarm system and the door being unlocked. That was the good. What the hell was the secreted door doing in the maid's quarters hallway and what purpose did it serve? Why were the latch and lock, that had been broken off the gate, left on the ground by the police? That was the bad. She needed to find the answer to those questions.

The drive up to Sacramento, where the old maid's family lived, was about two hours northeast of San Francisco. She left early, wanting to get a feeling for the area where they lived, and she needed to hit a burger joint for a late lunch on the way. She knew right where to go in Sacramento for the best hamburger in California. She made her way through the traffic in San Francisco, and headed up California highway 160 keeping her car's speed on the peg of the speed limit. She reached the outskirts of Sacramento and exited the highway. Her mouth was starting to water, thinking about the burger she was going to order.

McNally knew her way around the streets of Sacramento from all the times she had gone there with her dad on police business, when he was still on the force in San Francisco. She maneuvered her way to the corner of Fulton Avenue and El Camino Avenue. Harvey's Drive-In was at the corner of the two avenues. She frowned slightly when she saw a line at the order window. It was the middle of the afternoon, not lunchtime! She pulled into a parking spot facing the front of the burger joint, and switched off the ignition. It only took a few minutes of standing in line to reach the order window.

"What can I do for yah?" asked the young man with a tall white hat on his head.

Kat couldn't help herself. "I'll have the deluxe cheeseburger, an order of Suzie-Q-fries, and a cherry limeade."

The young man smiled and said, "It'll be right out. They'll call your name when it's ready. What's your name?"

"Kat."

"Thanks for coming to Harvey's Kat and enjoy," the young order taker said.

Kat went over to one of the picnic tables on a cement patio and waited patiently for her order.

Her name was called in a short amount of time. She went back to her car to eat. She put the cherry limeade on the dash board, and opened the paper container with the curly, spiral shaped potato fries. She unwrapped the gigantic hamburger with the works stacked on it. It was so large it was hard for her to bite a piece off. She started at the edge of the bun, and worked her way into the huge burger. The combination of cherry limeade, Suzie-Q fries, and the humongous hamburger, was close to Heaven!

Kat found the house that was on the contact list for the maid with dementia in a middle-class neighborhood on the west side of Sacramento. She drove around the block several times before parking on the street in front of the home.

She walked up the short walk to the two steps. There was a small porch to stand on and ring the doorbell. She could hear a soft scuffling behind the door, and then it was opened by a teenage boy.

"I have an appointment with Steve Henry. My name is McNally," said Kat.

"Come in, please. They're all in the kitchen sitting around the table waiting for you," the teenager told her. He turned around and walked through the living room. He stopped on the far side, and waited for McNally to close the door and follow him.

The teenager went to a kitchen counter and sat on a tall stool, without saying another word.

McNally wondered what was becoming of the new generation. The kid could have told the people at the table her last name, or that she was the woman that had made the appointment with the family about his grandmother. Social graces were slowly going by the wayside.

All of the adults at the table stood and introduced themselves to her. Steve Henry helped her with a chair at the table, and helped move the chair closer to the kitchen table. He sat back in his chair next to her. Maybe all the social graces weren't disappearing...

Martha, the wife of Steve Henry, and the mother of the teenage boy, asked her if Kat would have some coffee or water to drink.

McNally took the coffee. She waited for Mrs. Henry to seat herself, and asked them if they knew of the killing of the new maid at the Robinson mansion. They all started to speak at once. There was a pause, and Steve Henry was appointed the family spokesman. He told McNally that they had been contacted by the San Francisco police.

"I hate to drag your family through all this again, but Mrs. Robinson wants an in depth, private report to help clear her name to the public since she is a major owner of the San Francisco Globe newspaper."

"We understand that, Miss McNally. What we're concerned about is the questioning of our mother. She has been diagnosed with stage three dementia. That means she has mild cognitive decline. We've made an appointment to see her in an hour: her facility is close by. The two policemen that interviewed her were a bit gruff, and when mom figured that out, she shut down, like a clam closing its shell."

"I was going to ask about seeing your mother. Thanks for setting that up for me. But first, I'd like to talk with you folks a bit if that's okay with you."

"We figured you would ask us some questions, but we don't have a lot of information about Mom's work at the mansion."

"She didn't talk with you about her work?"

"She hated her work at the mansion, and what went on there, from time to time." Steve Henry told her in a rush of words.

"Wow, I didn't expect that! What do you mean about what went on there?" Kat asked him.

"I don't know much, because Mom didn't talk about specifics with us. She did mention the drinking and drug use, by the owner of the mansion."

"She was afraid of Mrs. Robinson; she would apparently go off on drunken rages about the smallest things, and then take Valium to come down from the drunken rage, she held Mom as a hostage in the mansion, because she was paranoid about Mom telling what she knew about her. Mom wanted to quit, many times, but she needed the money she made there, and was afraid of being ostracized by Mrs. Robinson. You know. From getting any other job."

"For not knowing much, you've painted a very dim picture of your mother's employer. Anything else you can relate to me about Mrs. Robinson or you mother's time working for her?" Kat asked.

"She did tell us about the men, and sometimes women that Mrs. Robinson entertained at the mansion. When she was entertaining Mrs. Robinson locked the door that allowed Mom to enter the main part of the mansion. She was told to not disturb Mrs. Robinson under any circumstance," he said.

Kat checked her watch, and suggested that Steve ride with her to visit his mom. "I forgot to ask your mom's name, Steve."

"Florence Henry," he told her.

The drive to the special care home where Florence Henry stayed was a short one; maybe a half-mile from Steve's home. It was a one-story facility, like a very long ranch style home. There were a couple of people sitting in wheelchairs under the portico at the front door. One seemed to not notice that he was outside, the other was bright and cheery, but unable to walk.

This was Kat's first trip to a special care facility. They checked in at the reception counter, and walked through another glass double door into the junction of three corridors. The halls were a like a traffic jam on the coast highway at seven-thirty in the morning, heading into San Francisco to work. Steve Henry told her that a woman sitting in a wheelchair mid-way down the right-hand corridor was his mom. They walked in that direction. Kat anticipated some recognition from Mrs. Henry the closer they walked to her. Steve touched his mother's arm, and told her it was Steve.

There was a look of recognition from Mrs. Henry then. She patted his hand with her free hand, but didn't say a word. She looked at him in partial recognition.

Before anything else happened, she said quietly, "I want to go home."

Steve tried to make his mother understand that it wasn't possible for her to go home, but it didn't seem to resonate with her. He told his mother that he had a friend that wanted to talk with her for a few moments in her room. He turned her wheelchair, and headed back down the hall to her room. The little room was a private one; it had only a closet, a dresser, a twin bed and a small desk, with a basic chair by it. There was a private bath through a doorway.

Steve helped her from the wheelchair to the basic chair. He stood beside his mother, Kat sat on the edge of the small bed, hoping not to appear threatening. It was under the one window that let light into the room. Steve told her that Kat was going to ask her a few questions about her work in the past. She looked over to Kat with a distant gaze in her eyes.

Kat wanted to get a couple of important answers to her questions, and thought the best thing to do was to keep her questions short.

"Did anyone ever threaten you while you worked for Mrs. Robinson?"

Florence seem to understand what Kat had asked. She didn't answer, she moved her head up and down in an affirmative fashion.

Kat asked her, "can you name the person or persons that threatened you?"

Florence continued to look off in the distance, but did not answer the question.

She smiled, trying not to offend or upset Florence Henry and asked, "did Mrs. Robinson ever threaten you?"

There was silence for a few moments, and then a sudden light came into Florence's eyes. "Keep my mouth shut." She ground her teeth for a minute, and then said with a fearful look in her eyes, and her hand over her mouth, "disappear."

Kat asked, "what was going to disappear, Mrs. Henry?"

Mrs. Henry didn't answer.

Kat waited a few moments, then asked, "were you afraid of Mrs. Robinson?"

Florence's face turned to a scowl with her eyes fixed on the light of the window. She sat like that, and then a heart-rendering tear formed in her right eye, and slowly crept down her soft wrinkled cheek to the corner of her mouth. Kat wiped the tear away with a tissue from a box on a tiny table, and patted her on her arm. She didn't want to continue asking questions of Florence.

Steve Henry suggested they leave, and patted his mother on the arm again. He asked his mother if she wanted to go out in the hallway.

She looked at him with those dim, sad eyes and said, "I want to go home."

On the drive back to Steve Henry's house he told Kat, "you have to understand that my mother was never a caring person: in fact my sister and I were a burden to her. She was missing the motherly gene, I guess."

Kat continued driving toward his house, not knowing what to say after his comment. Sometimes being a P.I. garnered more information than she expected. His comment did give her a better understanding of the atmosphere that surrounded the Robinson mansion. She was glad she was driving back to her apartment, after dropping him off. She needed the quiet of the drive to put things in the proper perspective, and decide where to go from there.

Before she reached the highway back to Emeryville and her apartment, she turned north on the highway to Eureka. She wanted to ask Mr. Windsor about the marks on his daughter's ankles and wrists. She wasn't sure when the trawler would come back from netting fish, but she wanted to be there when it did. The drive from Sacramento to Eureka took another five hours.

Kat drove through town directly to the harbor where the Gayle Pauline had its berth. The trawler wasn't at the end of the pier when she drove into the parking area. She continued out of the parking lot, and headed back to the hotel she had stayed in a few days earlier.

The clerk at the hotel remembered her from her last stay, a few days ago. He was able to give her the same room. She had planned on returning to her apartment after talking with Florence Henry, and had nothing packed for an overnight stay. She went to a nearby pharmacy, and picked up what she needed for a short stay in Eureka. She was hoping the Gayle Pauline would come back to port before the week was up.

For the next two days she went to the pier hoping to see the trawler at its berth, to no avail. She continued her daily check for the boat on the morning of the third day. She was thinking about leaving for San Francisco if the trawler wasn't moored at its berth. To her amazement, the trawler was at its berth, and there were men unloading the catch with an overhead net, and dropping the fish into a large cold storage semi-trailer.

She watched the process for a few minutes, and then saw captain Windsor come from the wheel house to watch the unloading from the rail, as the last of the fish were loaded into the large truck.

Kat started down the pier trying to get captain Windsor's attention. When he noticed her coming toward the trawler, his face turned to a frown, and he shook his head in disgust.

Kat climbed the ladder up to the wheel house, and told Windsor she had another question that needed to be asked of him. He responded by walking back to the wheel house and waving her inside.

"I thought I was finished with you and your questions, Miss McNally. Make this quick, I'm very busy at the moment.

"Do you recall your daughter ever wearing anything around her wrist or ankles that may have left a discoloration or stain on her skin?"

Windsor thought for a moment and told her no. "What's that got to do with my daughter's murder?"

"I'm not sure, at this point, if it has any bearing on her case or not."

Windsor stood quietly looking out the big glass window at the front of the wheel house and then told her, "I didn't know my daughter had joined a sorority until the police told my wife and I. They do some pretty wild stuff when the new girls are being hazed. Maybe they did something like you asked about."

Kat hadn't connected the possibility that the sorority might have something to do with the marks on Gayle Pauline's ankles and wrists. If they did, it would change her thoughts on the case, in more ways than one.

She left the trawler, walked immediately back to her car, and went back to the hotel to check out. She had come to Eureka with a question, and left with even more questions. She needed to get back to San Francisco as soon as possible.

CHAPTER SEVEN

Kat walked out of the classroom with the rest of her night school class, and headed for her car. She had missed a class in both courses while she went to talk with the Henry family, and the drive up to Eureka to talk briefly with captain Windsor. She didn't want to get behind in her course work, but finding the killer of the young maid was taking top priority at that point. It was still early in the evening so she took a chance, and drove across the bay bridge to the maid's university. She wanted to check with the sorority to see if they knew what the marks on her ankles and wrist were caused by. She doubted the girls at the sorority house would know anything about them, but she had to cross that off her list of things to check.

The Delta Zeta house was an older brick house that had been given to the sorority by one of its long-ago members. Kat pushed the doorbell and waited.

A young woman in her late teens or early twenties opened the door. After Kat told her what she wanted, she was invited into the living room where a number of young women were scattered around, trying to study with a radio playing, and the back-ground noise caused by others that were talking in normal voices.

The young woman that opened the door called everyone in the living room to order and told them what Kat wanted to know. Kat pulled one of the photos she had taken at the coroner's office from her wallet, and let her pass it around the room. She had picked them up earlier that day. The young women looked at the wrist photo showing the mark around it, but all of them were shaking their heads by the time the photo was passed back to her. They all agreed that the markings on the young maid's wrist weren't caused by anything the sorority would have put her through during rush. The young woman that seemed to be a leader told her how badly the sorority felt about the untimely death of one of their own, and the sorority was sending flowers to the church where her funeral was to be the next day.

Kat left the sorority house feeling like her visit was a waste of time, however it was something that she had to check out. She went back to her apartment thinking about what was next to check off on her mental list. She felt like the marks on the young woman's body were of importance to the crime, but why?

Her message light on her phone recorder was blinking off and on in the dark of her apartment when she opened the front door. She was tired from the all the driving and going to class; then to the sorority house. She threw her keys on the small desk by the front door, and went into the bathroom to take a long soak in the tub, before going to bed. She didn't think about the blinking message light, after all, it was probably someone wanting to sell her something.

She slipped into the sheets on her bed; put her head on her pillow, and tried to go to sleep. She kept seeing the damn red blinking light of the message recorder. She tossed and turned for a few more minutes, until she knew she wasn't going to get to sleep without knowing whether that message on the recorder was important or not. She figured, if it was a sales call, she would be so angry that she wouldn't be able to sleep, at least for a long while. If it was something important about the murder case, she knew she wouldn't be able to go to sleep either. She threw the sheet that was covering her and turned on her night stand light before her feet hit the carpet.

She left the living room overhead light off, and went to her tiny desk under the window to hit the play button on the message recorder.

A male voice said from the recorder, "this is Steve Henry. You talked to us yesterday, and talked with my mother, as well. I thought this might be important to you. When I went back to see how she was after you left, she had scribbled the words stand and fort. It took me a while to figure out what the words were, since her hand writing has become barely readable. This may have nothing to do with the murder of the young woman, but we thought you should know."

The tape began playing silence, and Kat McNally turned it off. She sat back in her chair at the desk wondering what the message could mean to her, or if it had anything to do with the murder case. Whether it did or not, she knew she wasn't going to sleep well that night.

Kat continued to toss and turn when she went back to bed. Her mind was working overtime on the words stand and fort. How did they fit into the questions she had asked Steve Henry's mother? Maybe they didn't have anything to do with the case. The two words scribbled on a used envelope could mean almost anything or nothing. She finally turned to thinking about something that had been bothering her since talking with Mrs. Robinson. She had told her that her husband had committed suicide by shooting himself. The police department by law has to keep those records until the deceased would be one hundred years old. Maybe she should go down to the records warehouse for the city of San Francisco, and try to talk her way into checking the file on Mr. Robinson's suicide. The first thing to do was to find out what his full name was and when he died. She finally went to sleep with that thought presenting a new item on her case list for the coming day.

The murder and suicide records of the city of San Francisco were stored in a large metal sided building in south San Francisco county. Kat drove along the west shore of the peninsula, taking in the Pacific Ocean on the way to the storage building. She turned east just before the county line and drove until she saw a large sign that said the San

Francisco storage building was inside a fenced in area to her right. The parking area was out front of the large building.

She had stopped at the information desk of the Globe newspaper to find out the full name of the deceased Mr. Robinson and the date of his suicide. The clerk had that information at her finger tips.

Armed with that information she entered the front door of the metal building where she gave the clerk her P.I. credentials. The clerk looked the license over, and handed it back to her.

"I'm sorry, the records in this building are considered confidential, Ms. McNally."

"Isn't there some way to get around that. I'm working on a recent murder case, and I need to see that file," McNally told the clerk with a smile.

"If there is a person that you know on the San Francisco police department you can sign in as a subordinate and pay a fee."

"Do you have Shay McNally on that list?"

The clerk flipped some pages on a clip board, and looked up with a smile. She told her he was on the list. "The fee is ten dollars, and if you want a copy of the file, it cost a dime a page to copy," the clerk told her.

Kat paid the fee, signed her name and asked, "how do I find the file? I can see row after row of files that take up the space behind your counter."

"I have a card file here. I'll pull the one for George C. Robinson. I'll walk with you so you don't end up lost out there in the record wilderness," the clerk smiled.

The clerk spent a few moments thumbing through a card file with the letter R on the front of the box. She pulled one card from the file, and put a sign on top of the counter saying she would be back in a few minutes. They walked across two-thirds of the rows of files and turned into a row half-way to the end. The file shelves were eight feet tall and required a rolling ladder to reach to the top shelve. The clerk went to the other end of the row and rolled back a ladder to where Kat still stood. The clerk climbed to the top shelve and pulled out a manila file. She handed the file to Kat at the bottom of the stairs and pointed a small gray metal desk at the end of the row.

"You can use that desk to go through the file, and leave it there when you are finished or until you find something that you want copied."

The clerk left her to walk back to the counter. Kat walked down the row in the opposite direction toward the gray metal desk. The desk made her remember the gray metal desks that were in the military police offices in Korea when she was still an M.P. in the army. She pulled back the metal folding chair and opened the file.

She spent the next hour reading the police investigation report, and looking at the suicide scene photographs. There were, she decided, parts of the police report that might sway a person reading it to the conclusion that Mr. Robinson had killed himself. She didn't want the police report conclusion to affect her investigation; she placed the paper report in the file, and left it on the desk like the clerk told her to do. She took all the photos of the suicide scene to the front counter, and asked that she be allowed to have copies made of them.

"We don't have the capabilities to copy the photos for you. Usually the officer checking photos out for duplication leaves his badge number so we can keep track of the photographs. In your case, I guess I could take your P.I. number, so we can keep track of the photos that way."

"Thank you." Kat handed her P.I badge over to the clerk so she could write the number down on her paperwork. The clerk placed the photos in a manila envelope and handed both the photos, and Kat's badge back to her.

"I'll have the originals back to you in a few days," she told the clerk.

CHAPTER EIGHT

T raffic was building when she reached the west side drive along the Pacific Ocean, so she pulled off at the first intersection, and drove over to the water where one of her favorite food joints was located. There was a large sign over the small drive-in. It simply read, 'BENNIES', and was the best hamburger joint in San Francisco.

She dropped off the photos she wanted copied at the same shop that had developed her photos of the dead woman's wrist and ankles. The owner of the shop told her the copies would be ready in two days.

She left the shop and drove toward the mansion. It was across town, but the traffic had thinned slightly from the noontime rush. The handyman-gardener was working in the mansion's flower beds along its side.

Kat walked over to him after she had parked in the small employee parking area. She stood craning her head back to look up at him. He was the tallest man she had ever stood next to. She raised her hand to shake his hand. He took his gardening glove from his huge hand and took her hand in his. Kat's hand disappeared in his.

"My name's Kat McNally, what's your name?"

"Name's Leroy Miss, Leroy Wilkins."

Kat showed him her credentials and told him, "I'm helping Mrs. Robinson with her desire to bring a quick and just conclusion to finding the person that murdered her maid, Gayle Windsor. I would like to ask you some questions about how you found the maid dead in her bath, and what led you to check on her initially."

"It was a Wednesday. A normal work day at the mansion for me. I work three days a week here and three days a week at another place a few blocks from here. I came here worried about the trees and taller plants around the mansion. It was the morning after that bad thunder and lightning storm came through here. It didn't have any hail with it, but the wind was something furious. I'm still repairing the damage from that storm."

"What caught your attention that concerned you? The first thing," she asked him.

"It was the door that opens on the hallway to where the maid lives. It was standing part ways open. I mean it was open enough to make me wonder if it had been left that way on purpose by the maid, or if it was damaged in some way from the storm. I worked around the bathhouse at the swimming pool, and kept an eye on the door for a while. The maid didn't come to close it, so I figured maybe she didn't know it was open. I went over to check the door. It looked alright to me, but you know, the latch on that door was never a good one. I meant to change it, but I never got around to it."

"What made you go inside the maid's quarters to check on her?"

"When I opened the door wider to check on the latch I saw some water, and in a few small places it had a tinge of red. I figured the water came from the door being open, and the blowing rain had come into the hallway, but I wasn't sure about the red colored looking stuff. I went a few steps inside the hallway to see if the water was farther down the hall. I couldn't, for the life of me, figure out what the red tinge was or how it got there. I went to the maid's door; the water and red tinge were even more visible there from under the door. I could see the water flowing from under the door. I knocked on the door several times; when no one came to the door, I tried the door knob. The door swung open into the flooding living room. I went right to the bathroom. That's when I saw the body in the bathtub with the water running over the side and flooding everything. There was blood all over the bathtub, the floor, everywhere. I ran to the phone in the living room and called the police. I went back outside, and ran to the front of the mansion to direct the police to the maid's quarters when they came."

"Did you notice anything else that you didn't think of to tell the police, Leroy?"

"I did notice something the next day, but haven't got around to talking with the police again. They stopped coming after the people came to photograph everything. The old gate at the back of the property that opens to a parking area for the park on the hill was standing open. The latch has been pried off the gate and its connecting post. It was something new to me. I don't ever remember that gate being open, particularly with the latch pried off and on the ground."

"That's very interesting Leroy. Can you think of anything else? How did Mrs. Robinson take the murder of her maid?" Kat asked.

"Mrs. Robinson wasn't here when the murder happened. She was off on some trip somewhere. She travels around a lot, I think."

"I mean when she came home from her trip? How was she acting?"

"I don't know Miss Kat. I like my job and I need the money to live on."

"What you tell me, will remain with me, Leroy. It's important for me to know how the people that were around the maid reacted to her murder."

"Okay, I'll trust you. Please don't tell anyone what I say. I'll deny everything."

"I won't tell a soul! I promise!"

"She was very angry that it happened, like she thought it was my fault that I let something like that happen at her mansion. She was in one of her terrible rages when she came to talk with me. She goes into those rage without anyone knowing why. I know she drinks a lot. The empty bottles of vodka stack up in the trash quickly, and the medicine containers with the labels for valium show up in the trash frequently as well. The bottles have different doctor's names on them. I'm afraid of her, so I stay out of her way. The only reason I know about the vodka and valium is that I am responsible for bagging, and putting out the trash on pickup days."

"You say you're afraid of her?"

"Yes, I am afraid of her. When she is in one of her rages she is, I believe, capable of anything," Leroy told her.

She told him she appreciated him telling her about how he had found the maid, and what he had seen at, or near, the murder site.

Kat walked back to her car, and sat there thinking for a few minutes before she headed off to her taekwondo class she was teaching. She had felt uneasy at her interview with Mrs. Robinson; it was something about the answers she gave her, and the Bloody Mary, and half-empty bottle of vodka. It was the sudden change in her personality from anger to calm, and then back to confrontational. Kat didn't understand why she had started looking into the suicide of her husband, but now she knew. Two totally different people, at two different times, had told her the same thing. Mrs. Robinson had rages that scared the living day-lights out of the people that were around her. Maybe her initial sense about Mrs. Robinson was right. She could continue that personal investigation into the husband's suicide, and Mrs. Robinson's role in it, while she dug around trying to find the maid's killer. She knew she could handle the search for truth about both unknowns, the murder and the suicide. She had to wait another day for the photo copies, so she went back to her apartment to spend some time on the weird message she received from Steve Henry.

CHAPTER NINE

Mrs. Robinson was madder than hell that the stupid little girl she had hired for show hadn't contacted her yet. It had been over a month since she had hired her. Why was she so upset about not hearing from the little bitch, after all, she was paying her to be the inept foul that she certainly was. That thought made her chuckle to herself. She poured another glass of vodka over ice with a twist of lime. She walked around the empty interior of the mansion, and stopped at the floor to ceiling metal door in the hallway to her bedroom. It was made to look like the wall, and had a hidden key lock for secrecy. She went to her bedroom to get the key to the hidden lock, and was half-way back to the secret room door when she stopped so quickly some of her drink spilled from her frosty tumbler. She wasn't in the mood to go in the pleasure room alone. She tossed off the rest of her drink, and went to change her clothes. She thought of the cretin she had hired for the fake investigation, and then threw the thought aside. There was no way she would learn about the secret door.

She dressed in tight fitting jeans and a linen, short sleeve blouse. The blouse was unbuttoned to let the full effect of her still great figure stimulate the young men and women that frequented the Ship's Bell. The Ship's Bell was known for its two dance floors; the back patio that had a view of the bay, and flirtatious young waiters and waitresses and the western bar with wait staff dressed in minuscule shorts and western design crop tops. The bar was set up like a sailing ship's deck, with a long, polished wood bar and worn wood floors. There were captain's chairs around tables that were made to look like map and chart tables from a sea captain's quarters. There were booths along the far wall in the saloon area that were made to look like berths on a ship with one side open for easy entry. It was frequented by young men and women that came to be part of the flower child culture for a night or two, and then went back to their other lives. A few always stayed and became part of the burgeoning drug culture. It was a place where the young came to mingle; share some smoke, speed or blow, and if they got lucky, hump something that was prime.

The Ship's Bell was Mrs. Robinson's new hunting ground!

She sat at the end of the long bar where she could watch the front door, without seeming to care who came in or who left the bar. The two dance floors were separated from the bar area with an open archway to each one. Each dance area played different types of music. She told the bartender she wanted a vodka on the rocks with a twist of lime. When he had placed a tumbler full of the clear liquor in front of her, she lighted a cigarette and started looking the young men and women over. She sat there like a lioness eyeing her pray.

She caught a well put together young man checking her out from the far side of the bar. He was standing by the archway to the western music dance room. She took a sip of her drink and looked again; over the edge of her tumbler, at the tall, dark haired, broad shouldered, well-toned, young man.

The young man, with deep blue eyes made a very small nod when the woman at the end of the bar looked at him the second time over the edge of her drink. She had a wisp of smoke curl up from her cigarette, making him think of the movie Casablanca. He thought it was a really sexy movie, with Bogart and Ingrid Bergman heating up the night. He had a feeling the woman at the end of the bar was hungry for a man. 'Why not him?'

He had smoked a joint before he came to the bar. It helped him relax and be more debonair, he thought. The woman at the end of the bar looked like she would like a seasoned young man and he was that! He had always been able to have sex with any woman he decided he wanted. It was something that made him who he was. He didn't wait any longer, he walked in the direction of the woman at the end of the bar doing his best impression of John Wayne walking up to a beautiful woman.

Mrs. Robinson knew the moment her pry left the archway to the dance floor that she was going to be able to control him, easily. She had to resist the urge to beckon him to come to her. She was steeped in the thrill of the moment. It was always the same when she captured a new lover. She couldn't remember the number of men that she had used for her satisfaction, but it didn't matter now. This young man was going to be easy for her to dominate!

The young man came to the corner of the bar, and stood there looking across the room at nothing.

Mrs. Robinson smiled and said to him, "Why don't we take one the booths so we can get to know each other?"

The young, good-looking man was startled by her suggestion. It took a moment for him to adjust to the sexy woman next to him, when she took control of the fragile meeting process that he was used to working through.

He picked up his drink, and helped her off her bar stool. He walked behind her toward one of the berth booths across the room. His heart was pounding in his chest as he watched her walk across the room in her tight Levi 501 jeans. She sat down in a booth and he sat down across from her.

"My name's Myra," Mrs. Robinson said in a soft, throaty voice.

"Mine is Jack, Myra. Nice to know you." Jack told her in a warm and inviting voice from deep in his chest.

"I'm glad you came over to me. I was watching you walk over. You move in a very sexy way. Did you know that Jack?"

"I was thinking the same thing, as I followed you over to the booth, just now," Jack answered her.

She reached across the booth's narrow table, and lightly touched Andrew's hand. "Would you call a waitress over: I'd like another drink."

Jack kept his hand where it was, and signaled with his free hand to a waitress that was standing by the bar, waiting for someone to wave her over to order more drinks. The waitress asked Mrs. Robinson what she was drinking, and when she had her drink order she turned to Jack.

"I'd like a Chivas and soda."

The waitress nodded and went to the bartender to fill their order. When she came back with their drinks, Mrs. Robinson waited for Jack to pay for them. The waitress left the booth, and went back to her place by the bar looking for anyone else that needed another drink.

"I think we should celebrate our meeting. It could turn into something very special for both of us."

Mrs. Robinson reached into her jean's pocket, and pulled out a small gold case with a tiny gold spoon attached to it. "I'm going to have a bump. I'd like for you to join me."

Jack looked around the bar to see if anyone was paying any attention to them. No one cared what they were doing in the darken booth area. Mrs. Robinson opened the small gold case, and scooped some of the white powder it held into the tiny gold spoon. She bent over the table slightly and sniffed the powder into her nose, expertly. She pushed the gold case toward Jack, and he followed her lead. Mrs. Robinson, the woman that called herself Myra, watched as the young man did the first thing that she wanted him to do. She found it exhilarating that he was taking the first step to her total control over him!

Mrs. Robinson asked Jack about himself, and then thought of what she could offer him to get him to the mansion. She found out he had taken a bus from a small town south of San Francisco to keep from having a car to worry about while he was enjoying himself around the Haight-Ashbury area of San Francisco. He had his travel bag behind the bar, since he hadn't checked into a hotel nearby.

He was perfect! No one would miss him or for that matter find him. She took her sandals off and carefully moved her toes over to the cuff of Jack's pants and lightly touched his leg with them. Jack sat very still for a moment and then relaxed. She started describing the private swimming pool at the mansion, and how much fun it would be to have a man like him share it with her.

She reached over the table and pulled him closer to her. She whispered in his ear, "get your bag and let's go enjoy the pool. You can stay at my place while you're in town. There's plenty of room."

She kept her mouth close to his ear and lightly breathed into it. She could feel him warming up to her. She flicked the tip of her tongue into his ear. He looked kind of confused, but when she said softly, "get your bag, I need to be alone with you, quickly." He scooted out of the booth and adjusted his crotch: he was starting to get an erection. Mrs. Robinson was pleased when she saw him adjust himself. She went to the entrance of the bar and waited for him.

Mrs. Robinson parked at the side of the mansion in the private parking area. She took Jack by the hand and led him by the hand to the pool area. She quickly turned on the swimming pool lights, leaving the area lights off. She picked up a couple of beach towels and a bottle of Tequila from a shelf in the cabana.

Jack was setting on the edge of the pool with his shoes and socks off and his feet in the water. Mrs. Robinson gave him a shot glass and poured it full of Tequila. She gave a sexy, throaty laugh when he shuddered from taking the entire shot down at one time. He looked up at her standing there with the bottle of Tequila in her hand. She tipped her head back, and put the bottle to her lips. She took two long pulls on the bottle and sat it behind her. She stood at the edge of the pool in front of Jack and started unbuttoning the rest of her blouse. She was enjoying how Jack was watching her. She had her blouse unbuttoned and pushed the sides back, exposing her perfectly formed breast to Jack. He reached behind him and took a slug from the Tequila bottle as well.

Mrs. Robinson let him take a good look, and then one by one began to unbutton the front of her Levi 101 jeans. She pushed them down around her hips and stopped. She smiled and said, "Jack, my jeans are tight. Will you help me push them down so I can go in the pool?"

"He stood at the edge of the pool, and pushed slowly down on the edges of her jeans, while Mrs. Robinson bent over him and kissed him in the ear again. She didn't have any panties on when he had pushed the jeans to her ankles. She kicked them off, and they flew into the pool. She couldn't believe she was so wet. It was starting to run down the inside of her thighs. She smiled at him, and told him she was going in the pool. She reached down and moved his erection over a bit.

She went to the nearby steps that went into the pool, and walked slowly into the pool, letting Jack get his eyes full. She moved along the edge of the pool and stopped by him.

"Take your clothes off. The water's great, and we need to do something about that huge hard- on that is about to rip a whole in your pants," she laughed, and swam to the other side of the pool.

When Jack swam up in front of her, she couldn't wait any longer. She took his throbbing erection in her hand, and worked the length of it. She wanted it thrust into her. She put her arms over his shoulders, and pulled up so she could feel his erection against her. She used one hand to slide his hard-on into her. She opened her mouth and let out a moan, as she opened herself to him, and closed her mouth over his with another moan. She had a quick orgasm and he thrust into her again. It wasn't something that had happened for a long, long time. She had another quick orgasm. She was screaming in delight. It took several more thrust before she had another orgasm. Her body felt like it was leaving her soul behind. He continued to thrust into her until she had another and another orgasm. She thought she might die and then he came. It was an explosion. She could feel the throbbing of his hard-on. It began to lose its size, but then she felt him reach down in the water and start to tap lightly on her clit. He moved it gently from side to side and then tapped more quickly. She was going to climax again.

OH, OOHH, OOOHHH! She came again, and again until she fainted in his arms. Jack pulled her to the steps at the edge of the pool, and laid her on her beach towel. He laid on his beach towel and started to pass out. He thought of his high school teacher that had taught him about sex, and its pleasures when he stayed after school,

95

or when she picked him up at his house to help him with his homework.

After three days of sex in the kitchen, the bedroom, and every other room on the first floor of the mansion, Mrs. Robinson grew tired of the same old thing. It was time to introduce Jack to what was behind the hidden door in the hallway.

CHAPTER TEN

The sheet of typing paper laid in front of Kat: staring back at her like it had a life of its own. No matter how she tried to apply her skills of communication and spelling; nothing she did with the two words that the old maid, Mrs. Henry, had scribbled made any sense. She walked around the apartment, trying to clear her mind.

Sometimes, when she went running by the bay, things she wanted to figure out began to crystallize into concrete actions she needed to initiate. She left the paper with all her scrawling on it and went to change into her running shorts and top. She slipped into her comfortably worn running shoes and left for the path, where she hoped she would find the answers to Mrs. Henry's puzzle.

The afternoon was clear with only white cotton ball clouds being pushed across the sky from the Pacific Ocean. She stretched at the rails that lined the cliff edge of the bay, at the beginning of the trail and started her run.

She ran with her mind working on the puzzle to the turn-around area. The end of the trail was on a high point that gave her a view of San Francisco bay and Alcatraz island. She looked out over the bay and watched a ship headed for the Golden Gate bridge. She turned around and looked to the east. She could see Sather tower, better known as the Campanile, on the campus of U.C. Berkeley in the distance. The tower reminded her of how pretty the campus was in the day time: she only saw it at night. She finished her run, but the only thing it had done was make her feel like the answer to the puzzle was trying to break through to her consciousness: there was no concrete answer.

She went back to her apartment and worked on her assignments for the following week for the courses at Berkeley. She clinched her teeth, shook her head to clear it, and started to work on her course assignments using all her will power.

The next morning was another California beautiful day. Kat had breakfast of cereal and a couple of cups of coffee with a touch of sugar. She never did learn to drink sugarless coffee when she was in the army. She left the dishes in the sink and checked the message light before leaving her apartment. It wasn't blinking.

The morning traffic was bumper to bumper on the San Francisco-Oakland bay bridge. Her trip to the photography shop was a long one. She arrived after the shop had opened for business. The owner of the shop came to the counter with an odd look on his face.

Something between an upset stomach, and a bad case of gas. Kat handed him her claim ticket, wondering what was bothering him. He reached under the counter, and brought out a film package that had her name on it. She paid the owner for the copies and started to leave.

The owner of the shop cleared his throat loudly and told her, "I don't know what you do for a living, but when you bring in photographs of dead men with their heads blown apart you must tell me. I found the young woman that runs my copier passed out and laying on the floor. She had started making the copies of the photos you wanted copied. I ended up doing the copying myself, and the photos bothered me as well."

"Those photographs are police property as you can see printed on the margin of each photo. I assumed you would see that and figure there might be some gruesome photos included in them. I'll make sure that I let you know when there are possibly troubling photos, so you can plan accordingly."

"Doesn't the police department have a photo lab of their own?" He asked.

"I'm not with the police department. I'm a private investigator. I need to have photos copied sometimes when I'm on a case. I'll warn you in advance about any photos that might be disturbing to a civilian."

"Please do that. I'll run the film through the copier myself. It's a tough job you have picked for yourself," he said.

"Someone's got to keep the wolves at bay. I figure I'm helping the average citizen, as well as, the police department. If I discover a person that is breaking the law, I think I have kept them from harming an innocent person out in society," she told him.

She left the photography shop understanding the owner and his sensitivities, but even more determined to continue her work. She was good at her profession!

The message light wasn't blinking when she opened her front door. She tossed the photo package onto a small table by the front door and went across the living room to her desk. She called a telephone operator and got the area code and number in San Antonio for the headquarters of the police department. She made a call to the main switchboard at the police department and asked to be connected to Lieutenant Ben Cooper. She reached a desk sergeant that told her the Lieutenant was out of the office. The sergeant told her to would leave her name and phone number, he would put a note on the Lieutenant's desk to return her call.

Kat sat at her desk tapping the point of a ball point pen on a yellow legal pad that she used to keep her case ideas on. She hated to waste time particularly when there was a killer running loose. The way she had it figured, the maid's murder might not be a one-off occurrence.

She dropped her pen and pulled her note pad from her hip pocket. Close to the top of the list was to talk with a weapons expert. She had to wait for Ben Cooper to call back and patience was not one of her better points. She had tried running to clear the fog: that didn't help. She decided to take a drive, sometimes that helped clear the air for her.

On her way out of the front door she saw the package containing the suicide photos on the narrow stand. She started to take the package to her desk and carefully check them over; for what she didn't know. The photos were gruesome. No wonder the clerk fainted at the photography shop. She noticed on the second to last photo that the Walther PPK pistol that was supposedly used by George C. Robinson was nestled in his right hand. She discounted the conclusion that the police report stated. How did they know if that was the gun that he used to kill himself? Maybe they were able to take the slug, and compare the rifling on it to that of the pistol in his hand. That would be the normal way, but who knew what steps they took when the suicide with that pistol was so obvious. She had a slight chill at her neck when she realized what she was thinking, but then, the police did make mistakes. She checked the last photo and for some reason went back to the prior photo that showed the pistol in the right hand of George C. Robinson. She felt there was something odd about the photo, but she couldn't figure out what it was. She sat the photos aside and started back to the front door. Sometimes, when she couldn't drag the answer from her mind she would leave it to germinate for a while.

CHAPTER ELEVEN

I t didn't take long for Mrs. Robinson to finish with the young
man from the Ship's Bell bar. She was more enraged than she
had been in years. She knew what was causing her aggravation,
it was that woman P.I she hired. She was to report to her on a regular
basis. It had been weeks and still no information from her. She
needed to know what she was accomplishing. If it was something
that had to do with her, she needed to tell her to stop what she was
doing or do some miss-direction. She couldn't fire her. If it became
necessary, she could hire the Mafia that hung out at the water front
to take care of her. That idea, even though it just occurred to her,
made her apprehension quieten down. She couldn't afford to have
the proverbial can of worms opened.

She made herself another vodka, ice and lime, and drank half of it
down in one long slug. She decided to spend a few hours driving
around the port area to try spotting some of the local Mafia members
that hung out down there. The Family was known to be active in the
port area. They were in her newspaper frequently. She finished her

drink, and made a roadie to take with her in the car. She needed some relief from all the stress she was enduring. She wanted to find a young man at a bar in the port area and bring him home with her. That might help too. The last one didn't last as long as she would have liked.

The port area of the San Francisco area was known as the Embarcadero, Spanish for pier, or in the case of San Francisco, pier area. She parked her car near the ferry pier and walked along the street that went in front of the piers on the east side of the peninsula. She went from pier to pier and from bar to bar, looking for someone that looked like a good candidate. She went into a saloon looking place that was also an Italian restaurant called Gambino's. She sat at the bar and ordered a double shot of vodka on the rocks with a twist of lime.

When the drink came she tried to start a conversation with the burly man acting as a bartender. His name was Frank: it was on his name tag.

"I've been looking for an authentic Italian restaurant in the Embarcadero area for a while. I hope this one will have good food. The last few I've tried didn't match the food I've eaten while in Italy," she told Frank.

"Do you know about the Family?" Frank asked her in a superior sort of way.

"I've heard that name mentioned from time to time and also in the newspapers," she answered.

"This restaurant is their favorite hangout when near the port area!" The bartender offered in a hushed voice. "They know good Italian cuisine!"

"I have pressing business to take care of now. If you would tell me what hours you work, I would like to come back, and have another drink with you. Maybe you could introduce me to some members of the Family. Would you do that for me? It would be a big thing for me to be able to say I know a member of the mob."

She put a fifty-dollar bill on the bar as a tip.

"Depends on which ones are here. I could do that with a soldier. Not a Capo. We have customers come in frequently and ask to meet a member of the Family. Like I said, a soldier is okay, asking to meet a boss is asking for trouble!" Frank told her as he picked up the fifty and stuffed it in his shirt pocket.

"You don't happen to know what restaurants or bars the crews from foreign ships frequent?" She asked him as she scooted her barstool back.

"That depends, as well. From what I have noticed since starting work here, they tend to go to restaurants that serve food that they normally get at home. As far as bars are concerned, they generally go to bars in pairs or small groups. They want to enjoy speaking their own language, while drinking American liquor."

She left Gambino's and drove slowly along the foreign freight piers watching for men to follow to a local bar. She watched several oriental men talking at the end of a pier. Both looked like ship's officers by the uniforms they were wearing. That gave her an idea. Chinatown was centrally located a few short blocks from the Embarcadero. She liked having an international flavor in her men from time to time. In fact, she went on international trips for that reason, at least once every six months. She was concerned when the woman P.I wanted to see her passport; she didn't want the P.I. to notice her frequent trips to foreign countries. Chinatown would offer men that fit right into her obsessions.

She turned toward Jackson Square and drove pass the financial district on Broadway. She went down Kearny street to Bush street. Dragon's Gate, the front entrance to Chinatown was up a few steps from there. There were large numbers of people entering and leaving the Dragon's Gate. Chinatown would be the perfect place to find a man of her choice. She drove back to the mansion to change clothes and wait for dark. Finding the right man in a crowded bar at night would be ideal. She wondered why she hadn't thought of Chinatown earlier. No matter, she fantasized about her new inspiration on the way to the mansion.

Mrs. Robinson hadn't been that excited about a potential conquest, since the last time she went to Europe to satisfy her international tastes. She showered, put on her favorite body lotion and a touch of fragrance, and dressed in a seductive evening dress that she thought would catch men's eyes when they saw her. The sun was lowering slightly in the west, casting its red, yellow and orange spears across the thin clouds over the Pacific Ocean when Mrs. Robinson left her mansion, and started off on her hunt for her newest prey. She parked her car a block away from Chinatown, and used a local entrance into the area. She walked around looking at each bar and restaurant for the one she wanted to try first. It didn't usually take but one stop for her to locate a good specimen to take back to the mansion with her.

A place at a corner on Beckett street caught her eye. The front door was open; it was dark inside and crowed. There was an outdoor patio area where you could drink, eat and watch, as other visitors made their way around Chinatown. She found a seat at the bar and ordered her usual vodka, ice, and slice of lime. It wasn't a large bar. The bartenders and waitresses were all young, good-looking Orientals. She took a sip of her drink when it came and turned to watch the close-knit group of partiers. She lit a cigarette and placed it in an ashtray on the bar. She noticed a man sitting at a table for four in the corner of the restaurant. He appeared to be alone. She continued to watch the other people that were standing around the bar, talking and laughing.

The man at the corner table had looked in Mrs. Robinson's direction twice while she watched the women and men with only elbow room, mingle with each other, like they were long-lost old friends. Mrs. Robinson noticed the man at the corner table was dressed better than most others in the bar. She wondered if he might be a ship's officer or an international traveler. There was only on way to find out. She ordered another drink, when it came she left her seat at the bar. She made her way through the crowd to the table in the corner and said to the stranger at the table, "mind if I sit down?"

"Please do."

She took a seat next to him facing the crowd and said, "I've been watching you for a while. "You're alone?"

"I am from ship. I don't know people here. I come to enjoy drink and rest. Sorry for my poor English."

"You speak English well. What is your native tongue?"

"What does word tongue mean?"

"It's another way to say language."

"Ah, my native tongue is Mandarin," the Chinese man smiled when he asked, "what is your tongue?"

Mrs. Robinson smiled and told him she spoke English. She asked if he would like another drink.

"I like another drink," he said.

They looked for a waitress for few moments; they all seemed to be busy. She told him she would go to the bar, and get their drinks. "What do you drink?" She asked.

"I learned to drink scotch and soda."

"Scotch and soda, it is. I'll be right back."

"By the way, my name is Myra, what's your name?"

"My name is Lei. Mean's thunder in English," he said proudly.

She made her way back to the bar and asked for another drink for her and a scotch and soda for her friend. She reached into her tiny purse to get the money to pay for the drinks. She paid with a twenty-dollar bill. The bartender left to make change; Mrs. Robinson took a small peach colored pill from her tiny purse and dropped it into the scotch and soda.

Lei was slightly unstable when they left the bar together. Mrs. Robinson had hooked her arm though his to help steady him. She walked him the short distance to her car, and drove him to the mansion.

Lei took a seat on a comfortable, stuffed love seat that faced a huge fireplace while Mrs. Robinson made two more drinks. She wanted the man compliant, but not passed out. They sat snuggling on the love seat, sipping on their drinks between kisses, and feeling each other up for a short time. Lei had the top of her dress down and was kissing her nipples, it was making Mrs. Robinson want him to pull up the bottom of her evening dress and use his finger on her. That would be a good start for her. Like he was reading her mind, his hand went slowly down her evening dress, and pulled the edge of her dress up to her waist. He was delighted to find that she had no panties under it. He didn't use his finger to enter her, he felt along the lips of her vagina and found its hood. He began slow movements around the edges of her Clitoral hood, then stopped suddenly for a couple of seconds and did the same thing again, but in reverse. He could feel the tiny clitoris beginning to swell from the increase in blood to it. He started to lightly tap on it. Then he changed the frequency of the taps, then the force of the taps, until he knew which she liked the best. She pushed hard at his finger, and waited in a stressed position for a minute. She rested for a moment, and then she suggested they go to her boudoir so Lei could show her some new Chinese positions. He was very excited to do exactly what she wanted which happened to be what he wanted as well!

Lei helped Mrs. Robinson to settle into a position she had never experienced, the second time they had sex. It wasn't long before she reached orgasm and a moment after she felt a second, more deep orgasm. The one that followed the second orgasm made her feel like the life was being sucked out of her. She was exhausted when Lei took himself away from her. He was aware of the multiple orgasm that Mrs. Robinson had experienced, but he was use to women reaching super orgasms in the position he had shown her.

They didn't say anything to each other; both were deep in their own thoughts. Mrs. Robinson was thinking of Lei in one of her favorite positions, but that would happen later!

CHAPTER TWELVE

Blink, blink, blink! The damned message light on Kat's recorder was going wild when she opened her front door. She walked across her living room to the recorder and hit the play button. It was Lieutenant Ben Cooper, returning her call. She wrote down the number that he left in the message and then dialed it. The phone rang several times and was picked up.

"This is Lieutenant Cooper."

"Lieutenant Cooper this is Kat McNally in San Francisco. My father Shay McNally recommended that I call you."

"Shay McNally! How is he doing? I heard he had retired from the force a while back."

"He's fine Lieutenant. He told me you were the best ballistics man anywhere. I'm in need of information about a suicide pistol. I hope you can take a few minutes to tell me about the Walther PPK.

"Are you on the force, now that your father has retired?"

"No, sir. I went another way. I'm a licensed Private Investigator."

"That's good. Please call me Ben."

"I will Ben and my name is Kat."

"What caliber is the PPK?"

".380."

"The Walther PPK is known as a blowback-operated weapon. I'll tell you about it without using too many technical terms, but if I lose you tell me to explain, okay?"

"That'll be fine, Ben."

"A blow-back semi-automatic pistol operates by using the energy of the expanding gas from a fired bullet to load the next round in the chamber and cock the weapon. It helps hit what you're shooting at to hold it with two hands."

"The one I'm dealing with was used apparently with one hand for a shot in his mouth through the top of his head and was still in his right hand when he hit the floor."

"San Antonio police have actually done a study on head shot suicides. Their study indicated that seventy-five percent of the time the pistol that was used fell several feet from the body. That was with revolvers and other semi-automatic pistols. With the Walther PPK, the recoil would make it loosen in the dead person's hand. If the dead person fell to a floor, or to the ground, the hand used to hold the pistol would be open, not closed. With that and the blowback, the pistol would fly a short distance from the hand/body. The percentage of the PPK being away from the body and out of the body's hand would go close to one hundred percent. That would mean someone had to place the pistol in the hand of the body they had murdered, making it look like a bonified suicide."

"Hot damn, that confirms what I was suspicious about. The suicide photo of the body has the PPK laying loose in the man's hand," she told him.

"The chances of that happening are nil, almost impossible." Ben told her.

"Thanks for helping me, Ben and I'll tell dad that you asked about him."

"That's great Kat, and if you ever need my help again, you have my phone number now."

"I'll keep that in mind, Ben, and thanks so much."

"You're welcome and keep your head down!"

Kat pushed her chair back, and started to pace the living room. What Ben had told her was another piece of a very baffling puzzle. Ben had indicated there was basically zero chance of the suicide weapon staying in the dead man's hand. The copy of the photo that she had, showed the gun in his hand. What was odd about the photo? The police had missed it. She couldn't put her finger on what the odd thing was, so she took that photo from the rest of the suicide photos, and sat down at her desk to look it over carefully. It was there, somewhere on the photo, an oddity that wouldn't be quickly noticed. Something that she hadn't looked for in the suicide record were figure prints on the pistol, but, of course, the gun was registered to Mrs. Robinson, and the weapon should have her prints on it, as well as, Mr. Robinson's. She put a note in her pad to check the suicide record one more time, looking for any lab reports that may indicate who handled the pistol when it was used by Mr. Robinson to commit suicide.

Kat went to her classes that evening. She was shocked when she pulled into the student parking area and parked. She had driven to the university crunching all the little facts that she had gathered so far about the murder of the Gayle Pauline Windsor. For all the driving around the state of California and the search and research she had been able to complete or was in the process of completing, she seemed to be gathering circumstantial knowledge of Mrs. Robinson, without trying to do so. Nothing she had discovered helped with the murder. It was showing that Mrs. Robinson was an out-right liar: there was nothing illegal about that. She tried to clear her mind of all the questions that were piling up. Did Mrs. Robinson have something to do with the murder of the young maid. Had she been hired as misdirection away from her? She took off her backpack, sat down at her assigned seat with her psych book open. It was time to switch gears!

Kat hit her pillow for the umpteenth time, and glanced at the clock looking back at her on a nightstand a few inches from her face. This was a bad one. She had trouble sleeping on a regular basis. She had realized when she was in the army that her brain liked to work at night as much as it did in the daylight hours. She knew what was keeping her awake, but had tried to get some sleep, instead of chasing ghosts around on a bad black and white police crime photo. She gave up when she read the time on the bedside clock. It was 2:18 a.m. She threw back her cover and went into the kitchen to brew some coffee. She knew from experience that she would be awake until she figured out what was wrong with the photograph.

She turned the adjustable gooseneck table lamp on, and moved it so she could see the stack of police photos on the edge of her desk. She found the photo that was zeroed in on the hand of the body and the Walther PPK that filled it. She positioned the gooseneck lamp over the photo that she had placed in front of her chair at the table and walked over to her kitchen counter to get her first cup of camp coffee. In the army it was said to be strong enough to float a combat boot.

Kat sat the steaming cup of coffee to the right side of the base of her lamp and pulled a shallow drawer open from the desk. She shuffled things around until she found what she looking for trapped in the very back. She closed the drawer and put the magnifying glass next to the photo. She scanned over the photo with the magnifying glass moving it very slowly from point to point on the photo. When she had negotiated the entire photo, she found nothing that caught her eye. In her exhausted sleeplessness her anger took over; she swept the photo, magnifying glass, and lamp off the desk in one quick sweep of her hand and arm. She stood up and paced around the small living room about to blow her stack. She grabbed her coffee cup as she passed the mess she had made at her deskj and filled it again with black, strong coffee.

She took the fresh coffee to her desk and started picking up the mess she had made. When she put the photograph of the gun in the dead man's hand back on the desk she glanced at it and then looked again. The photo was upside down, but she immediately saw what was wrong in the photograph. How the hell had all the police, and now her, miss such a simple screw up!

"That was it!" She grabbed the magnifying glass, and looked at the spot on the photo that held her attention. She smiled to herself and realized what was wrong in the photo had opened up a can of worms if it turned out to be right.

She knew she wasn't going to sleep after figuring out what had been bothering her about the photo. She walked with a fresh new step into her bedroom and dressed. There was an all-night Mexican restaurant a short trip away; she was going to have her favorite breakfast to celebrate.

While she was eating her breakfast, she thought of something else that she should have looked at in the photographs of the suicide. There was a photograph, she remembered, of fingerprints that were taken from the Walther PPK, the weapon that was the apparent suicide weapon. She broke the last of her pan dulce and added fresh cream butter and honey to both halves. She had another cup of coffee and finished the two halves of the sweet biscuit. Her breakfast was enough to keep her running for the entire day.

She left the all-night restaurant and drove back to her apartment. She was going to check the prints out one more time before making the drive to the Globe Newspaper.

She grabbed a can of Dr. Pepper from her fridge, and headed for her desk and the stack of police photos. When she was having one of the sleeplessness periods she used sugar to burn until she finally caved, then she slept for a long time. She searched through the stack until she found the two photos of the fingerprint dust on the Walther

PPK. She looked both images over carefully and then went over them with the magnifying glass. She saw the notes that were on the legend of the photos, as those of Mr. Robinson, but no other prints belonging to anyone else. She was expecting to see the prints of Mrs. Robinson on the Walther, since the gun was registered to her. That piqued her interest enough for her to make a note of it in her note pad.

It was after rush hour in the morning when Kat drove away from her apartment toward the bay bridge, and downtown San Francisco, where the Globe Newspaper headquarters were located. She parked in a nearby parking garage and went to the information desk on the ground floor of the Globe building. There was a different person at the desk than a few weeks earlier when she had been there to ask about the deceased owner's full name and date of birth. The lady at the desk this time had her gray hair up in a tight bun at the back of her head. She had those blue eyes that tell you she knew her business, and wouldn't put up with any crap.

She turned in her swivel chair to asked Kat what she wanted. Kat asked her if there was anyone that she knew that was working at the Globe when Mr. Robinson was the president and owner. The woman smiled a croaked smile and informed Kat that she might be able to help her out, if the question wasn't too specific.

"I was here a short time ago, and wanted to find out the full name of Mr. Robinson, and his date of birth. I forgot to ask if he was right or left handed," asked Kat.

"That one's easy. I was his secretary until his death. Now I'm assigned to whatever position is open for the day, week, or sometime for months. I've held almost all the non-professional jobs at the Globe over the years. The answer to your question is that he was left handed."

She had a look on her face, like she was in the past: seeing Mr. Robinson at his desk writing something important with his left hand.

Kat started to leave her, staring off into space. Her mind was racing a thousand miles an hour. Mr. Robinson was left handed. Someone had placed the Walther pistol in the wrong hand, not knowing that the gun shouldn't have been in his hand at all!

She left the older woman still staring off in the distance with that glassy look in her eyes. She went back to her car, saying to herself, "holy shit, holy shit, there might have been another murder in the Robinson mansion that no one knew about." Was she going to spill the information the lady at the newspaper had given her to her employer or not. That was the question!

She drove down several floors of the parking garage to the exit where she paid for the parking and kept the receipt as she had been doing since she had been hired by Mrs. Robinson.

She was hitting a brick wall with no sleep. She stopped at a gas station to buy
 a large cup of coffee. She sipped the coffee on her way to tell Mrs. Robinson what she had figured out, and see what her reaction would be. She checked to make sure her pistol was still riding at the small of her back.

CHAPTER THIRTEEN

Lei woke up with Mrs. Robinson doing a spoon with him. She moved her left leg over his legs, and tried to pull him closer to her. He moved from under her leg, and started to sit on the edge of the bed. It was the largest bed he had ever seen, and they had sex on every inch of it, in a multitude of different positions. She was driven to have sex in a new position each time they fucked. He felt the nails on her hands touch his back and then slowly move down until they reached his butt. The pressure she used was slight at first and then increasingly more painful until he was sure they were making bloody scratches on his back. He was worn out, but apparently his wood had a different idea. It was laying comfortable over the front of his nuggets. He could feel the very light flush of new blood that made his dick fibrate slightly. It started to come to life; like a Willow tree, and then as a young sapling, as he felt her sit up behind him, and start to rub her tits against his back, up and down, and then all around. She reached around his waist and slowly, softly moved his beginning erection up and down playing with its head at the same time. His cock quickly became engorged, and hard as the trunk of an old oak tree. She continued massaging it until she felt him shudder and his cock popped up and down from reaching his climax.

They rested like that for a few minutes, when Lei told her it was time he was leaving for his ship. It had to be loaded by today, and its scheduled departure time was early in the afternoon.

"Oh," she said, "but you haven't seen the exaltation palace. Let's go there now, while there's still time. We don't need to get dress and you can shower with me before you leave for your ship. You'll make it in plenty of time."

She moved to his side and walked across the large bedroom to a small decorated music box that was on her writing table. She made sure she moved sensuously for him, as she moved to the table. She turned the key at the side of the music box; music began to play. At the same time the lid to the small box sprang open. She took something from the inside of the open box and left it playing while she moved seductively back across the room to took Lei's hand. She noticed he was getting hard again. He had great stamina she thought. She walked him down the hallway from her bedroom to the bar and made two drinks; his with an added little peach colored pill.

They walked together back down the hallway to the hidden door. She slid the thin camouflaged cover off the lock and used the key to unlock the hidden door. It moved between the wooden wall studs and was essentially a hidden door. She took Lei's hand, and led him into an ornate iron cage that was only big enough for them to stand against each other's naked bodies. It reminded Lei of the tiny metal lifts that he had been in London and other European countries that his ship used as ports.

Mrs. Robinson had a look on her face that for some reason scared Lei. She rolled in the code to the rotary lock at the side of the cage that was behind Lei's head. She always entered the cage so her prey would not be able to see what the code was for the one-story elevator. It jerked to a start, and in a few short seconds stopped a floor below the main floor of the mansion with another jerk. She reached behind Lei's head and push the combination to open the back door of the tiny wrought iron lift. The door slide into the wall, like the one on the main floor of the mansion.

Mrs. Robinson took Lei's hand and moved into the exaltation palace. Lei was aghast at what he saw before him. The door to the tiny lift silently closed behind him. He didn't hear the lock click close.

CHAPTER FOURTEEN

K at looked at the clock on her bedside table. The time was
10:14 a.m. She sat straight up in bed and looked out her
bedroom window. The sun was shining brightly across
the landscape and other apartment buildings in the area. Her problem
was she didn't know what damn day it was. She had been exhausted
from lack of sleep and working only on coffee when she finally made
it back to her apartment. She went directly to her bedroom, then laid
down on her bed with all her clothes on to take a quick recharge nap.

The coffee pot was waiting for her in the kitchen. She dumped in
enough coffee to make it stronger than normal, which was usually
like Atlas holding up the world. She shuffled over the tiny desk, and
dialed the time and date number. A female voice told her the exact
time and date. It was worse than Kat had thought. The recharge nap
lasted for twenty-four hours, a new record for her.

There were so many things that she needed to do. She checked a
calendar on the fridge door where she kept appointments and

important notes. There was a note in red for the day's date. She felt a sudden jolt and wished she hadn't slept so long, but it wasn't as bad as that guy in the story that slept for twenty years! What the hell was she going to do? She'd have to put everything aside, even her work on the murder case!

The semester final exam for her Tuesday night psych class was that night. She poured a stiff mug of coffee and took a drink. She pulled the course book from her backpack and the notes she had made along the way in the semester. She was going to cram for the exam, that was her only chance to pass the course that she had been shoving to the side while she was busy digging into all things Mrs. Robinson.

Her cramming session went slowly, but the hours went rapidly down the drain. She stopped for a pit stop; some left over pizza that had been in the fridge since Jesus was a little boy, and a can of Dr. Pepper, throughout the day. When it was time to head over to the class to take the exam, she had bee's buzzing around in her head instead of feeling ready for it.

The exam was short answer, matching and fill in the blank. She was the last one in the classroom when the professor came to her and told her the time for taking the test had expired. Kat felt like she had expired; not the time for the exam. She left the classroom feeling like pulling her hair out but thought better of it when she was sitting in her car. She knew what the problem was. She had let the murder case take over her life. The psych course was finished, she had one more final on Thursday night, and then she could go full throttle ahead.

It was early Friday morning, both the exams were finished and Kat thought she might be finished at the university if she did as bad as she thought she had on each of the exams.

Traffic was heavy early on Friday morning going across the bay bridge into San Francisco proper. She had her radio on and was driving in the slow-moving traffic. It seemed like she was only making a few feet each time she took her foot off the brake and inched along for a foot or two, and stopped again, like a slug moves across the ground in the damp grass and undergrowth, in the not so far away forest. When she finally broke out of the downtown traffic, she was able to drive the speed limit through the city streets. She could see a wall of dark rolling clouds at the horizon. It looked like a summer pacific storm was headed for the area.

CHAPTER FIFTEEN

Lei's ship wasn't at the pier when Mrs. Robinson drove down the Embarcadero on the way to her now favorite Italian restaurant. She took comfort in knowing the large Chinese freighter had left the port for who knew where. She remembered Lei for just a moment. After all, he was one of her best sex partners ever. She parked in a lot a block down from Gambino's and walked to the restaurant. Frank wasn't behind the bar when she took the same seat at the end of the bar, and waited for the new bartender to notice her.

She asked for a menu when she ordered her drink and asked if she could be served at the bar. The bartender told her she could eat at the bar and went to make her vodka with ice and a slice of lime. He brought a menu with him when he served her the drink. She looked around the dinner area looking for Frank the bartender. Maybe he was waiting tables today. She didn't see Frank anywhere in the restaurant. That was too bad, she was looking forward to meeting a real soldier of the Mafia. She had a feeling she might need quick help from them if it was necessary to end the P.I's employment. "How cool would that be?"

She finished her drink and signaled the bartender that had gone to the other end of the bar to serve another customer. She ordered her favorite Italian dish and asked if the restaurant had Castello di Ama Chianti wine. She drank it when she made her trips to Italy. It was the best wine with Italian food.

"We do have Castello di Ama. I'll have to pull the cork on a new bottle if you decide that is the wine you want with your dinner," the bartender told her.

"I like the idea of a fresh bottle of wine. Do that for me please and I'll have a glass while I'm waiting for my dinner to be served," she answered.

The dining area was starting to fill when she checked the area the next time. She saw Frank walk through the batwing doors that went into the kitchen area. He was dressed as a waiter in dark slacks, a white shirt and a dark waist coat. He walked to the waiter at the front door to check on the most recent customers to be seated. The couple had their menus open but had nothing to drink. He quickly took two glasses of water to the booth they were sitting in and took their order. He stopped at the bar to tell the bartender what they wanted to drink and went through the batwing doors to place the couples order. He came back out and walked to the end of the bar where Mrs. Robinson sat.

"I'm glad to see you again. Are you having dinner with us tonight?" Frank asked.

"Yes, I am Frank. I thought you only worked behind the bar," she told him.

"One of the normal waiters called in ill, so I was told to be a waiter tonight. The guy behind the bar knows drinks but he hasn't ever waited tables."

"If you have someone drop in that has the connection that we talked about while I'm here, it would be a thrill for me to meet him."

"I'll keep my eye out for one."

The bartender waved him back to the other end of the bar where he had two glasses of wine ready for Frank's customers.

She finished her meal while on her third glass of the Chianti. It brought back memories of a young Italian man she had become involved with the last time she visited Naples. She had rented a villa a short way up the coast. It had a number of well-kept lawns and gardens that bordered on the cliffs of the Mediterranean Sea. The cone of Mount Vesuvius, only a few kilometers to the east hung in the sky, like a giant monster from the early ages. She had noticed a young Italian man doing the gardening and lawn care around the property. He sometimes had his shirt off while working and his firm upper body attracted her to him like a bee to a flower.

He had the body of the naked statue of David she had seen in Tuscany. She spent a week at a villa near Florence. The statue was so dramatic, so provocative, that she spent hours idly walking around the square looking from each angle at a perfect copy of a man's body. She went back to the rented villa after each time she had spent time absorbing the statue and fantasized over it until she climaxed.

The young gardener became her David as she watched him work around the villa. She starting to plan on how to have the young gardener as her David. She started going down to the pool, which was in the middle of the garden area, with only a towel over her shoulder and a white minimal top and bottom thong bikini. She was well tanned from sun bathing at her pool in San Francisco. She kept a careful eye on the young gardener while she swam and dried herself and sunbathed laying on a pool lounge chair.

The second afternoon she took off her top, and let him have a look at her perfectly formed breasts. She stood there looking around the gardens, but always keeping him in the corner of her vision. She caught him looking at her and turned to let him know she approved of him watching her. She jumped in the pool and swam in the warm water of the pool. She lost sight of him, while she was in the pool.

She pulled herself up on the edge of the pool, and dried her hair with a pool towel. She looked around the garden area for the young gardener but didn't she him. She was disappointed that she hadn't attracted him closer to the pool and her partially nude body. She wondered why he hadn't come closer to watch her? She had always been able to draw men in by exposing herself to them; by knowingly giving them an enticing look at her body.

The next day, following her morning trip to Naples to see the sights, she went to an area on the edge of the bluff that overlooked the Mediterranean Sea. There was a small terrace built under an overhanging tree and a steep set of switchback steps down to the sand beach below. She took a bucket of ice and a new bottle of vodka that she had purchased that morning in Naples to the terrace and relaxed while watching the surf roll in on the beach. She made herself a drink and stood at the edge of the bluff where the switchback steps started. She watched as a man in the Italian version of Speedo swim trunks came from an outcropping in the bluff and ran into the surf that was breaking on the sand beach. He seemed familiar to her somehow. It must be the body. It made her think of the David statue; then she realized who the man in the tiny tight Speedo was. It was the young gardener. She picked up her ice bucket and bottle of vodka and started her way down the switchback steps to the beach and the perfect male body.

She didn't speak Italian, he didn't speak English, but they did both spoke body language. For the next four days, they met on the beach, or the pool and enjoyed each other, totally. The day she was to leave the young Italian gardener didn't show up at the beach or the pool. She kept a watch out for him until she had to leave to catch her plane back to Rome and then back to San Francisco. She never knew what happened to him or why he didn't come to see her off. She was pissed off that she didn't have the opportunity to end their relationship permanently; like she always did with her other prey.

Frank woke her out of her play back of her fling with the young Italian gardener when he tapped her on her shoulder.

"I sorry to bother you, but you told me to let you know if a member of the family came by," Frank said. "See the man at the other end of the bar, drinking a beer? I know him, he's a Family member in good standing, as far as I know. Would you like me to tell him you want to meet him?

"Yes please, Frank. Ask him, if he will, to come down here and talk with me. I have something special to ask him and I don't want to look like a pick up in a bar," she said to him.

"I understand." Frank left to make a round of the tables and booths that he was serving and then she saw him stop by the man drinking the beer on the other end of the bar.

CHAPTER SIXTEEN

Kat stopped at a gas station for coffee and gas. After she had the coffee and her tank was full, she went to a outside telephone booth to call Mrs. Robinson. The phone rang several times without being answered. Kat let the phone ring.

"I don't want any! A slurred, angry voice said over the phone."

"Mrs. Robinson don't hang up, it's Kat McNally."

"Well, well." You've taken you time in keeping me updated on your progress!"

"That's why I calling you Mrs. Robinson. I'd like to come by, and give you a report today. I'm near your mansion now."

"No, I'm waking up and need to eat breakfast. Two p.m. will be much better for me. Come at two p.m," the phone went dead.

It was Friday and she taught her Taekwondo class on Friday. She would have to make her report to Mrs. Robinson short and sweet if that was possible. She went to the coast road and drove over to a small café on the beach.

Snoopy's café had the best fish and chips in the San Francisco area, with a large outdoor patio and a long pier running past the surf line. She ordered fish and chips at the counter with a cold beer to drink. She took a seat on the patio and watched the fisherman along the long pier cast their lines in to the surf. Her beer with frost on the bottle came a few minutes before her lunch. She savored the lunch and enjoyed another frosted bottle of beer. The time whipped by: it was twelve-ten when she checked her watch. She called her waiter over to pay for the second beer. She left Snoopy's and headed for the police storage facility to return the police photos. There was plenty of time to do that and still make the appointment with Mrs. Robinson.

Kat's trip back to the San Francisco storage facility was a quick one. She returned the photos to the clerk, and asked the clerk if she might read the police report one more time. The clerk turned to a desk that was behind her and picked up the folder on the George C. Robinson suicide and handed it to Kat.

Kat put the photos back in the file while the clerk watched her. That way no one could say she didn't return the photos. She took the file back to the desk down in the rows of files and started to read the report again; in case she missed something the first time.

There was a better way to the mansion that was faster. She had stayed too long at the storage facility and might be late to the appointment. She reached highway two eighty north bound and then made a connection to one hundred one highway north bound when she was getting close to the city. The she was pushing above the speed limit and watching for highway patrolmen as she passed Stanford University campus on the right side of the highway. The two hundred eighty-five feet high Hoover Tower stood above the tops of the trees hiding the rest of the campus. It was named for President Herbert Hoover and housed his presidential library. She switched her eye scan back to the highway traffic and the cars she was passing. It was two in the afternoon when Kat parked in the guest parking area in front of the mansion. She was going to tell Mrs. Robinson most of what she had found, but not all. She wanted to see her react to some of the information she had learned, since she saw her last. She grabbed a manila file holder that was on the right-side front seat and took it with her.

Mrs. Robinson opened the right-side door of the mansion entrance a moment before Kat pushed the button for the doorbell. She must have been watching through the drapes at the side of the door. The smell of alcohol and cigarettes almost knocked Kat over.

Mrs. Robinson started bitching right off the bat. "Our agreement was for you to report on a regular basis, you idiot! I don't think several months was in our agreement. I hope you have made some progress."

"I have some information for you and some questions for you. The next time you call me an idiot, I'll knock you on your ass!" Kat told her.

"You don't need to be ugly about it. I need more coffee and a cigarette, let's go out to breakfast area in the kitchen. I have everything there, and you can calm down," smirked Mrs. Robinson as she stumbled on the way to the breakfast room.

Kat followed her back through the large living room, while she listened to Mrs. Robinson's shoes echo through the huge room. Mrs. Robinson poured a cup of coffee with a shot of whiskey and sat down at the breakfast table; it had a view of the large patio and pool. She didn't offer Kat anything to drink so Kat poured her own coffee from the pot on the counter.

"What have you found?" Mrs. Robinson snarled at her.

"I don't know who the person is that murdered your maid, yet. I have some questions for you that I believe will help me find him or her."

"Or her?" What the hell do you mean? You think a woman might have slashed the maid's throat?"

"No. However, I must leave that option open until I know for sure who the killer is. I spoke with the maid's father. He indicated that his daughter's attitude changed drastically after she came to work for you. He told me they had called you several times to inquire about their daughter, but the calls were not returned."

"I don't remember them calling or leaving any messages. I can't remember every damn call that comes in. I'm a busy woman! There is a private phone in the maid's quarters, after all. If the maid didn't return her parent's calls, that would be up to her. I think young students at university often change the ideas that their parents have instilled in them from childhood. Don't you?"

Kat didn't bother to answer her question. She left out all the derogatory comments that most of the people she had interviewed had used in describing Mrs. Robinson. She wasn't ready to go there.

"Mrs. Robinson, your old maid, the one that has dementia, wrote a note after I talked with her. She scribbled, stand fort, on an envelope. Does that mean anything to you?"

"I don't recall anything with those words. They could mean anything or nothing. Is this the type of information that you have gathered over the past months? If it is, I think you're doing a damn poor job of investigating. If you can't give me more pertinent information about the murderer, I don't need you."

"I'm interested in your input about the information that I have garnered. I hoped something as simple as two words from your old maid might jumpstart your memory, and help me figure out who the killer is."

"I have no idea what the damn words that an old woman scribbled on a piece of paper could mean."

"Was Miss Windsor dating anyone at the time of the murder?"

"I knew nothing about the maid's social life," stated Mrs. Robinson in anger. "I only know she didn't do a very good job keeping my home clean!"

"By the way, I came back to check the maid's room again and found a hidden door in the hallway that leads to the main part of the mansion. Any idea why that is camouflaged to look like the wall or where it might lead?"

"I am the second owner of the mansion. I find things that were done by the original owners from time to time. There being a hidden door doesn't surprise me in the least. Why were you in my home without my knowledge?"

"You hired me to find the murderer of your maid. That in its self leaves your mansion as a site of investigation, with or without your permission. On the other hand, you are never home, and when you

138

are home, you don't answer your phone or doorbell for days on end. You are drunk all day long, and are bumped up most the time by drugs from doctor shopping or off the streets. How am I to investigate the murder if you're constantly in a fog, and won't truthfully answer my questions."

"Now you're calling you employer a liar? That's grounds for me to fire you right now! You bitch!"

"Fire me! It really doesn't matter to me who the killer is. I have discovered that the police have made mistake after mistake. They'll never find the murderer, and you will never be able to clear you name. People will continue to drive by to look at the mansion where the young maid was slaughtered, until the end of time!"

Mrs. Robinson sat quietly, in a drunken daze. No one had ever talked to her like this little private investigator did. She knew she was in a fix. Neither choice; keep her on the case or fire her seem like a good option. She was sitting in the power seat for the time being.

Mrs. Robinson put a bird in a cat's paws look on her face and told Kat that she was overstressed, and on pins and needles, about when she would find the murderer of the maid and who it might be.

Kat assumed that meant she was still on the case. She threw the receipts she had in the file on the counter and said, "I have another appointment very soon, so I'll need you to pay my expense receipts."

Mrs. Robinson wrote a check to reimburse her.

"Kat held up several photos that she had taken from the folder after giving the receipts to Mrs. Robinson. I have several very interesting photos and I would like your opinion regarding them. She handed the photos the her.

Mrs. Robinson glanced at the photos and lost total control. "WHAT IN HELL'S FIRE DID YOU SHOW ME PHOTOS OF MY DEAD MAID FOR? ARE YOU CRAZY OR WHAT?"

"No mam, I'm not crazy, unfortunately there might be people involved in this investigation that are crazier than a hoot owl. Look carefully at her wrist and ankles. I want to know your idea of how those marks were made."

"Mrs. Robinson looked more carefully at the photos, and then threw them on the breakfast table. I'LL NOT LOWER MYSELF TO YOUR LEVEL. THE PEOPLE YOU MUST DEAL WITH EVERYDAY HAVE UNDOUBTEDLY TAINTED YOUR ABILITY TO FUNCTION ON A NORMAL HUMAN BEING'S LEVEL. HOW THE HELL SHOULD I KNOW WHAT CAUSED THE CUFF MARKS! YOU GET THE FUCK OUT OF MY HOME AND FIND THE PERSON THAT KILLED THE MAID. STOP BRINGING THIS TRASH FOR ME TO SEE! I'LL MAKE YOU VERY, VERY SORRY IF YOU CONTINUE DOING THIS SORT OF THING! NOW GET OUT!"

Kat didn't blink an eye about the onslaught from Mrs. Robinson. She started to walk into the kitchen when she stopped, turned around, and asked Mrs. Robinson if her deceased husband was right or left handed.

"YOU FUCKING LITTLE BITCH! WHAT THE HELL DOES THAT HAVE TO DO WITH WHAT YOU WERE HIRED TO DO?" Mrs. Robinson screamed.

"Probably nothing, but it's something odd that I've picked up along the way: no one can tell me whether he was right or left handed."

"HE WAS RIGHT HANDED! NOW GET THE FUCK OUT OF MY HOUSE, OR YOU MIGHT NOT GET OUT AT ALL!"

"If that is all the fucking information you have for several months investigating, I don't think you're worth a damn. Have the murderer identified at our next meeting or I'll fire you on the spot."

"Sticks and stones, Mrs. Robinson."

Kat smiled at her and continued to walk across the kitchen into the large living room. She waited on the covered entry to see if Mrs. Robinson would rush out in her rage and fire her. She pushed as far as she dared. Now she wanted to see if there was any immediate action that might include a slip of an enraged tongue. Mrs. Robinson was lying about her husband being right handed, or she had forgotten over the years. The tell in the photo was the callus on his left index finger from using a pen or pencil to write all the time. If she had shown her that photo, Mrs. Robinson's rage might have turn to attempted murder. There was something else that she said about the marks on her maid's body that spiked her interest. All she heard through the tall front doors were what sounded like things being broken.

CHAPTER SEVENTEEN

T he recruits were separated into two groups: A through M went through several distribution centers where they were issued everything from mattresses to put on their metal framed bunks to several new army fatigue uniforms. N through Z went to get their heads shaved at the barber shop at the base PX. It was the army's way of keeping head lice under control.

Once all the gear was stacked on their metal racks the A-M group went to the barber shop. The N-Z group went to get their gear to be stacked on their assigned racks in the barracks they had been assigned by their new drill sergeant. The two groups were lined up and marched to the mess hall for dinner that night and then followed the instructions of the drill sergeant on how to fold clothes and place all personal items in the foot locker at the end of each bunk. The next morning, they wore their new uniforms to roll call and then marched to the health clinic where everyone received several shots in their right shoulder to ward off weird diseases that occurred around the world. Several of the recruits passed out during that process which made the slender, fearful draftee proud of himself for not being one of the recruits that fainted.

After that line, they were marched back to the barracks and allowed to work on their gear until the following morning. He was trying to get all his military issue stuff into the footlocker that he had been issued. There had to be some secret to getting all the stuff in the footlocker but he didn't remember what it was. It was something simple.

The Staff Sergeant that was N-Z platoon's drill sergeant, with Fowler on his fatigue name patch, stopped at his bunk with a clip board in his hand. He told the recruit to roll everything; it would all fit in the footlocker. Then the sergeant said, "you belong to me, Fuck-up. You are no longer the son of anyone, the husband or boyfriend of anyone. You, Fuck-up are mine!"

The young frail recruit's body shook with fear of the drill sergeant that was standing in front of him. He didn't know what to do or say. So, he said nothing. He wanted to close his eyes and make the sergeant go away. He tried that and it didn't work. It did bring down the wrath of the drill sergeant, again.

"Don't close your eyes when I'm talking to you, recruit," drill sergeant Fowler yelled. "You didn't answer me Fuck-up. DO YOU BELONG TO ME?"

"Yes sergeant," the thin frail recruit told him.

"WHEN YOU SPEAK TO ME, CALL ME SIR OR SERGEANT. YOU SAY, SIR, YES SIR, OR SIR, YES SERGEANT. DO YOU UNDERSTAND THAT FUCK-UP?"

"Yes sir!" The shaking recruit said in a normal tone.

"NEGATIVE, FUCK-UP. YOU WILL ADDRESS ME BY SIR, YES SIR, OR SIR YES SERGEANT. TRY THAT AGAIN FUCK-UP, WITH SIR IN FRONT," the drill sergeant yelled at him.

"YOUR NAME TAG WILL BE MADE WITH FUCK-UP ON IT. THAT WILL BE YOUR NAME WHILE YOU ARE MINE, IS THAT CLEAR? YOU WILL ANSWER TO THAT NAME DURING ROLL CALL, WHEN YOU ARE SPOKEN TO BY A SERGEANT OR AN OFFICER OF THE UNITED STATES ARMY!"

"Sir, yes Sir. I will be called Fuck-up from now on."

"IF YOU WORK HARD AND BECOME A WORTHY RECRUIT, I MAY CALL YOU BY YOUR LAST NAME," the drill sergeant turned on his heel and marched to the young man at the next bunk to start all over again.

145

The scared frail recruit thought he had been yelled at before but never like that. He started trying to make his bed tight enough to bounce a quarter on it, but his hands were shaking so badly from his brief confrontation with the drill sergeant that his blanket slumped in the middle. He was afraid of what would happen to him if the sergeant noticed the slump in his bed. He was shaking on the inside too. What in the hell was going on. The yelling and screaming, and malicious talk from all the non-commissioned officers, like drill sergeant Fowler.

The next few weeks the men in N-Z platoon started to learn to march in line with a specific cadence. Fuck-up couldn't figure out why marching was such a big part of killing people. Doing calisthenics every morning gave him an appetite for the first time in his life. The mess hall food wasn't particularly good, however it was packed full of carbohydrates. He started to see muscle building on his thin frame, and his energy level was up.

 Sergeant Fowler continued to call him Fuck-up, because he couldn't do as many pushups as the rest of the recruits in his platoon. Fuck-up started to try to hide from the drill instructor. Every time sergeant Fowler saw him, he made him do more pushups.

The fourth week of basic training they were issued their M-14 rifles. The recruits took their assigned rifles with them everywhere. Even to the latrine! The N-Z recruits were stacking their rifles prior to starting morning calisthenics when Fuck-up let his rifle fall to the ground. The drill instructor was on him like a fly on shit.

"What's the matter with you Fuck-up, are you too weak to keep your weapon from falling to the ground? Get down there in the dirt with your rifle and hold it in the air over your body while the rest of the recruits do morning calisthenics."

"I'll deal with you when they are finished. Don't let your rifle hit the dirt again Fuck-up," sergeant Fowler said.

After calisthenics, the drill sergeant made him field strip his M-14 and clean it thoroughly. The drill sergeant checked his M-14 rifle; and then yelled at Fuck-up that he had latrine duty for the next week and that he had to sleep with his rifle and learn to love his rifle because it was what was going to keep him alive.

Starting then, Fuck-up was isolated from the rest of the men in the N-Z platoon. He was beginning to hate someone like he hated lightning and thunder. He was made to sit alone in the mess hall, the other men weren't allowed to talk with him. The latrine had to pass inspection every morning. The drill sergeant made sure he found something wrong with its cleanliness to belittle Fuck-up even more.

On the third day of latrine duty, the drill sergeant found a burned match outside the butt can at the door to the latrine. He called Fuck-up over to the door. The drill sergeant checked out in the hallway to make sure no one was coming to the latrine. When Fuck-up stood in front of him at attention, the drill sergeant hit him as hard as he could in the stomach. Fuck-up doubled over and fell to the floor, howling in pain.

"YOU FUCK-UP! YOU LET A BURNT MATCH STICK FALL OUTSIDE MY BUTT CAN, FUCK-UP. WE'RE GOING TO THE RIFLE RANGE TODAY. YOU WILL MARCH AT THE BACK OF THE PLATOON WITH YOUR WEAPON AT PORT ARMS ALL THE WAY TO THE RANGE. UNDERSTAND FUCK-UP?" Screamed sergeant Fowler.

Then Fowler pushed him over on his back. He wanted to make eye contact with the recruit and let him know how pissed off he was. Fowler stepped back in fear when he saw Fuck-up's eyes and face. The corneas of his eyes were a luminous yellow, the irises were bright red, like an ember in a campfire, and the pupil was a large densely black orb in the center. His mouth was like that of an angry cat and a low hissing sound came from his throat.

Fowler stumbled back in shock and tripped over the cigarette butt can, knocking cigarette butts and sand over the sparkling, clean latrine floor. He didn't know what to think of what he had just seen, but he knew he wasn't going to tell anyone. They would just think he had been down to the local bar and gone on one of his payday drunks. He moved quickly into the hall and went into his room directly across from the latrine. He shut the door and stood there for a while. He had been through the Korean war and close quarter combat, but what he had just seen in the latrine scared the ever-living shit out of him. He knew he couldn't say anything about it, or he would be classed as a nut case himself. He thought it would be a good idea if he let up on Fuck-up the last few weeks of boot camp.

The blow to his stomach sent the frail recruits mind to the edge of his Dark Persona. It took over; starting to make plans for his abuser. His Dark Persona made him want to be a perfect soldier for the duration of boot camp. He could stop the abuse by being a perfect soldier. He would make sergeant Fowler pay for what he had tried to do to him. The blind urge to kill raged within him. He could see in his stark, acutely warped mind how he would make the drill sergeant bleed. He'd feed on his blood and absorb his power.

CHAPTER EIGHTEEN

Fuck-up struggled to his feet and leaned against the latrine wall. He wondered where the drill sergeant had gone. From the time of the blow to his stomach, to the moment he was able to stand again, he knew he had been in his Dark Persona and then he remembered the drill sergeant running across the hall to his room and slamming his door shut.

There was a switch, like turning on a light, and the darkness became light and he knew he must wait for the proper time. He was amazed at his precipitous restraint of his secret Dark Persona.

He spent the next hour cleaning the old cigarette butts and sand from the latrine floor and finished just before reveille sounded. While he was scrubbing the floor on his hands and knees, he tried to decide what to do about the incident with the drill sergeant. He figured it would be best if he denied any of it ever happened. It would be his word against the sergeant's if he told anyone about it. He still didn't realize that what he called his Dark Persona actually made physical changes in him.

He went to calisthenics and wasn't singled out by the drill sergeant. He marched to the rifle range at his position in the N-Z platoon, not behind the platoon like the sergeant had threatened the night before. He gained confidence from these small things that happened because the drill sergeant was in denial that anything had happened in the latrine. Sergeant Fowler was certain he experienced a nightmare.

That Friday the N-Z platoon was given their first off-post pass. Some of the men that lived close to Fort Ord took busses from the local bus station and went home. Others spent time at the base post exchange or the movie theatre on base. Fuck-up stayed in the barracks and cleaned his M-14. He went to the base laundry mat and worked at getting the slump out of his bed cover. He polished his boots and made sure his foot locker was in perfect condition.

After evening mess call, he followed the drill sergeant off the base and watched him go to a local bar at the end of what was called the strip. He went back to the barracks and waited for the drill sergeant to return. It was near one o'clock when the sergeant came staggering back to his room at the far end of the barracks. He fumbled with the lock and key to his room's door and finally made it into the room. Fuck-up noted the time and went to sleep, smiling to himself for the first time since he had been inducted into the army, six weeks earlier.

He went the next day to the bus depot and brought a round trip ticket to Castroville a short distance north of Fort Ord. He bought a hunting knife and a new set of civilian clothes. He returned to the strip just off Fort Ord that afternoon and walked along the sidewalk to the Full Clip bar where the drill sergeant had been drinking the night before. He found what he was looking for behind the bar. There was a fenced in trash area where the bar left the trash for pickup. The entry door was unlocked. He looked around to make sure no one was watching him as he went into the fenced off trash area. He stashed his new cloths behind a large metal trash container and put his hunting knife inside the boards of an old wood flat leaning against the fence wall. He left the trash area with a quickness to his pace. He didn't want to be seen leaving the area. There were only two weeks until N-Z's graduation from boot camp!

With his newly found desire to do well in boot camp, the last two weeks went by in a rush. The N-Z platoon did the obstacle course for record and everyone passed, including Fuck-up until he missed the rope at the water pool and fell into it. He passed all other parts and after a second chance he grabbed the rope properly and swung to the other side. He passed the obstacle course with the rest of the platoon. He ran the mile run with full gear and finished in the middle of the platoon. Next was the live fire course where a machine gun fires live ammunition over the recruits' heads as they crawl under barbed wire barely over their heads. He was really concerned about getting shot with real ammunition but so were all the other men of the N-Z platoon. It was very loud with percussion bombs going off at the sides of the course. The extremely loud noise caused his Dark Persona to try to take over. He managed to fight it off with his desire to finish the live fire course in good shape. He did so.

The last week was spent at the rifle range. He consistently scored in practice in the sharpshooter ranking. Then sergeant Fowler sent a corporal that was an instructor to him to check his mechanics of firing the weapon. The drill sergeant was afraid to get anywhere near him. The corporal told him he wasn't holding his breath when he applied pressure to the trigger to shoot.

"Not holding your breath will cause the bullet to raise up or down according to what part of your breathing cycle you pull the trigger in. Try this, take a deep breath, let some out, and slowly pull the slack up on the trigger. Let it surprise you when the M-14 goes off," the corporal told him."

He followed the suggestion with the corporal kneeling next to him. The very first round that he fired hit the bull's eye. The next day the platoon fired for record. He shot expert, the best ranking for the rifle course qualification test.

On the last day of basic training the drill sergeant had N-Z platoon circle around him inside the barracks and told them everyone had passed the basic training course and then read off by name what their new military operations specialty was. It was simply called MOS in the army. Most of the platoon were given a 11B MOS. They were headed to advanced combat training and then would be sent to Vietnam.

Sergeant Fowler didn't make eye contact with Fuck-up when he told him he had been assigned the 11B MOS, but had been assigned to the parachute jump school at Phan Rang Airforce base in Vietnam and then to 173rd airborne brigade. After successful completion of that course he would be sent to a sniper school south of Na Trang. He was to be sent directly to Vietnam after a week's leave for completing basic training. To attend the sniper school he had to be the minimum rank of private first class while the rest of the recruits were leaving basic training as privates.

"You'll get your advanced combat training with the soldiers on the front line, Fuck-up!" Drill sergeant Fowler snarled at him. "Your odds of being killed were one in three as an 11B. As a 11B sniper it goes up, way up! Maybe two in three for you."

The rest of the day was devoted to packing gear into a duffle bag; turning in their M-14's for the next group of trainees to use, and preparing for the graduation parade taking place the following morning. He couldn't figure out why he had been selected for the advanced training as an airborne sniper, unless it was because he was the only man in the N-Z recruit platoon that had a college degree and he had shot expert with the M-14 rifle and with the M1911 A1 pistol. Or maybe the drill sergeant had told someone he was a loner. He wasn't accepted into the recruit platoon like all the rest of the men.

He figured he would be assigned to some journalistic MOS with his college degree in that field, nevertheless the army could assign him wherever they had the most need. He shook his head in marvel how the army worked. His Dark Persona would like being out in the jungle on his own and killing people with orders to do so!

It started to rain as the men were heading for the mess hall for chow. When he returned to the barracks from the mess hall, there was a thin plastic army drab pull over rain coat on each bunk. A form had been placed on the information board at the entrance to the latrine that indicated the soldiers should were the rain coats over their uniforms for the graduation parade. He figured he could use it for other purposes too.

The next morning all of the soldiers from N-Z platoon were given their travel orders and a week's pass before the report date for their further training or for travel to their newly assigned post. He was the last to leave the barracks that day. He wore his dress uniform with a rain coat pulled over it. It was gradually raining harder as the day passed. He left Fort Ord and walked the short distance to the strip. He walked passed the Full Clip bar and waited in the rain at the side of the building. When he was certain there were no eyes on him he shouldered his duffle bag and went back to the fenced in trash area. He stood his duffle bag in a corner of the fence and moved some of the wood flats to make cover for him while he waited. Night came quickly with the help of the rain clouds that were sweeping by overhead. He watched toward the west. That would be the direction that any lightning and thunder would first appear. There would be no moon that night. He went to get his hunting knife and bag with his new civilian clothes in it. He didn't need the clothes to change into since he had the plastic pull over raincoat to protect his uniform from getting blood all over it.

Gradually he allowed his Dark Persona to take him over. It felt like a long-lost friend returning. It wasn't concerning to him if the drill sergeant was coming to the Full Clip bar. On this night he would be wanting to celebrate getting another platoon through basic training with his friends at the bar. He kept checking his watch looking for the perfect time to go to the front corner of the bar and wait in the alley between buildings for the drill sergeant to leave. The sergeant was bound to be drunk. That would make things perfect. There were no loud noises like thunder and lightning, nonetheless the Dark Persona remembered the taunting, the punch to his stomach and the rest of the terrible abuse the drill sergeant had done to him throughout the eight weeks of hell.

He waited until twelve mid-night and moved like a shadow from a dark spot outside the fenced trash area and waited in the rainy night's darker shadow at the back of the building. He started to get ready. He had taken the hunting knife from its sheath and kept the butt of it tightly in his right hand. The Dark Persona started the feeling of euphoria all over his body. He had missed that feeling, barring for a short moment in the latrine that night.

He crept along the side of the building in the heavy rain and stopped short of the corner. He knelt down in the wet grass next to the building and waited. He had to make sure he could get his left hand over the drill sergeant's mouth to stop any sound he might make, first and foremost. No, better yet, he would trip him. He would fall easily being stupid drunk. That was it, he would reach out with his left hand and trip him by grabbing one of his legs. The Dark Persona liked that idea. He smiled to himself.

Drill sergeant Fowler of N-Z platoon sat at a small table in the corner of the Full Clip bar and talked with the drill sergeant for A-M platoon of recruits. They were both Staff Sergeants in rank and had been drill sergeants for raw recruits for three years.

The A-M drill sergeant told drill sergeant Fowler that his platoon that graduated that morning was one of the best he had seen come through basic training in the past three years. Fowler didn't answer his friend. He was still in denial about the happening in the latrine two weeks earlier.

"Why are you so sullen tonight? All the other times we have graduated a class of recruits you were ready to celebrate and get drunk with me," asked A-M platoon drill sergeant Bill.

"I don't want to talk about my platoon of recruits or how they did. They all made it through training and that's good enough. All I want to do is to get drunk and forget about them," said N-Z platoon drill sergeant Fowler, as he swallowed a drink of beer and tossed down a whiskey chaser. He could feel the alcohol numbing his body and mind. That's what he needed he figured. A numb mind!

"Man, something has really got you bugged! I'll get us another beer and whiskey and maybe you'll lighten up some," said Bill as he went to the bar to order another round.

Bill brought the drinks to their table and continued trying to get his friend out of his funk. Fowler was a heavy drinker when he was off duty. He was drinking with a purpose. He hadn't slept soundly for two weeks. The piercing glare of the recruit's eyes that night kept him from sleeping; and if he did sleep, he had nightmares about those eyes, those crazy eyes, and that cat like snarling from his mouth. He felt a cold shiver run over his body, and his entire body shook from it.

"Hey, buddy? You getting sick from marching in the parade in the rain?" Asked Bill.

"Nah! It's nothing, just the whiskey going down hard," answered Fowler.

Bill tried to get his friends mind off whatever it was that was bothering him. He started trying to talk about the woman he had met the last time they had come to the Full Clip and that he was going to meet her tonight at her trailer outside of town.

"She sure was aggressive that night! I liked that a lot. She's called me several times on the phone in my room at the barracks. She's hot and she's ready. As far as that's concerned, so am I!" Bill told Charlie Fowler.

Fowler didn't answer. He didn't even hear what Bill had said. He kept turning his shot glass of whiskey in a circle and staring into it like there was an answer to what was bothering him somewhere in the honey colored drink. He tossed it off after he took a drink of his beer and went over to the bartender for another shot. Bill watched him go and shook his head. He was going to leave his friend and head over to his newly found girlfriend's trailer before he got too drunk.

When Fowler came back to the table with his next whiskey shot, Bill told him he was leaving to go to the trailer park where the woman lived. Fowler just kept staring off in the distance.

"They were the eyes of a crazed animal. The snarl of a demented man-eating animal." Fowler wailed into his glass of beer.

Bill thought he heard Charlie right, even so he asked him to repeat himself.

"This recruit that I called Fuck-up turned on me. There's something evil about him. That look he gave me will stay with me for the rest of my life, Bill. The rest of my life!" Charlie threw down the rest of his whiskey and took a long draw on his beer.

Bill left him like that still staring off in the distance. He had never seen anyone so distracted as Charlie was that night. He figured Charlie Fowler was having some sort of mental breakdown from running so many recruits through basic training.

Fowler sat at the table and continued to down beer and whiskey until he had trouble walking over to the bartender to get the next whiskey and beer. He watched as some other men came into the bar still dressed in their fatigues. He could see out the entrance that it was still raining, yet much harder than earlier. There was a flash of light and a loud clap of thunder from the coast area. A more severe part of the rain storm was coming over the coast and would be hitting the area shortly. He didn't have his rain coat with him; he decided to call it a night. He hoped he had time to get back to his room in the barracks before the thunder storm hit. He checked his watch. He was so drunk he couldn't focus on the dial of his watch. He went up to the bar to pay the tab in his drunken state. He paid the barkeep his tab and asked him what time it was.

"It's one-twenty sergeant," the bartender told him. "The bar closes at the usual time tonight at two o'clock. You'd better get back to the fort before that thunder storm hits. You're not driving tonight are you, sergeant?" The bartender asked him.

"Nah, I don't even own a car. I'm going to beat that storm though."

Fowler staggered across the bars interior and pulled the heavy door open with some effort. There was another brilliant lightning strike along the coast and then a deep roaring clap of thunder. It was so strong that he thought he could feel the sound waves hit him. The heavy entrance door to the Full Clip bar shut behind him. He shivered again and then started to walked along the sidewalk toward the corner of the building. He was using one hand against the exterior of the building to keep from staggeringc and falling down on the sidewalk. He thought he was going to have a hell of a hangover in the morning.

CHAPTER NINETEEN

Running along the bay helped Kat's mind move off the terrible thoughts she was having about the confrontation with Mrs. Robinson. She was considering quitting the case, however there was a bunch of circumstantial evidence against Mrs. Robinson and her husband's suicide. She decided to stay for the time being on the maid's murder case and put up with all Mrs. Robinson's crap in case she turned out to be involved in her husband's suicide. She saw the tower on the campus of U.C. Berkeley off to her right as she came to her turn around area. The tower jolted her thinking back to the old maids scribbling. She made her turn and started running back to her starting point. What was it about her scribbling that bugged her so much. She was trying to figure out why the U.C. Berkeley tower struck her like it did when she made her turn.

She had finished her run, and was getting in her car when she again had a glimpse of the tower in the distance that made her weak in the knees. She fell into the driver's seat of her car and hung onto the steering wheel for a moment. It was the Stanford University Hoover tower she saw on her way to the mansion that was blowing her mind.

The old maid's note flashed before her eyes. Her words Stand Fort could be Stanford for Stanford University. That campus had the Hoover tower that she had seen from the highway, as well. She needed to figure out if Stanford had anything to do with the killing of the young maid, or, if she was making a mountain out a molehill.

When Kat opened the door to her apartment she went over to her desk under the window instead of changing from her running cloths to street clothes. She pulled the typing paper over to her, and looked at the two words. They could fit in with Stanford University or did they fit into some totally different thought the old maid had, after all, she did have class three dementia. She tried the two words separately and together to see if that popped anything into her head. Nothing rang her bell when she did that, even so the university name was always at the back of her brain. She waited for a few moments and then tried again. The waiting period didn't have an immediate ah ha moment.

Kat decided to drive down to the university and see if there were any recent graduates with the last name that was on the draft notice. Stanford University offices were closed when Kat got there. The university had only day classes. She was used to attending the evening classes at U.C. Berkeley. Stanford was a private university maybe they didn't need more classes to accommodate the masses. It was an hour or more distance south of her apartment on I-280 south and it was late when she started the drive down to the Stanford. She turned around to drive back to her apartment.

The drive across the bay bridge and onto I-280 south was crowded. Kat didn't mind the drive. It was a beautiful drive across several counties to where the university was located. She enjoyed the scenic drive with the windows down on her car and the fresh cool air of spring blowing in from the ocean. It took a bit over an hour to reach the campus and she wasn't in any hurry either. She parked in the visitor's parking area and went to the administration building. The walks around the front part of the campus were crowded with young university students going to their next classes. There was a special office for student transcripts down a long hallway from the main administration offices and up one floor. Kat showed her credentials to a clerk that came to a window like a bank tellers window. The clerk took her badge and license in Kat's leather folder to a slightly gray-haired lady in a small office within the office. The clerk and the older woman talked for a few moments, then the clerk came back and asked Kat to come behind the counter and talk with the head of the department.

The department head stood as Kat entered her office to introduced herself. She went straight to the point.

"We have a privacy policy at Stanford, Ms. McNally. Unless you can justify your wish to see a student's records, I will have to decline your request."

"I am employed by the student's parent and the check of his record will be important to finding him."

"Is he lost?" The department head asked.

"He hasn't been seen by the family for a long time," she was fudging the truth, but she wanted to know if the old maid had meant for her to find someone or something there, or maybe the scribbled note was about something else entirely unrelated to her investigation.

"I understand Ms. McNally. I will make a concession for the family. I'll let you see the records for the past year and you may make notes, however you may not have the record to take with you or have us make a copy of the record. If that is agreeable to you, I will have the clerk go to the file area and get any records that may apply to your request."

"That's agreeable to me. The family thinks he was enrolled here last year, or the year before that, for sure."

"It seems odd to me that you don't have a first name for this missing person, Miss McNally."

"I'm hopeful that he hasn't changed his name. I'm not even sure that he came to this university. It's just one more thing that I have to check on."

"I see. You're fishing. Is that it?"

"I guess you could call it that," she said.

The department head waved the clerk back into her office and told her to get the record file for the student that Ms. McNally wanted to see, but to stay with her while she checked over the record and to allow only hand-written notes to be made.

Kat and the clerk left the department head's office. The clerk asked Kat for the name of the student and what years he or she had attended the university.

"His name is Robinson. He would have been enrolled here in the last two years."

The clerk told her it would be sometime before she would retrieve the record that was on another floor of the building. She suggested Kat might want to visit the student union for an hour or two.

Kat left with the clerk and went down stairs when the clerk went upstairs and followed the clerk's instructions on how to find the student union building. She had a snack at the union food bar and shopped the unions gift shop waiting for two hours to pass. She left the union twenty minutes early and went back to the student records office. She was hoping the clerk would be back when she started up the steps to the records office.

The clerk was back and behind the counter. She told Kat to come around the counter to the desk where she worked. She pointed to several folders on the desk and told Kat, "those are the Robinson records we have in that time period with the Robinson surname. One of them is a female. I brought it out just in case."

Kat stood by the desk for a moment thinking of Mrs. Henry, the old maid, and remembering the tears in her eye. She remembered, but couldn't tell Kat. There were three male student's files, one of which graduated recently. She wrote what contact information there was for each of the three students and left the university. Her hopes for a connection were fading rapidly.

Kat didn't bother looking at the academic grades, or courses the three had taken, she did copy the addresses around the university where they lived. There was an address for an apartment in San Francisco. That was thirty-five miles from the campus. No family members were listed on the record. It did give his date and place of birth.

Kat made her notes on her pad and thanked the clerk for helping her. She went back to her car and started her drive back to San Francisco and the Bureau of Vital Statistics. She had copied the birth date from the records at Stanford, of the student that lived in San Francisco. She wanted to validate who his parents were before doing anything else.

The Bureau of Vital Statistics was like most other government office buildings in the downtown area of government buildings. It was getting close to closing time by the time she had filled out the request form at the records department. The clerk told her the records were all on microfilm. Having the birthdate and name of the person she wanted to check would make it much easier and possibly take a few minutes to pull that information up on the viewer for her.

The Bureau clerk returned in a few minutes and told Kat she didn't have a birth certificate under that name.

Kat asked her to try under the father's name. The clerk came back shortly and told her she found one under that name. She escorted Kat to a viewer for microfilm. She put her eyes up against what looked to her like a pair of binoculars and saw a magnified version of what was in miniature on the actual film. She didn't have to write down what she saw, it was plain as day. George C. Robinson, was on the father line and Myra Jean Robinson was on the mother line. That would be burned into her memory. There was no need for the note pad. She paid the fee and left the Bureau of Vital Statistics. There was no name on the newborn's name line.

On the way back to her apartment Kat couldn't decide if she was pleased with what she had discovered, or if it was a disconsolate discovery of a family torn apart. Either way, it glared at her, like a beam of light from a tall lighthouse sitting on a rocky promontory. The birth certificate had to be filled out before the baby left the hospital. It was a state law, however the parents had up to a year to add the name of the child. Many parents forgot to finish putting the child's name on the certificate. It wasn't all that unusual. Maybe the baby didn't live? That could be why Mrs. Robinson lied about not having any children. She opened the door to her apartment to a quiet, dark room that made her feel even more lost in the darkness of all the twists and turns the case was taking.

CHAPTER TWENTY

Fuck-up's Dark Persona had totally taken control after the first flash of lightning and thunder from the coastal area of Monterey Bay. He kneeled down at the corner of the sidewalk and the Full Clip Bar, covered in his thin plastic raincoat, waiting for his prey to stumble by him. Every ounce of the Dark Persona's sadistic will was focused on a single thought. The killing of drill sergeant Fowler. It would elevate his mind from the crippling fear of the lightning and thunder and the all-encompassing hatred of Fowler. It would give him the euphoria that he had grown to embrace, each time he killed someone. The heavy rain that was drumming down on the plastic head cover of the cheap army raincoat added to his exuberance. He wanted the euphoric high that he got from the killing of his prey, like heroin addicts achieved as the needle went into their veins.

He heard the entrance door to the Full Clip bar bang shut over the roar of the rain, and the flashing lights of multiple lightning strikes with the horrific clap and roll of the subsequent thunder. He gripped his hunting knife more tightly in his right hand and waited.

He saw the dark form of a man leaning against the front wall of the bar with one hand, obviously trying to steady himself. He couldn't make out the man's face. He was dressed in an army dress uniform. He waited, his rage increasing each and every second. Where was the damn lightning when he needed it?

There was a blinding flash of lightning that threw enough light on the shadowed drunk form inching his way toward his waiting nightmare to let the Dark Persona take in a split second of light and recognize the face of his prey. He waited until the wet figure of the drunk sergeant Fowler had to moved his supporting hand from the wall of the building, then struck like a pit viper. His left hand moved to the drunk's closest leg and grabbed it like a vise holding a piece of steel pipe. He pulled on the leg, and the rest of the drunk followed. The drunk let out a sudden scream that wasn't heard by anyone. After all, who would be out on a night like that?

The Dark Persona covered in a dark thin plastic raincoat leaped like an attacking tiger on to the fallen drunk. There was a flash of brilliant light off the blade of the hunting knife as it flashed toward the drunk's neck and the soft tissue under the sergeant's chin. It sliced, but met a resistance that the Dark Persona hadn't anticipated. There wasn't the smooth separation of throat tissue as the blade went through it like a hot knife through a stick of butter.

Another flash of lightning let the Dark Persona see that the drunk sergeant, even though he was intoxicated, had raised his arm in front of his neck. He had been trained to do the move when protecting his throat from an enemy's knife attack. The Dark Persona saw what had happen and sliced down to the bone of the drunk's forearm. There was another scream of pain as the arm was pulled away from the drunk's neck by the psychotic strength of the Dark Persona's left hand. His right hand made another attempt at severing the sergeant's neck; and exposing the two large carotid arteries. The shining white sheath covering the cervical spinal cord of the drunken sergeant was exposed as the hunting knife cut deep into his throat. The last things the drill sergeant saw were the two blazing yellow and red eyes burning into his dying brain, like red hot steel coming from a blast furnace. He heard that horrible hissing sound as he had in the latrine. He knew for that second who was killing him; but not what was killing him!

The Dark Persona pulled the dead man's arm to him and cut off the distal phalange of its left index finger. He had forgotten something to keep the short piece of finger in, so he tossed it to the back of his throat and swallowed. He cupped his hand next, and gathered blood from the pool that had formed in the open cut of the dead man's throat. He used that to wash down the small tip of the finger he had cut off.

He leaned back, while still sitting on top of the dead body and looked up into the heavy rain while he waited for a strike of lightning. When it came he let out a loud call of euphoric satisfaction like a Hyena over a fresh kill. No one would hear it: the thunder was far too loud. With the strength of a wild animal he dragged the body through the mud and grass to the back of the fenced trash area and closed the door to the fence after him. The rain would wash away any signs of the attack and the dragging of the body to the trash area. The Dark Persona was quickly dissipating from his body and mind, however the euphoria that went with the killing of his prey during a lightning and thunder storm was still with him. He stuffed the empty shell of the body into the bottom of a large metal trash container. A trash truck would take it to the trash dump and dispose of the body. He left the plastic raincoat to let the rain would clean it off. He walked out onto the strip with his duffle bag over his shoulder. He walked to the end of the strip where it joined to a state highway. Even in the rain, cars driving toward San Francisco would stop to pick up a hitch-hiking army soldier. He had a week of leave before he had to report to the transient depot at Travis Airforce base. He would fly to Vietnam on a C-141 Star-lifter jet aircraft, and serve his twelve months in hell.

CHAPTER TWENTY-ONE

rill sergeant Fowler wasn't reported AWOL until he didn't return to his training company on Monday. There was no immediate search for him. Sometimes drill sergeants over stayed their weekend passes when a training cycle was completed. It was a very stressful job. The main gate guards were given notice of his absence without leave and told to take him to the stockade when he tried to re-enter the fort and to notify the training battalion commander.

A young man driving a huge compactor trash truck pulled up to the back of the fenced in trash area behind the Full Clip bar. He jumped down from the high seat of the truck cab to open the double doors that gave the trash truck easy access to the metal dumpster at the back of the fenced trash area. He came to this particular dumpster on a weekly basis, but he had been delayed a few days from his normal routine by the severe lightning and thunder storm that had occurred last Friday and Saturday. He jumped back up to the seat in the cab of the huge trash truck and backed it around to load the trash from the metal dumpster container to the truck's lift at the back. He hooked the trash container to the lift and threw the leaver that would hydraulically move it to the top of the truck's large compactor. He made the lift shake several times to make sure everything was shaken out of it and into the compactor. He hit the compactor leaver after the trash container was back in place and started to jump back in the cab. He stopped on the step of the cab when the smell from the back of the truck hit him. It was the worst smell he had ever encountered in the year he had been driving the trash truck.

He wasn't going to put up with the dumping of something that smelled that bad. He came off the step of the truck and walked toward the back door of the Full Clip bar. He was becoming angrier as he went. It was against the law to put anything in the trash container that was food stuff. The county land fill prohibited anything other than solid waste trash; meaning no damn food or meat of any kind could be dumped there.

He caught the bar owner at his office and without knocking or any other acknowledgement, he confronted him while the owner sat behind his desk with his shirt sleeves rolled up going over the night's usage of liquor and beer.

The young man stood in front of the man behind the desk and said in a rather gruff voice, "What the hell are your people doing dumping stuff that rots in the trash container. You know that's illegal. That'll get yah a mighty big fine from the county."

175

The owner told him he wasn't aware of anything like that taking place. "Maybe it was one of the other businesses that serves food. They have food that goes bad, and I know they have to put it in special containers that they have at the back of their businesses, nevertheless sometimes the containers are full before your company comes to empty them. The Full Clip bar doesn't serve anything that would spoil and smell bad."

"I don't have time to stand here and argue with you about who did what." The young trash truck driver said.

"I'll take it to the landfill and empty the compactor. The landfill people will find whatever is smelling bad and dispose of it properly. They will know where it came from by what it is and if there are any identifying papers with it. Then the county will jump whoever did it."

The young trash truck driver stomped out of the bar, jumped to the seat in the cab of the truck and went directly back to the landfill, without completing his daily route. He drove his trash truck to the weigh station and jumped from the cab of the track.

He went into the small office at the weigh station and told the manager, "I dumped the container at the Full Clip bar and immediately there was this awful smell that was coming from the back of the truck. I went to the bar to tell the owner about it, and he denied dumbing anything that would spoil in the trash container. He tried to blame it on one of the other businesses close to him. I guess that's possible that some other shop dumped food stuff in that container. Do you want me to take it over to the area that you keep for this sort of thing?"

The manager shook his head affirmatively and went out to the truck with the young trash truck driver. The putrid smell coming from the truck almost knocked the manage over. He signaled to the young truck driver to drive the truck over to the food waist area, and he walked along behind it. He could smell it all the way to the segregated area where they separated that type of trash problem from the rest of the landfill.

The manager and the young truck driver watched as the trash was dumped from the compactor. It wasn't very full: the driver didn't complete his route. The driver shook the leaver that emptied the truck compactor a few times to make sure all the debris was knocked from it. He went to the back of the truck and looked in the compactor to make sure all the trash had been dumped.

Hung up on the rod that pushed all the lower trash out of the compactor was a body. A body in an army uniform! The smell and sight were more than the young man could handle. He clung to the back of the trash compactor and started to retch from his toes to the top of his head. The manager ran back to his office to call the county sheriff's office to report the dead body in the back of one of the trash trucks.

The sirens of several police cars could be heard coming to the landfill from far away. The manager waited at the weigh station while the young driver had been brought into his office in a faint. One of the other drivers was administering first aid to him.

The first sheriff's office car slid to a stop at the weigh station. The back door opened and the manager slid into it.

"Where's the body?" The sheriff asked.

"You see that trash truck over there to the right, by the bluff? That's it," the manager told him.

The sheriff's car peeled out and roared to the far side of the landfill where the trash truck with the compactor still raised in the air was located. The driver slid the car to a stop parallel to the truck and all four doors sprang open simultaneously. The sheriff and his two deputies ran over to look at the now empty compactor and came to a screeching halt. The sheriff told one of the deputies to get the coroner out to the landfill.

"Call the office and have the Homicide team come out here before someone screws the scene up. Have the local police send out their team as well."

The truck remained as it was until the murder team had taken all their photos and had lowered the compactor down to its normal position.

The murder team and the coroner had arrived. The murder team went into the level compactor first, aided by several ladders the landfill had. When they had inspected the scene, they asked the coroner to come up and check the body. He eventually came back out of the compactor and stood by the sheriff.

"The murder squad is examining the body's cloths for an easy identification. His head was totally cut from his body. His spinal cord was showing. It looked like he tried to defend himself with his arm. It was badly cut in a way that the assailant would have used to cut the man's throat. The last part of his left index finger has been cut off. The beginning of rigor mortis and the decomposition of the internal organs have begun. I would guess he has been dead between twenty-four and seventy- two hours," the coroner told the sheriff.

"The smell comes from the decomposing organs. It's always bad for the uninformed person that discovers a body. You'll get a complete report in about two to three days."

The sheriff turned to one of his deputies and told him, "You'd better contact Fort Ord and let them know what we have so far. The body had a military I.D. on it. The name on the I.D is Charles Fowler. Tell them this will be a civilian case since the soldier was apparently killed off base."

CHAPTER TWENTY-TWO

The apartment was in an area centrally located for many of the universities around San Francisco county, and they were slightly more upgraded than the normal apartments on or near university campuses. Kat stopped in front of the building that had the address she had copied from the student file at Stanford University and went to check the exact location of the apartment. It was along a narrow hallway on the ground floor. She passed the stairwell leading up with a small elevator adjacent to it. She came to apartment A-3 on the right side of the hallway, midway down the hall. It was dark and cool in the hallway at the apartment door, even with the sun shining brightly outside. There was some flyers and papers shoved under the door part way into the apartment that she pulled out and checked for the address and name on all of it. The name on the envelopes was Robinson. She wasn't surprised, this was the first of the three Robinson's that had or were attending Stanford, according the records office. It turned out to be general advertising and months old free papers from the university. The outdated material made her wonder if the occupant had moved or was on a trip of some duration. She walked back to the front of the building and wrote down the address and phone number for the rental office. She wanted to check with them before making a move to gain access to the apartment.

Kat didn't have a clue where the apartment rental company was located, so she did the smart thing and stopped at a gas station to get some coffee. The attendant there gave her directions to the company's office. She left the gas station with directions to the rental office, but no coffee. The morning rush had emptied the coffee pots; more had not been made. She bought a Dr. Pepper instead and drove back to the apartment building, from there it was a quick two blocks away with a right turn at the end and she was parked in front of the apartment rental company.

Flying by the seat of her pants was normal for Kat. She had no idea how she was going to talk the rental people into letting her check the interior of apartment A-3. She sat in the car for a few minutes before going into the reception area of the office. She was going to fall back on the thing that worked for her in such situations. She was going to bull shit her way into the apartment.

The office secretary welcomed Kat and asked how she could help her.

"My cousin has an apartment rented through your company at the University Towers apartment building. The family is very concerned about him. It's been months since he answered his phone and when members of the family try to get him to answer the door he doesn't respond. His car is missing, but they don't want to get the police involved yet. I was hoping one of your agents would let me in so I could check on him."

The secretary told her to take a seat while she checked with general manager of the rental company. The secretary came back shortly with a medium height man with the top of his bald head covered with a rather bad comb over.

"Miss Devens has informed me about you wish to check the apartment of your cousin for the family. My name is Tanner. I would normally try to help you, but there is a problem of a good number of months past due rent of that apartment. It's A-3 in the Towers building, is that right?"

Kat decided to try her timid, soft spoken, young female cousin character on him.

"Yes, sir. I understand sir, I thought you might make an exception for me. How much is the total past due rent?"

"I'm not sure I can tell you that, Miss?"

"My name is Susan Clark and my father's his uncle."

"What's the renters last name, Miss Clark?"

"His name is Robinson, and I'm sure you will be paid any past due rent by his parents. They don't know I'm here. I just thought I might find something in his apartment that would help in lowering their anguish. They think maybe he is laying in there dead, or something bad like that."

"I'll have to have you sign a waiver stating who you are and releasing the company from any responsibility, right, or claim in this matter. I have such a waiver in my office, if you are willing to sign it?"

"Oh, yes sir." Kat told him, "That would be most appreciated by the family."

In a few minutes Kat had signed the waiver with the fake name Susan Clark and had a pass key in her hand, which she was to return when she had finished checking the apartment. There was a second key on the ring that had the A-3 key on it. Kat hoped it was a key to the mail box for apartment A-3.

She drove to the apartment building, and parked near the front entrance in the building parking lot. She had a cold chill go over her body when she put the apartment key in the door lock of A-3: like the saying that someone had just stepped on her grave. She left the door closed for a moment while she reached to her back and pulled out her Smith and Wesson .357 Magnum pistol. She stood to the side of the door and turned the door knob to open the door. She pushed it open while she stood to the side of the door frame. She glanced inside and stepped into the living room in a crouch moving the pistol with her eyes checking the living room for trouble. The room was empty and unkept. It had a smell of being closed up for a long period of time.

CHAPTER TWENTY-THREE

The new Private first class checked into the transient company at Travis Airforce base the day before he was due to fly to Vietnam. A list of names scheduled for a flight to Ton Son Knut air force base northwest of Saigon, Vietnam at 0700 hundred the following day was posted the day before near the door leading to the stairwell down from the third floor of the transient barracks. His name was on the list.

When he stepped off the C-141, he was told to pick up his duffle bag and get in line. He stood in line at the reception center until it was his turn. The corporal at the desk with his last name letter over it had his papers in a stack of other men's papers with his last name letter. He was given transfer papers to the jump school at Phan Rang airbase and told to go the front gate where a deuce and a half truck was waiting to take personnel up highway 101 to the north from Saigon. The trip up to Phan Rang was uneventful, except for heavy military traffic and the check points along the way.

He was checked into the jump school that night and assigned a bunk in a metal Quonset hut. He learned the next day at rollcall the school was an intensive course. It only lasted eight days and then he would be sent to the sniper school near Na Trang before getting to the 173rd airborne brigade, his permanent duty assignment.

Jump school was a little like an extremely short boot camp. He was assigned a number and that was what he was called the entire eight days he was at Happy Valley. That's what everyone that was permanently assigned to the base called it. His first jump had his stomach in his throat when he stepped out of the plane, like he was taught to do. he hit the ground and rolled to his side like he had been taught. Everything went well. He completed one more day jump and then one at night. After that he was given his new transfer papers to sniper school and had an airborne insignia over his left jacket pocket of his jungle fatigues. He was proud of that.

He caught the daily deuce and a half truck that was going north and checked into the sniper school near Na Trang. He was checked in at the orderly room for the 173rd sniper school and was immediately told that there was a fifty percent failure rate at the school and if he failed he would be sent to the headquarters of the 173rd airborne brigade as an 11B combat infantry man. The school was eighteen days long. He was taught ambush techniques, camouflage and characteristics of each weapon he might use. He was taught distance shooting with the M-14; the Winchester model 70, and the Remington model 40. He liked the model 70 best. It was lighter and had a greater effective kill distance than the other two. He passed the course and was given a sniper patch to sew on his shoulder above the 173rd patch that he would be issued when he reached his new unit.

That time he rode in a deuce and a half truck to Dok To in II corps. The Central Highlands of South Vietnam composed most of II corps. Dok To was close to the border of Laos and an easy way for the North Vietnamese Army to infiltrate into the south. He was told he was being assigned to a LRRP detachment, a long-range recon patrol, there were no separate sniper's units. A private that was acting as a runner for the company that had the LRRP patrol, called a Lurp patrol, took him to the platoon where he was promptly assigned to a five men unit led by a sergeant first class. Lurp units normally were made up of six men, however one man had been killed in an ambush a few weeks before his arrival to Vietnam.

Fuck-up was re-named when he joined the five men of the Long-Range Recon team. The five men called him FNG for Fucking New Guy from the moment he reported to the leader of the team. The five men in the team were like most in country veterans. They considered a new soldier to the country, and to their team, was a bad thing. New men didn't know anything about combat in the jungle and that meant they were a danger to the rest of the team. New men were known to walk into ambushes and get people killed. They tripped wires across jungle trails that set off mines that killed them and others near them. They walked into punji stick traps and generally endangered the rest of the team. The five men of the

187

specialized team spent two weeks off the normal two patrols per week in trying to get the new man familiarized with how they did things, and what he could expect while out in the boonies.

FNG and the team leader were called to the company commander's hutch at the end of his first week in the company. Both men were a bit uneasy about being called to the company's headquarters. The team leader knew that it usually meant someone was going to get their asses chewed. Normally the team was left to take care of itself. It was the code of deniability. A master sergeant checked with the company commander before he let the two men enter the sectioned off part of the Quonset hut. The two men saluted the captain that was the company commander. The company commander didn't waste any time with informal talk.

"Sergeant, the new man assigned to your Lurp team will be the only sniper assigned to a Lurp team in South Vietnam. He will from time to time get special orders and your team will supply him with all necessary cover. He will from time to time have orders that will take him out of contact with your team and all other military forces. Do you understand, sergeant?"

"Yes, sir!" The sergeant answered.

"We have been sent a weapon from the sniper's school that you finished a week ago. I have no other information, except that this weapon is for your use," the commander said.

The commander picked up an M-14 that was leaning against the table behind his desk, and handed it to the new Lurp team member. It was brand new and still had storage grease visible around the trigger housing group. The commander put two cardboard boxes on the corner of his desk.

"Sergeant, you don't need to check the contents. I have, the top one has extra magazines for the M-14 and the other has a variable distance scope and a mount for the scope that fits onto the M-14. I know you are taking a short time off your normal duties to train him in. One of the things he'll need is a rifle range to zero in the new rifle and scope. You and the team need to give him time to accomplish that before you take the team out to the bush again."

"Yes, sir. Consider it down, sir!"

"That's all Sergeant and good hunting Corporal!"

The NFG and the sergeant turned around in unison and FNG said, Sir, I'm a Private first class."

"Not anymore. You're a corporal, and E-4 paygrade. With the training you have and the specialty you have, it requires a minimum grade of corporal. All the rest of your team still out rank you. Don't get a big head about being special or any of that bullshit! Understood?"

"Yes sir!" The two men said in unison; they did an about face, and marched side by side out of the Quonset hut. The corporal carried his new sniper rifle, and the sergeant carried the two cardboard boxes back to their isolated tents that the Lurp team lived in, when they were on the base. No one from the base came to visit; only those under orders went there. The Lurp team was talked about a lot, but very little was actually known about them. They were known as very hard men! Nothing about the Lurp teams was military. They were men of the jungle. They changed clothes for the type of terrain they were heading into. If they were going into open areas, they wore died black jungle fatigues to look like Viet Cong.

CHAPTER TWENTY-FOUR

Before she started looking, for what she didn't know, she cleared the bedroom, bathroom and the small kitchen. The rooms were all messy and smelled the same as the living room. There was a window in the bedroom and one in living room, but none in the kitchen or bathroom. She went first to the living room to start checking the papers and books that were carelessly tossed about the room. Then she started to take the cushions from the furniture and checking under them all. No big surprise there.

She went to the bedroom next. She tore the bed apart and turned over the mattress looking for anything hidden there. She knew in her still tingling body that there was something in the apartment that would steer her to finding the son that never was. The bathroom had a combination shower and bath tub with a small linen closet and some storage under the sink. She went through the linen closet and storage below the sink like a small tornado hit the area. Still nothing that struck her fancy. The closet was next. The hanging clothes were in neat order, hung by type and color in sections. It was too neat for

Kat's taste. Something else bothered her about the closet. She looked at the shoe rack on the floor for a minute. The shoes were all polished with shoe horns in them. There was still something bothering her about the closet. She left it for a few minutes and went to the dresser. The underwear, t-shirts, socks, were all neatly folded. She returned to the closet and stood looking at the neatness of the entire closet. It hit her like a slap in the face. The person that lived there had Obsessive-Compulsive Personality Disorder, better known as OCPD. She smiled when she realized her psychology courses had just kicked in. Why wasn't the entire apartment like the bedroom?

She went to the kitchen and started checking the two cabinets over the small kitchen counter. It was about the same size kitchen that she had at her place, except her kitchen was open to part of the living area. This one was a separate space from the rest of the apartment. The fridge had old milk in a plastic bottle that had curdled. There were several frozen dinners and some awful smelly stuff in the freezer compartment: the electricity had been turned off. She slammed the fridge door closed in disgust. She turned to go back to the living room and stopped short. There was a trash can at the end of the counter on the side away from the fridge. The trash in it was overflowing and some of it had ended up on the floor. The trash on the floor is what caught Kat's attention.

She dumped the trash on top of the counter and started looking through it with care. There were opened envelopes, unopened envelopes and a few letter-sized papers, one in particular caught her eye right off the bat. The heading was a government heading with the state of California seal on it. It stated that his draft number had been picked by the lottery and he was to take the enclosed document to the local army induction center for processing into the army.

Kat folded the letter and put it in her hip pocket. There was a long cardboard container with a plastic cover attached stuck inside of the trash can. It was a sales container for a double-edged butcher knife. Kat laid it aside to make sure she took it with her. She went through the drawer that held the utensils. There wasn't a double edge butcher knife in the drawer. She continued her search, but found nothing further that she felt was interesting. Then she remembered the other key on the ring with the apartment key. There had to be some mail in the that box. It seemed like it had been many months since anyone stayed in the apartment; therefore the mail box hadn't been checked for that long as well.

The second key on the ring sank into the mail box lock that was marked A-3 in the small lobby at the front entrance. The mail person that was for the building had managed to poke, shove, push, and cram months of trash advertising, letters from collection agencies, past due notices from the apartment rental company, and a bunch of other envelopes that were stuff so tightly in the mail box she couldn't pulled the mess from the metal mail box. Quite a bit of force and ingenuity had been used by the mail person. Kat formed her hand into a blade, and hit the jammed mail with all her might. She gained

193

enough depth to clasp her thumb on a newspaper and pull it out. After that the rest of the bulky mess of mail came out easily.

A few pieces of mail dropped as Kat was trying to bundle all of it into her arms to carry into the apartment for sorting and reading. She squatted down and was able to pinch each piece with her thumb and forefinger. Without dropping any more of the bundle, she placed each piece that had dropped between her teeth and held them there. She made her way to the apartment door and twisted the knob with the same two fingers to open it. She went to the middle of the living room and dropped the huge bundle of mail from her arms to the floor and then spit out the envelopes she held between her teeth.

There were two piles of envelopes and plastic covered advertisements sorted on the living room floor. Kat had separated all the stuff in the mail box into a pile of junk mail and a pile of mail with the renter's name. She stuffed the junk mail into the trash can in the kitchen and started on the other stack. There were several letters from Stanford University about his graduation and a package with invitations for relatives and friends to his graduation ceremony. There were a few past due notices for his rent. She opened several bank statements with his name and address on the envelope. The account had a huge sum of money in a savings account and another large sum in the checking account under the same name. She wondered how those two accounts received all that money. Both accounts had balances of more than five hundred thousand dollars.

She kept the most recent statements. She tossed everything else into the trash but kept the draft notice.

She put the draft board's letter to him about his induction into the army in her pocket. There were three past due notices from an auto long-term parking facility in Modesto, California. Those were of interest to Kat. She kept one and put the other two in the trash can. She found an investment account that was recent. She did some quick math in her head; she was never very good at math, quick took a few moments. The total was something over two million dollars. That put her panties in a knot! How in the hell did he get all that money? Kat put that statement with the other two envelopes she had in her hip pocket. She saw nothing else in the stack that struck her as important she trashed those too.

 Kat sat in a cushioned chair by the front door and tried to put together what she had found in the apartment. She didn't know what she was going to do with the bank statements but she was going to keep them. Her best shot seemed to be the past due bills from the long-term parking and storage company. She was going to drop off the keys to the rental company, and take a drive over to Modesto to see what would pop there. Maybe she would get lucky.

CHAPTER TWENTY-FIVE

The FNG had another week to get his equipment ready: before his first indoctrination patrol. The team was very upset about him being with them. He was left alone at the base camp. Even when he went to the base firing range to zero in his M-14 at one hundred yards, there was no interest shown by the other four men on the team. FNG came back feeling good about having zeroed the M-14 a one hundred yards, but the most important thing was that the M-14 felt good to him. It fit his shoulder well, the trigger slack at just the right amount, and the scope was dead on. It was easy to change the windage, but he needed to figure drop of the bullet for long ranges. He got a jeep from the company motor pool; and asked the team leader, and the lead scout, that was also the team's RTO, radio telephone operator, to come along as spotters and target distancing.

FNG kept the RTO to train as his spotter, and gave four standard range targets to the team leader; and told him to drive the jeep to a place .22 miles down the rutted dirt cart path they had found and put one of the bamboo stakes he had made with a standard range target on it in the ground away from the road, so he wouldn't inadvertently shoot a local. He told the team leader to then drive to .45 miles, and repeat the process, and again at .56 miles down the path.

FNG took his time placing several sand bags on a rice paddy walkway and made himself comfortable. There was no wind to speak of, so he told the man acting as spotter to simply tell him what ring he was hitting by looking through the spotting scope he had commandeered from the base rifle range. The spotter laid down a couple of feet from FNG to watched as the team leader put the bamboo stakes out and drove back to where the shooter and spotter were lying on the ground.

FNG racked back the bolt and jacked a round into the receiver. He settled in to fire at the closest target which was four hundred yards away. He took a deep breath; let part of it out, he then took in the perfect amount of slack on the trigger, and very gently let the bullet go to its target. The spotter waited a second and told him the shot hit the center of the bull's eye. Another round was already chambered. He had the M-14 on single shot, the option was with a small switch at the back of the receiver. Flip the switch and the M-14 was on automatic.

He took the next target that was at eight hundred yards, and aimed slightly above the bull's eye on the target. He squeezed off his shot, and the spotter told him the shot was high. He settled in again and fired. This time not allowing for as much bullet drop. The spotter reported a hit that was high. The FNG took another shot at the target this time just one ring of drop for the bullet. The spotter told him his shot was in the ten ring or the center of the bull's eye. He mentally marked the drop for the M-14 at .45 miles at one ring.

He shot at the one-thousand-yard target. The bullet hit the center on the bull's eye. The spotter rolled over on his side and looked at the FNG.

"You just hit the ten-ring with you first shot from a new rifle at a thousand yards. That's over a half-mile away."

FNG settled in without saying a word and in a few seconds fired another round at the thousand-yard target. The spotter shook his head, after looking in the spotting scope, and told him he hit the side of the bullet hole from the first shot. Both in the ten ring or the bull's eye.

The three team members rode back to the base with the team leader and the RTO talking up a storm about the shooting of their new team mate. The M-14 he was using for a sniper rifle was going to add more security for the team as well. It could fire on automatic and was more accurate than the Ak-47's the rest of the team were using. FNG dropped the team leader and the RTO off at their little Lurp camp and drove over to the company motor pool to return the jeep. By the time he had walked back to the LRRP bivouac, the other three men were talking to him and shaking his hand. He knew that the team leader and the RTO had told the other two about his shooting ability and that it made them more confident in his skills. He still had a lot to learn by experiencing Lurp patrols and combat, but at least he was being accepted into a very select group of warriors.

The day after sighting in his M-14 the team leader took him into the jungle outside of camp and told him he was going to teach him how to take out a sentry and to do it silently.

"Do you have a knife on you now?"

"I have a Ka-Bar stuck inside my belt at my back." FNG said.

The team leader reached into a small backpack he always carried with him. "Take this Randall hunting knife. A guy that rotated back to the world gave it to me. I have one like it myself. You can get them from the Special Forces men if something happens to that one."

"I like the looks of the knife. Is it any better to use than the Marine Ka-Bar?"

"The Randall will cut through muscle and bone if the bone isn't too large. The Ka-Bar was made for combat, the Randall is made to kill people quickly with no noise at all. I'm going to teach you how to make the proper moves to kill an enemy silently. Turn around, I'll let you see and feel the moves that you need to make into an automatic series of motions."

FNG turned his back to the team leader and stood still, as relaxed as he could be, under the circumstances. FNG didn't hear the team leader approach him from the back. He didn't smell him. He didn't sense him in any way. An arm came around the right side of his neck and in one motion the hand clamped down on his mouth and nose, so he couldn't breathe or yell out an alarm. The team leader grabbed a hand full of hair with his left hand and pulled his head back using the power of his right hand. The team leader sliced with his Randell in one swift motion. The blunt side of a knife crossed from the right and made a hard swipe across FNG'S throat. The team leader waited like that for a few seconds.

"That's the way to kill a sentry silently or for that matter an enemy that you need to kill in close quarters combat," his team leader told him. "Now you try it on me."

They changed position with the team leader in front and FNG with the knife. It happened like flipping a switch. FNG's Dark Persona took over in the bat of an eye. He flipped the Randall knife around in his hand for a couple of times and then moved in quietly. He held his breath so the leader wouldn't hear him coming and struck with his left hand forcibly over the leaders nose and mouth. He pushed back with force from his left arm and hand. His right hand at the same time cut across the team leaders throat with the blunt side of the blade. He stood like that for a moment in a moment of rapture.

The team leader threw FNG's arm away from his neck, and turned on him in a crouch with his Randall knife drawn and pointed at FNG.

"What the hell are you doing, troop?" The team leader said to him angrily.

FNG's switch flipped. "I was trying to get all the movements down into one motion, team leader."

"I think you're a natural. It seemed almost like you had done it all before. You had all the moves down and made the kill like a man that had done it before. You'll be the main man, other than me, to take out sentries or to do silent kills for the team, if I'm not available. Consider the lesson on sentry killing with a knife completed."

CHAPTER TWENTY-SIX

Kat left the envelopes from the apartment laying on the rider's side of the front seat while she drove back toward her apartment. She decided half-way to her apartment that she had time to drive back across the bay bridge and drive to Modesto. She had to cross the bay bridge to get to her apartment anyway. Modesto was southeast of San Francisco, however it was an easy drive along I-580 east. The drive to the auto storage building took her a little over an hour. The office was still open when she parked her car in the office parking area.

She showed the envelopes from the storage company and asked the clerk where the car in question was parked. The clerk looked in her file cabinet and brought out a manila file folder with the parking space number on it. She looked through the folder first.

"I'm sorry but that vehicle has been sold for salvage. It was towed to a salvage company a week ago."

"I need the address of that salvage company. Is it in Modesto?"

"Yes. I'll write it down for you."

"If you have a description of the car, would you write that down also?"

"Sure thing. I don't think the salvage company would have had time to salvage it or to sell it for an as is auto. I looked at it as the tow truck left the building, it was a nice car."

Kat asked the clerk if she could go up to the parking space that the car had been at to look around the area before she went to the salvage company.

The clerk gave her a piece of note paper with the address of the salvage company and told her it would be alright for her to check the parking space out before she left.

The parking space was on the third floor in a darkened place under a ramp up to the next floor. Kat parked away from the parking space where the car had been stored. There was nothing to indicate that the car she was looking for had been parked there. She drove back down to the bottom of the ramp and out of the storage building. The salvage company was on the northeast side of Modesto. She hoped she would be there before they closed for the day.

The traffic was light, and allowed her to make the drive through the center of town at thirty-five miles an hour. The traffic lights were set for that speed. She hit every one of the lights on green. Sometimes it's the little things that made her feel the happiest.

She parked outside the salvage company office, but walked to the wire fence that served as a sliding entrance to their back lot of salvaged cars and trucks. She saw the car she was interested in still setting chained on the back of a tow truck. She hurried back to the front door and pulled on it, hoping it was still unlocked. The door swung open with the tinkle of a small bell that hung on the door sill.

The room she entered smelled of engine oil. She could see a young man at a counter looking her way through the chaotic stacks of used auto parts. There were baskets and boxes of smaller parts, and large parts were laying on the dirty floor edging a walkway to the counter that was just as grimy as the rest of the place.

The man at the counter asked what she needed. She pulled her credentials holder out and flashed it at him.

"I'm investigating a murder case. I need the title information for that Ford coupe out there in your yard that is still chained on the tow truck," she told him.

"The boss is gone for the day," he told her. "Can you come back tomorrow?"

"This is very important! Somewhere a killer is loose, and I'm trying to stop him before he kills again. Don't you have access to that information in case some buyer comes along while the owner is away," she asked him.

"I don't guess it will matter to the boss, since it's a police matter."

He went through an open door that was covered in oily hand prints and smudges. She watched as he pulled a drawer open in a tall metal file cabinet. He worked his way through a group of folders and pulled a new one out. It was actually clean of oily finger prints. Kat figured it was the one that had information for the car on the tow trunk, since it was obviously new. He handed the file to Kat and then said, "what's a pretty young woman like you doing on the police force?"

Kat wanted to jump down the guys throat, but ignored him as she opened the file. The one piece of information that she wanted was right on top of other paperwork pertaining to the car on the tow truck. The owner of the salvage company had requested a copy of the title to the car using the license plate number. The owner was listed at the top. The address was that of the apartment that she checked out earlier. She took her note pad out and made those entries.

"I need to look the interior of the car over. Is it locked?" She asked the man behind the counter in a very police sort of way.

The man took the file back and re-filed it. On the back wall was a cork board with hooks on it for key placement. He found the keys to the Ford and gave them to her.

"Don't fall off the tow truck cutie."

The guy was starting to get to her. She walked out of the office through a side door that went to the salvage yard. She walked around the tow truck at first looking for anything that would catch her eye. It was a nice, clean, new car. She stepped on the hub of the rear dual wheels of the tow truck and pulled herself up to the flat bed where the car was chained. She walked around the exterior not sure what she was looking for. The key she had opened the driver's side door, and she slid in under the steering wheel. There was an odd smell to the interior. She thought it might be from having been closed up for a long time. Everything seemed to be in good order in the front of the car. She was disappointed. She had been hoping to find something that would tie the owner of the car, to the murdered maid. She pulled the lock up on the back door of the car and went around the open front door. She saw a plastic trash bag immediately. It was stuffed part way into the space under the driver's seat. Before she removed it, she looked over the rest of the back seat. She walked to other side of the car, opened the door, and checked under the front seat on that side of the car. There was nothing unusual there. She went to the trunk and unlocked it. The spare tire was the only thing there, in fact she thought she could still smell the new car odor.

Kat's heart was beating rapidly when she pulled the plastic bag from under the front seat. It had a tie twisted around the top that wasn't doing a very good job of keeping the odors in the bag. It smelled of desiccating tissue. She held her breath and opened the bag. The smell almost knocked her off the tow truck. She let go of the bag and turned to face off the bed of the truck. She thought she was going to throw up.

It took a few minutes for her to regain control of her senses before she tied the twist tie around the bag again. This time she made it as tight as she could, but there was still a stench about it. She closed the car doors and locked them all. The trunk lid was already closed. She dropped the plastic bag down to the gravel covered ground, and stepped carefully down to the hub of the dual wheels again. She dropped down to the gravel beside the plastic bag.

It was a short walk back to the salvage office. She had the bag in one hand and the car keys in the other when she walked up to the counter.

The man behind the counter gave her another look, like he was undressing her. She slammed the car keys on the counter and turned to leave.

"You sure did make that old tow truck look good while you climbed around on it. You want a job driving the truck? I bet you'd knock the guys out that you had to deal with every day," the lecherous asshole said.

Kat didn't look back, she didn't say anything, she made it to the front entrance before the man at the counter asked, "What's in the bag? Something in that bag smells terrible. You can't take stuff off the salvage yard without approval."

Kat went back to the counter and looked the man in the eyes. "What you smell is the decomposition of human tissue. I've checked it out. There's a penis and a scrotum with the testicles still in it. The killer must be a woman. The woman that did the cutting must have got fed up with dumbass jerks like you. In fact, I'm getting fed up with the stupid shit behind the counter at the salvage yard. I've got the knife that did the cutting, maybe I should do some cutting on you. I'm taking the fucking bag with me!"

After Kat started her car, she sat for a minute trying to calm down. The combination of the horrible smell and the greasy worm behind the counter were a bit much. She went by a local pharmacy on her way back to her apartment and purchased some surgical gloves and a mask. She stopped at a dumpster behind the pharmacy and opened the bag up. The mask helped a lot with the smell.

There were a shirt and pants crammed into the bag. They had dried blood all over them. There were blood covered shoes and socks. A towel with blood coagulated on it. At the bottom of the bag there was a large kitchen butcher knife with dried blood, and some pea-sized pieces of tissue on the double sided knife handle. It was the same make as the cardboard and plastic cover she had recovered from the trash can at the apartment. Something moved in the corner of the bag when she pulled the knife out. She couldn't see what it was, but she could feel it, even with the surgical gloves on. She took it out with her finger tips and let it roll into her palm. It was a fingertip. The first joint of a finger had been severed from a hand. She took the gloves and mask off and ran back into the pharmacy. She came right back, and put new gloves on with the same mask. She tore off a piece of the Scotch roll tape she had run back to the store to buy. She gently put the piece of the finger in her palm and applied the sticky side of the tape to it. She pulled the tape off after she had made sure it was in good contact with the fingertip. She had a perfect finger print to use for identification of the body it came from.

She took off the gloves and mask and went back in the pharmacy to buy a box of plastic bags to put the clothes and the knife in. She threw everything else in the dumpster. The tape with the finger print went inside one of the envelopes she had lying on the driver's side seat.

She drove away from the pharmacy certain she was about to learn the true identity of the maid's killer. She was going to take some of the dried blood to a local blood bank and have it typed as well. That she would do in the morning. No, she wouldn't. 'Damn,' she thought, tomorrow was Saturday. She'd take it over Monday morning.

She left the clothes and knife in the new bag in her car trunk when she reached her apartment. The first thing she did when she walked in the apartment; other than checking for the blinking light on the recorder, was to go through the papers she had from the coroner's office. She found what she was looking for two pages down. The maid's blood type on the coroner's report was AB negative. A rare blood type, for sure. She couldn't wait for the blood bank to type the dried blood from the clothes and knife handle.

CHAPTER TWENTY-SEVEN

There was another week of intensive training by each member of the team; with the last two days of the week going out in full gear with the entire team and patrolling a non-secure area around the base. At the end of that week the sergeant called him over to the team's quarters, and told him he was going to be the slack man; the last man in the line of the Lurp team for the first few times he went out with the team. The sergeant told him there was less possibility of him screwing up back there and killing other team members or for that matter the whole team. He was told to keep his eyes and ears open for movement as the team moved in front of him. The enemy liked to wait until the Lurp teams passed by them and then close the back door on the trail. He was told there would be a briefing the next day.

He was issued a marine Ka-Bar fighting knife, and a used M-1911A1 .45 caliber semi-automation pistol. His back pack was filled with extra magazines for the M-14, several smoke grenades and anti-personnel grenades, two Claymore mines, a medical pack and C-rations to eat.

The leader of the team, at the briefing, told the team they were going out for a short hump, to break-in the FNG. The four other team members nodded their approval. The entire team was airborne qualified, but they were walking into the bush for the training patrol for the FNG. They would be out for five days to find a new unit of NVA operating in the area.

The team leader told them, "This is a hunter-kill operation. Communication security people have detected an increase in enemy radio traffic northwest of here. If there are a large number of NVA at the camp, we call artillery in. If it's a smaller recon group, at our discretion, we take them out. If it's a group we can take out, our sniper will take out officers first. Keep your distance, lock and load when we leave the perimeter of our camp. Remember the objective of this patrol is for all of us to survive."

The Lurp team headed through a small concertina wire gap that acted like a hallway into and out of their camp. The team leader headed northeast along a trail into the jungle's edge where it had been cut back to make a free fire zone around the camp. He headed northeast first, in case there were Victor Charlies monitoring the movements of their team from the camp. There was a slight mist floating down through the triple canopy jungle. It made the point man's vision like he was looking through a thin layer of fog. It was the first month of monsoon season in the highlands of South Vietnam.

The team leader held up his hand with his fingers together and it was passed down the line to FNG at the slack position. He stopped behind the scout at a distance of about six meters. It was the distance he was told to keep when they were moving through the jungle. He kept his head on a swivel looking for anything that was out of place; the wrong color, smelled bad or movement. The team leader waited a few minutes to check his compass, and then turned to the RTO putting his arm out in front of him and pumped it up and down at his elbow. It was passed down to the slack man again. That was the signal to move forward. When the FNG made it to where the team leader had stopped the small column of men, the team leader had made a ninety degree turn to the northwest and headed for the area where the NVA were reported to be located.

The point man position was rotated between the four experienced team members. FNG remained at the slack position. It was on the third day out when the point man stopped and raised his left hand, with fingers together, to his ear. As the signal was passed along, each man stood quietly checking for noise, an unusual smell, and looked carefully into the surrounding jungle. A few minutes passed, until the point man moved his left hand to shoulder's height and moved his forearm from the elbow up and down rapidly. The point man had made visual contact with the enemy off to his left. He quickly put his hand to the collar of his fatigue jacket and moved the corner up and down rapidly. The team leader, who was in the third slot, moved up to him quickly.

There were sounds of an enemy camp and a smell of burning wood on the slight wind working its way through the jungle. The team leader held up his hand with three fingers showing. The team member in the third position moved past the other team members to the team leader's position. He was the team scout. They conferred in whispered voices, and the scout moved out toward the left of the team; looking for the camp where the smoke and noises were located. He was back in ten minutes.

FNG saw the team member in front of him give the signal to go to the leader. He advanced slowly to where the other members of the team were gathered loosely around the team leader.

"The enemy has what looks like a permanent camp down in a valley shaped like a bowl with hills around it, to the left of us. I'm sending the scout back to get a head count, so we know more or less what we're up against. The rest of the team will form a loose half-circle defensive position on me and wait for the scout to return," the team leader told them.

No one said a word. The scout left the team again and the other four men, including the FNG, spread out in a semi-circle around the team leader's position about six meters from where he stood. When they were at the positions they picked, the team leader went to his knee, and moved his left arm up and down telling his team to go flat to the ground.

The scout came back several hours later and reported to the team leader. It was a company sized unit. The team leader called FNG and the RTO over to his position, and told them to be set up by night fall in a position to take out the ranking officer at the camp. The team set up around the bowl placing their Claymore mines where they would do the most damage, and made their hides accordingly. FNG would take out the highest officer, and that would be the signal for the team leader to call in artillery. The Claymores would be used only if about to be overrun.

FNG nodded and whispered for the RTO that was his spotter to follow him. He went to the top of the ridge that partly surrounded the bowl and moved through the dense jungle like he had done it a thousand times. He found a place that gave him a clear line of fire into the camp. There was one larger tent, with a guard casually standing by the entrance. FNG figured that was the tent of the commanding officer of the company sized NVA unit. The RTO started helping him set up before the sun went down: it disappeared rapidly in the dense jungle.

Slowly through the night, NFG could feel his Dark Persona taking over. He could feel the adrenaline pulsing through his veins. He made sure he didn't look in the direction of the RTO spotter. His eyes were changing to the yellow-red colors of the Dark Persona. He wasn't scared, he wasn't nervous, he was exhilarated! He had placed his rucksack at the front of his hide to act as a rest for the barrel of his M-14. He knew he wouldn't sleep the entire night, for that reason he let his Dark Persona take him back to his killing of drill sergeant Fowler. Now that his new team leader had taught him the best way to make a silent kill, he knew he was lucky that the drunk sergeant didn't yell out the second before he slit his throat. He knew he would do better the next time. Then he smiled to himself at the thought of slitting another throat, and sipping the blood of his prey. He began to think of the four men in his Long-Range Recon team, as his protectors. With them around him, no harm would come to him. All was quiet around the bowl, except for the light clicks of metal on metal from the camp, as the guards walked around the perimeter of the camp.

The first gray light of the morning came slowly through the thick growth of trees, giant ferns, and low brush. NFG was settled in with his weapon, waiting for the perfect moment. His breathing was slow, he senses were acute, his eye sight was clear and perfect. He was his Dark Persona!

His RTO spotter whispered, "the troops are starting to come from their tents. A flap on the front of the larger tent has been thrown back; an officer with three yellow chevrons on a red background, a captain started giving orders to the guard at his tent. The captain in front of the tent is your target."

FNG already had the captain in his scope. He waited a hairs breath, thinking there would be other officers reporting to the major about their men, and what their assignments for the day might be. He was right, another officer, obviously a minor one, went to the captain and saluted, two more came, and saluted. A conversation was started.

The Dark Persona put the cross hairs of his scope at the top of the major's head and slowly, ever so slowly, let his breath out, and took the slack up on the M-14's trigger. There was a release of the trigger, a crack of the bullet firing, and soft thud, as the bolt closed on a new round. He knew he had killed the captain when he pulled the trigger. The captain's head blew apart like an egg dropped from a ten-story building. He moved his sight to one of the other officers that were standing still around the falling major, and shot him in the back, through the heart. There were two more shots in rapid fire succession, and the last officer and a top enemy sergeant fell to the ground, dead. It had taken ten seconds for the FNG to take out three enemy officers, and one high non-commissioned officer. The Dark Persona was elated with his results. He could feel the ecstasy rushing through his body.

He realized that the RTO, his spotter, was shaking him by his shoulder.

"Come on man, come on. Grab your rucksack and let's get the fuck out ah here!" The RTO said.

Just then there was a loud noise overhead as the rattle, rattle of artillery shells broke over the ridge and fell on the enemy camp. The shells sounded like tin foil being wadded into a ball and then the blast came. By the time the team had gathered at their pre-arranged spot in the jungle the camp below them was being torn apart piece by piece, and body by body.

The RTO told the rest of the team about the NFG methodically taking out the four enemy soldiers, including three officers in less than ten seconds.

"I couldn't believe it, there was a crack, crack, crack, crack and the four guys were dead. I think we need to change his name for FNG to Slack."

They started to move out, working their way back to the base by a different way to stop any chance of an enemy ambush. Two days later they made it back to the Lurp camp and all the team members were calling FNG, Slack, by then.

Slack kind of liked his new name! He found that shooting people, and watching their heads blow apart, like a watermelon hitting a cement walk, was very pleasing to him. Cutting their throats, and watching them bleed out, was like a climax to him. That was it, a climax!

CHAPTER TWENTY-EIGHT

The weekend of rest and relaxation did wonders for Kat. She had placed the Scotch tape finger print in a stamp folder for safe keeping and used some more tape to attach the small folder on the inside of the front cover of her murder file. She had taken the time to put on another pair of surgical gloves and cut a narrow splinter of wood with clotted blood on it from the handle of the butcher knife, and then laid the knife on the cardboard package that she found in apartment A-3. It fit perfectly. She covered it with the clear plastic cover and taped in closed. It went into a cloth bag that was on the floor under her small desk. She cut the largest glob of blood from the front of the shirt and put it with the splinter of wood. She put the small cloth bag on the console table next to the front door; she didn't want to forget it when she left for the local blood bank.

Kat parked in a space in front of the blood bank. Her car was the only one there. She had been waiting for two days to get the blood typed from the plastic bag. She went to the front door and tried to open it. The door was locked. She went back to her car and waited. A woman in scrubs unlocked the door a few minutes later. Kat went to the reception desk where the same woman sat and asked if it was possible to get a blood type from dried blood.

"It doesn't take much. We put a saline solution on the clotted blood to make it into a more liquid form. We only need a drop. It is a fairly common request. Mom's worry about their children, especially when they get hurt in some why and bleed from a cut or scratch. They usually bring it in on a used bandage."

"How long will it take to type it?"

"Generally, twenty to thirty minutes. You're the only one here, so I would guess on the shorter time," the woman in the scrubs told Kat.

"Do I wait?"

"You can wait. There are chairs over by the door. You'll need to pay in advance for the service. Once you have done that you can leave and come back to get the results."

Kat showed her the blood clot on the wood splinter and the larger glob on the piece of shirt material. The nurse told her they should be able to type one of them. Kat paid and went back to her car. She had passed a Dunkin Donuts on the way to the blood bank.

By the time she had finished her cup of coffee and a glazed donut, it was time to return to the blood bank, a few blocks away. The same woman in scrubs was at the counter when she entered the blood bank.

"You're right on time. The results of your blood typing came out to me just a few minutes ago."

She handed Kat a form with the blood banks name at the top. It had Kat's name next and then some medical information about the clot that she didn't understand. At the bottom in a special box was the blood type the test had revealed. It was AB negative.

"We would appreciate the person that has that blood type donating blood from time to time. AB negative blood types make up only four percent of the people living in the United States. It's very rare, and we try to kept track of nearby donor's, in case of an emergency. Do you think this person would sign up to donate if they are contacted by our blood bank?" The woman in the scrubs asked.

"I'll have to talk with her first," returned Kat.

"That'll be great. Let us know please."

Kat walked back to her car and sat with her hands on the steering wheel. She had a body chill as she realized what the blood type meant.

She had looked up the local draft board location for San Francisco county over the past weekend and drove through the Monday morning traffic to the south side of city. It was next to a new post office building. The parking lot in front of the draft board office was completely filled. She parked at the post office and walked over to the front door of the draft board's office. There was a line of young men moving slowly down roped off corridors that eventually allow them to reach one of the clerks behind a counter that looked much like a bank.

It took almost an hour for Kat to reach one of the clerks behind the counter with a glass divider between the clerk and Kat.

"Where do the men that are drafted from San Francisco county take their basic training?" She asked.

"For the Marines, they go to Camp Pendleton. For the Army they go to Fort Ord."

Kat took the envelope from her hip pocket that was from the draft board and asked if there was any way to tell if it was the Marines or the Army that the person named on the envelope was inducted into. The lady took the envelope under the glass divider and circled a number that was immediately below the address. That number means he was inducted into the Army.

The woman behind the glass enclosure looked to the line behind Kat in the rope corridor and shouted, "NEXT."

CHAPTER TWENTY-NINE

Mrs. Robinson sulked in her living room. She was deep in alcohol depression and decreased coordination caused by Valium. She hadn't been out, looking for a new pry in weeks. The Chinaman was great and lasted the longest of any man she had seduced in recent history. There were those in the past years, starting before her husband's sudden demise: she smiled at the memory. The men around the globe were like American's as a whole. Some better than others.

What she was missing was a close to hand female lover that would play with her when she wanted. It wasn't that she missed the young maid: she had become her on demand lover and was starting to really enjoy their time in her special room. It took time to introduce people to B.D.S.M. Mrs. Robinson had no special play part, however being a Dominatrix was the basis of primary control over any of her lovers; be them male or female.

Gayle Pauline had answered her ad in the Globe newspaper for an in-house maid. Mrs. Robinson interviewed several young women: that's what she really needed, a young woman. The old maid had been difficult at times. She wasn't a totally willing partner. She needed another young woman as a maid to train to be her partner in everything that was; Bondage, Discipline, Submission, Sadism, and Masochism!

She started to stagger into bedroom to take a shower. She didn't have time for an ad to come out and then go through the interview process, she needed one quickly, she was tired of men and their incessant desire to use their dicks.

She was taking off her clothes and stepping into the large walk-in shower when the word dick made her think of the stupid little private investigator she had hired. She was so inept that she couldn't find anything to report to her about. She was off on some damn tangent looking for who knew what about the killer of the maid. She didn't expect her to find anything. She was lathering herself up in the shower and began to feel the need for a sex partner. What about the private investigator, she was cute and had a body made for sex. Stupid, but sexy. Was that a good combination for her possible training in the finer art of sex and play? 'Not so much,' she thought.

She gave up on that idea by the time she was out of the walk-in shower and was dressing to attach attention at a local lesbian bar. She had noticed a lesbian club while she was in Chinatown seducing Li.

The front of the club looked inviting, and there was music she like coming from the open front door. Maybe they had a dance floor. She fought through her valium sedated unawareness and remembered its name. The G Shop. She grinned to herself over the name. She loved to dance with other women, they were always much smoother in their dancing than men were.

She went to her dresser and sorted through her t-shirt collection. She picked out a folded black T that had the word Bitch written in cursive across the front. She held it up in front of her near perfect breasts and smiled. She put it aside and continued looking through her t-shirt drawer. She picked up a light green T with the word Beast written across the front in bold print letters. It was perfect for how she felt after the alcohol, Valium, and the long cold shower.

She stood in front of her mirror and slipped the Beast t-shirt over her head and pulled it over her breast. She felt her nipples harden with the subtle caress of the soft linen green t-shirt. There was a special pair of blue jeans that she thought would be perfect. She went to her walk-in closet and moved down long row of clothes until she reached the blue jean area. All the jeans were hung with no wrinkles in them. The young maid had always taken care of washing, drying and hanging all her clothes. There was no ironing necessary on the pair she picked. There were ragged holes over the knee areas. There was a vertical rip at the corner of the right rear pocket that allowed anyone looking at it to see she wasn't wearing panties. The jeans were some of her favorite Levi's with a button up front. She tucked the

Beast t-shirt into the jeans; she liked the way it showed off her naked breast under it. She thought about putting on a belt but decided against it. She braided her hair and stuffed it under a ball cap and put on a pair of soft leather western high heel boots. She left all her make-up off.

She walked over to a full- length mirror: she liked what she saw. She brushed against her nipples with one hand and tapped on the lip that covered her clit, lightly. It didn't take a minute or so, thinking of a young lesbian woman naked beside her in bed to cause the turning point from pleasing excitement; to a sense of arousal that she had no control over. She let herself go, she continued the slight tapping and brushing, until it felt so damn good she couldn't resist what she knew was starting to happen. She trembled as an almost electrical charge went over her body. She grabbed for the edge of a dresser to keep her from falling, and almost fell anyway, her legs were weak. She relaxed there, feeling refreshed and excited for what might occur later that night.

Mrs. Robinson left her bedroom, and ambled over to the bar to make a double dry Martini, before she left for Chinatown. She drove at the speed limit and stopped at all the stoplights and signs. No need to get a ticket on the way. She parked in the same lot that she had used when she went hunting for Li, the last pry she had enjoyed. She timed her arrival perfectly. It was dusk over the ocean, and the lights along the street that The G Shop was on hadn't turned on yet. The bar lights she could see as she walked up to the entrance were subtle, but multi-colored. The music was coming from a Juke box, and the soft sound of social talk whiffed by her like an exquisitely scented candle. She had that tingle that she loved so much when she was about to begin her hunt.

There was a butch, acting as a bouncer, standing inside the door to check ages for entry. In San Francisco, the drinking age was twenty-one, but she was also looking for anyone that might cause trouble. The city let them stay open as long as there wasn't a problem that required a police officer. Lesbian bars weren't allowed to operate under existing city law.

Mrs. Robinson stepped inside the bar and stood to the side for a moment while her eyes adjusted to the light cast by the colored lights placed around the bar in a artful way. She wasn't about to walk in and stumble over something. When she could see comfortably again, she walked over to an empty barstool at the end of the bar that faced the tables and dance floor. It was her favorite place to begin her search for a new quarry.

The Juke box started playing Goodnight Sweetheart, by the Platters. There was a shuffle of butches asking femmes that were unattended to dance. She remained seated at the end of the bar and looked over the femmes that ended up on the dance floor with a butch. The butches that had a femme on the dance floor were busy chatting their dance partners up, while making the soft, subtle body movements that each one thought might attract her femme on the dance floor to want to become better acquainted with her during the night of drinking and dancing.

There were some very pretty femmes on the dance floor, but none of them drew Mrs. Robinson attention for more than a passing moment. She had through the years formed a sexual fetish that she focused on when searching for a new conquest. She watched the dancers come and go while finishing a few more drinks, and then she saw her.

She was a young femme and appeared to be somewhat uneasy about walking into the dancing area. She was slim, with just a slight hint of a well-formed body under her casual clothes. Makeup was minimal, which was fine with Mrs. Robinson. The young femme, trying out her sexuality, maybe for the first time, was gorgeous with no covering up of anything. Mrs. Robinson's heart beat a bit faster when she thought of the young woman naked with her in bed, letting Mrs. Robinson teach her what she liked most.

Mrs. Robinson waited for a while to see how the young woman accepted the advances of the butches hanging around the dance area. She waited for the right moment and when it came, she walked across the dance floor as Unchanged Melody started to play on the Juke. This was not her first rodeo. She smiled at the young woman and held out her hand, inviting her to take it, and go with Mrs. Robinson out to the dance floor. She held the young femme softly with a gentle hand guiding her around the dance floor, like a professional dancer would do. She made sure there was slight, brief touching of their bodies, at the right times during the song, nothing overbearing or clinging about it. She was a pro.

When the song was over, she walked the young woman over to the small table where she had been sitting and asked if it would be alright if she asked her again for a dance when one of her favorites was played. The young femme told her she would look forward to it.

Mrs. Robinson had made up her mind. The young woman was exactly what she needed. She reminded her of the young maid that she trained over time to become her private lover. It took her forever to train her to like the dark side of sex. This one would be more willing to learn from her, and she would groom her more carefully, particularly in the finer ways of lovemaking and sadomasochistic sexual pleasures. Her favorite.

She danced another time with the young femme, letting her take her time about asking if Mrs. Robinson would like to sit with her at her table. They began talking about nothing and ended up later that night, as new friends. Mrs. Robinson, the predator, knew that with this one was going to take some time, but she felt in her bones that it would be worth the effort. The young femme made her excuses and left the bar, promising to come back several days later to meet her new acquaintance for a drink and to get to know Mrs. Robinson better. That was exactly what Mrs. Robinson wanted. The predator would have licked her lips in anticipation; and howled at the moon if she wanted to do so, right then.

She made her way back to the mansion and did one rail of cocaine before she went to sleep to dream about her new pry, and what the future might hold for the young woman as she grew to love her Dominatrix.

Mrs. Robinson sat up in bed in the middle of the night from a drugged sleep, and realized she didn't know the name of her new subjugate.

CHAPTER THIRTY

K at made a quick trip back to her apartment and packed an overnight bag with what she thought she would need for a short trip down to Fort Ord, California.

Highway one ran along the coast, it was a pleasant drive on any day. She drove across the bay bridge and caught highway one on the southwest side of San Francisco. Fort Ord was located a few miles east of Monterey, some of the most beautiful coast line was between Monterey and Big Sur. She was going to enjoy the trip to Fort Ord as much as possible. There was a state highway that ran from Big Sur to Fort Ord. From Monterey to Big Sur was one of the most famous drives along the California coast.

The drive to Monterey was an easy two hours. Kat was being a tourist and driving below the speed limit so she could take in the coast's beauty. She watched in her rear-view mirror as an orange colored Dodge Charger Daytona muscle car followed along behind her. The car had the normal black trim of a muscle car: the driver was driving erratically. He ran to within a few feet of her car; and then slowed down suddenly, and then back again, like he wanted to pass her, however he couldn't decide when to do it. It bothered Kat that the driver of the other car was driving so badly that she had to use all of her attention on driving down the narrow two-lane highway; while not watching the green and blue water of the surf.

She decided to slow down even more. The speeding Dodge Charger kept pace with her. She was able to see two men in the car in the rear-view mirror when the racing car came roaring up to the rear of her car. She started to tap her brakes just enough to get the rear lights to glow red. The racing Dodge Charger pulled up to the rear of her car; swerved to the side, and raced up beside her, fortunately there was no on-coming traffic. The orange and black car started to edge toward the side of Kat's car: like the driver was going to hit her car on purpose. She hit her brake hard and slid almost to a stop. The other car did the same.

Kat wasn't about to stop on the coast highway in the middle of the day and let the two men get away with endangering her life for fun. She dropped her car into a lower gear and floored the accelerator. She swung the steering wheel to the left. Her car raced pass the orange car, and was past it before the other car's driver could react. The charger raced up behind her, and again pulled along-side of her car. The man in the shotgun seat had his window down and was waving a pistol in her direction.

She reached to the small of her back with her right hand, and pulled her .357 Smith and Wesson pistol out. She was either going to scare the crap out of the idiot waving the gun or get in a gun fight while driving down the highway on a bright sunny day at the beach. She held her pistol in her right hand while driving with her left and pointed it at the man with the gun. He ducked lower behind the car door. The driver floored the muscle car and roared away down the highway like a scare rabbit. Kat continued to drive down the highway after she had put her pistol back in its place at her back. She was shaking from the experience, and had no idea what or why the two men were acting like they wanted to make her first crash her car, and to threaten her with a gun was more that she was willing to allow.

The episode with the orange Dodge Charger took all the pleasure out of her drive down highway one along the coast to Monterey. She was calming down from the incident when she reached Monterey. She was going to finish her pleasure drive from Monterey to Big Sure and then turn inland to Fort Ord despite what happened earlier in the afternoon.

At first, she didn't notice the car that was following behind her at a normal distance, as she was leaving the city of Monterey on highway one headed for Big Sur. She was driving the speed limit when several cars passed her going toward Big Sur. That let her see farther behind her in her rear-view mirror. The orange Dodge Charger was once again behind her. She saw a road sign that indicated the Bixby Canyon Bridge was coming up in a mile. She knew about the bridge, but had never been over it. It was all concrete with a three-hundred feet drop to the jagged rocks and cliffs along the coast road. She raced her car far beyond the speed limit; not wanting to get jammed up, or shot while on the bridge.

The orange Dodge Charger raced up suddenly, and began to pass her as she started onto the high bridge. It swerved like it was going to push her against the low cement railing of the bridge. The man on the rider's side looked at her with a grin on his face and gave her the finger. She slammed on her brakes, swerved into the on-coming lane trying to get away from the other car. The driver of the orange Dodge Charger under corrected as he raced into the south bound lane in front of Kat, trying to cut her off or make her hit the bridge. The orange Dodge Charger's right front tire clipped the bottom of the low cement rail. An instant later the tire blew out. The racing car flew into the air; flipping as it went over the top of the low cement rail, dropped three hundred feet to the rocks below where it immediately exploded into fire, like a napalm bomb going off.

Kat didn't look back. She drove as fast as her car would go for several miles and then slowed down. She was shaking all over. 'What the hell just happened?' She wondered.

There was nothing she could do about the wrecked car that flew over the rail. She continued to Big Sur and turned east to Fort Ord. She was still wondering why the two men were trying to kill her when she reached Fort Ord.

Kat pulled into the parking lot of a nice motel just a block away from the main entrance to Fort Ord. It was a two-story stucco covered building with parking out front and a red tile roof. The office was at the end of long building across from the swimming pool. She checked in for one night. She thought she would have the information she needed by then.

Kat was still jumpy about the attempt on her life. It wasn't reasonable to believe that it was a random act. Was it possible that another try would occur? There was no way of knowing for sure. She made sure the room's door was locked and chained before she went to bed. She put her .357 Magnum under her pillow. It seemed like an absurd thing to do, but she had learned to plan for the unfathomable while in the army.

She was starving when she checked out of the hotel the next morning. A small chain café was around the corner from the motel. It had a sign up saying they had world famous breakfasts. That sounded like what the doctor ordered.

The coffee was strong, but she liked it that way. The pancakes and eggs with a side of bacon had filled the empty spot she had from not eating for twenty-four hours.

She drove directly from the café to the main entrance guard house, and told the soldier on duty there that she needed a visitor's pass to the headquarters offices for the basic training command. He checked her in and started to give her directions.

"It's okay. I did my basic here a few years back. I know my way around the base, soldier," she told him.

He walked over to the cross bar that blocked entry to the base and pushed the weighted end of the long pole down to get the rest of the pole to rise and let her drive passed the tall wire fence with concertina wire on top.

The main command headquarters were close to the entrance she had been checked through. The army didn't want civilian traffic driving around in the training area, disturbing the new recruits. She parked in the visitor's parking area and locked her pistol in the glove compartment. She wasn't authorized to be carrying her civilian gun on Fort Ord.

She checked in at the reception desk and asked to see the officer in charge for that day. She told the young private first-class what her business was concerning and waited while he went down a long corridor to find out if the OIC, Officer in Charge, would see her.

The reception clerk walked her down the corridor to an office with the hallway door open. A captain that was sitting behind a gray metal desk with his back to a large window overlooking a parade ground.

He remained seated when she walked up to his desk, as a show of power, she figured.

"What can the army do for you Miss?" The Captain asked in a tone that told Kat he was impressed with himself.

"I'm ex-Staff Sergeant and former CID, Criminal Investigation Department, agent, Kat McNally. I am now a private investigator. I'm here in search of information about a recruit that was processed through the basic training program in the past six months."

"We don't normally give out military information to civilians, Miss McNally. I'm sure you know that being ex-CID."

"This man is a possible murder suspect, Captain. He was a civilian when the murder happened and I happen to know, since I'm ex-CID, that the military tries to co-operate with civilian criminal investigation if it might involve a presently serving soldier. I'm here to co-operate with you about this matter, or I will be forced to request a meeting with your commanding officer, Captain."

Kat's comment got the attention of the young captain. "We do our best to facilitate military and civilian criminal investigations. What's the name of the soldier, and when did he take basic training here?" The Captain asked her.

Kat handed the draft notice envelope to the captain, without any explanation. "I'm not sure of the exact dates that he may have passed through Fort Ord. Probably, in the last three to six months, according to the induction date on the draft notice," she told him.

"That's a lot of time to have to check through, Miss McNally. It might take weeks to locate their records," the Captain told her.

"Captain, I know your files are in alphabetic order, and that you have a staff of young privates that do nothing but deal with records request for basic training soldiers. They are kept separate from all other soldier's files for just that reason. Some of them always seem to have warrants for their arrest when they come here for basic training. They are trying to run from their past indiscretions."

"Miss McNally, since you seem to know about our separate files on recent inductees, I will simply ask you to return tomorrow. I should have the information you need at that time. Now if you don't mind, I'm a busy man," the Captain said with a very busy tone.

"I'm sure you are, Captain. I'll tell the private first-class at the reception desk that I will need a pass to enter Fort Ord tomorrow to get the information that I need. And a good day to you, sir."

She was given the pass from the soldier clerk and left the post. She checked back in the motel for another night. Kat didn't sleep well;

she was re-playing the attempt on her life by the two men in the Dodge Charger.

She had an early breakfast at the same café. The waitress nodded her approval when Kat ordered green tomales with hot green chili sauce on the side. She needed something to kick start her morning since she didn't get much sleep the night before.

Everything starts early on a military post! Kat took a cup of coffee to go and drove over to the main gate at Fort Ord. She presented her pass to the security guard on duty there. He waved her through the pole gate that had its own soldier to raise and lower it.

The private-first class clerk ushered Kat into the not so friendly captain's office, as soon as she arrived. He was still sitting behind his desk, but this time he motioned with his right hand to the coffee pot sitting on a gray metal tray with wheels. Everything in the army was colored gray. Why that was the case, Kat didn't know.

There were no pleasantries between the captain and Kat. She took a seat in front of him at his desk and waited. The captain had a manila folder file in front of him, and he was obviously aggravated about something.

"This is the file for the basic training graduate that you requested. After graduation he was sent to advanced training in Vietnam as a sniper. His awards during basic training were the expert marksman badge with both pistol and rifle. He graduated with the rank of private-first class, which is very unusual. His travel orders were for air travel from Travis Airforce Base, direct to Tan Son Nhat air base outside of Saigon, Vietnam. He was given a week's leave after finishing basic training.

"I would appreciate it if you would let me look over the recruit's record while he was stationed at Fort Ord. Is there anything classified in his folder that you might need to remove?" Kat asked.

The captain folded the front of the folder over and put his hand on top of it, like it belonged to him, and only him. After a period of waiting with neither one speaking the Captain pushed the file across his desk with a disgusted look on his face.

Kat took the next few minutes leafing through the few sheets of paper that were attached to the file folder with two metal clips at the top of the file. The file was as the captain had presented it to her. There were several awards for marksmanship that he was allowed to wear on his uniform, and a copy of the general order that promoted him from private to private-first class.

She finished leafing through the attached documents in the folder, however as she closed the file a corner of a folded piece of paper slipped from under the last page of documents. It was folded in half and simply stuck up under the other pages in the folder. She took it carefully from under the other paperwork and unfolded. She read the title to the document and stopped for a moment. Her heart was racing, and she could feel her hands shaking. She continued to read the document; slowly, carefully, until she was finished. She wanted to get up and dance around the room but regained control quickly. The document explained to her in no uncertain terms that the ghost she had been chasing, wasn't a ghost at all.

She slid the folder back across the desk.

"That's all I need to see, Captain. I will get out of your hair now," she rose from her chair and started to turn to the closed door to his office.

"Just a minute Miss McNally, I have one more piece of information that I think I should pass onto you. What I'm about to tell you is not in that folder, but I thought it might be of interest to you."

"Go ahead Captain, I'm listening."

"Staff Sergeant Charles Fowler, a basic training drill sergeant, who was the sergeant in charge of your recruit's training platoon was murdered the night of the platoon's graduation from boot camp. I remember you telling me you were investigating a murder that might involve this recruit.

"Can I see the murder sheet on the case you just told me about?" Asked Kat, trying to keep her excitement out of her voice.

"You'll have to go to the Monterey county sheriff's office for that. The sergeant was murdered off base and is therefore under the jurisdiction of the civilian justice system.

CHAPTER THIRTY-ONE

S lack had been accepted by the other four men in his Lurp team. He had been assigned one or more targets regularly since he had reported to the Lurp team. When he went out on an assigned assassination he took his spotter with him, the brass somewhere up the line of command liked to keep track of his kills. Each kill was identified by a rank and was verified by the spotter when they did the debrief at headquarters. All the other enemy he killed weren't counted by the brass; but Slack knew exactly.

He had started leaving at night when he had an assignment. He figured the NVA had people watching for men or patrols leaving the base area day and night. It was a lot harder for them to see the two men sniper team leave when it was dark as a Viet Cong tunnel. The team was use to him disappearing, and then showing back up in a day or two looking tired, strained and detached. They didn't question him about blood on his jungle fatigues. His team thought he was like a guy that always wanted to take point on patrol; they lived on the adrenalin, and Slack did as well.

It had started raining early one morning, and continued through the night, and into the next day. The Lurp team leader had told Slack that it was the beginning of the monsoon season in the central highlands. Slack left the team area late that night and started his trek through the jungle. He moved like a ghost, making his way to a spot on a narrow trail about ten miles from the base. It was near a village called Ben Het, where a special forces camp was located. He broke out of the jungle into the hills between Dok To and Ben Het. The rain was coming down so hard it was difficult to see through it. The hills were covered with low growth brush and trees, nevertheless it was more open than the jungle. It took him most of the night to reach a path that connected a small gathering of bamboo huts not far from the special forces camp. He had watched a young Vietnamese woman walking from the camp where she brought fresh eggs to sell. Slack found a stand of bamboo for a hide next to the trail that crossed the local rice paddies and began his wait.

His Dark Persona had started to take over after the rain had started two days earlier. Sunrise brought with it a low to the ground gray cloud day. The rain had slowed slightly and made the visibility better. His Dark Persona was slowly taking over, but couldn't force total control of Slack. There was no thunder or lightning to drive his Dark Persona into total control.

It was still early in the morning, when the young woman with her conical leaf hat keeping the rain from her head, came into view. She had a bamboo stick across her shoulders with what looked like vegetables in a basket hanging from one side and chicken eggs in the basket on the other end of the stick. She walked beside the trail to keep her sandals out of the mud. She was going to pass right by Slack.

The Dark Persona edged its way, trying to take control of Slack. There was still no thunder or lightning to consummate its control of him. He must wait until there was thunder and lightning to take her. He had a sudden thought. He wondered how her blood would taste. His Dark Persona gave him the drive to taste her. It was getting stronger and more acute, as she walked passed him on her way to the U.S. Special Forces camp.

She passed by then, and the Dark Persona partially subsided. It would be there until the young girl returned from selling her eggs, but the Dark Persona had to have the brilliant light and the crashing sounds of the storm to complete its takeover. Slack could wait. The Dark Persona would be there when the time was right.

Slack didn't know how long he had slept. A sudden clap of thunder and bright light that penetrated his eyelids brought him back to full awareness. He glanced at his watch. It was the middle of the afternoon. His Dark Persona roared into control. Had he missed the young Vietnamese girl while he dozed? The Dark Persona cried out for the killing and the blood. The lightning and thunder had come, as it knew it would. There was little patience with the Dark Persona in control of Slack. He stood up, and worked his way slowly to the very edge of the bamboo where he had been hiding, and waited for the young girl pass. The Dark Persona was near its peak!

A sound of feet swishing through the tall went grass along the edge of the path to the village alerted the Dark Persona. The rhythmic swishing was coming closer to the Dark Persona from the direction of the Green Beret camp. He could feel the exhilaration from the surge of adrenalin coursing through his body. He waited for the right moment, but he was becoming more agitated as each moment passed. He saw the young girls right sandal step into the wet grass right in front of him. He struck like a Cobra!

He grabbed her foot, and pulled with all his power to make the young girl fall in the wet grass. There was a startled cry, and then he was on her. He went over the prone girl, and stuck his sharp pointed knife into the side of her neck. He knew the correct move to slice the girls throat. He clamped her nose and mouth closed with his free hand, and jerked with all his dark strength across the young girl's throat. He could barely hear the flush of blood shooting up into his face. He could taste it. It was a bit salty, and had a similar coppery taste like the one he killed at the mansion. He jerked his knife with brute force and severed her head from her body. He reached over to her hand to cut the tip of her index finger off and stuffed it in his jungle fatigue jacket. He cut a slice of meat from her breast and stuff it in his mouth. It was delicious! He wanted to stay with the body and consume more of the young girl, but there was a sound of other feet coming rapidly through the tall wet grass near him.

The Dark Persona rolled off the body. There was a snack, snack a few yards down the path. The Dark Persona knew what made that sound. It was the charging arm of an AK-47. The Dark Persona scrambled off the path and came to his knees with his knife held low with the cutting edge of the blade up. A dark figure came through the rain like a ghost through a dense fog off a swamp.

The Dark Persona lunged at the figure of the Viet Cong dressed in black, loose fitting clothing, and a conical hat that had rain running off it in large rivulets. He hit the Viet Cong with a rush and knocked him to his back. The Dark Persona ripped the Viet Cong from belly to chest and continued in one motion to slice his neck to his spinal cord. The AK-47 fell into the mud and water that was pooled on the side of the path. He jerked the weapon from the dead man's hands and started to move quickly away from the dead V.C. and the body of the young girl.

The V.C. had spoiled the Dark Persona's plans to enjoy the young girl more. He was a mile away from the path where the Dark Persona took over before it started to subside. Slack knew it would stay with him all the way back to the Lurp camp in the morning. He clung to the Viet Cong's weapon. It was going to be proof of what he had been doing out in the thunder and lightning that night.

The team member that slept in the bunk next to Slack heard him come in from the rain early in the morning. It was still raining heavily, and the thunder and lightning could still be heard as the storm moved to the east. The team member didn't think much about him coming back from one of his night excursions. He had started going out at night by himself a few months ago. The team member rolled over and tried to get back to sleep.

The team member that slept next to Slack's bunk was up at first light, as was the habit for the Lurp team. He went around the tent that the team slept in, and shook each team member awake. He motioned for them to come over to the bunk where Slack was sleeping. They stood at the end of his bunk and stared at the bloody mound of fatigues at the head of his bunk. Even his jungle combat boots were smeared in blood. There was an Ak-47 laying on top of his footlocker. It was covered in mud and blood as well. It wasn't the first time that Slack had returned from one of his night recons with blood on his uniform or an enemy weapon of some sort. The team quietly dressed and left the tent for breakfast at the base mess hall.

The team sat off to themselves like they always did, talking in hushed voices about what they had seen earlier that morning. All of them agreed that Slack was an unusual troop. Very few men liked going out on patrols, particularly night patrols or ambushes. Slack seemed to thrive on them.

"Haven't any of you noticed that he goes out on one of these one-man ambushes at night, and in the worse kind of weather?" The second radio-telephone team member asked the other three members of the team sitting at the table.

The team leader told them, "I'll admit that there is something special driving Slack. He's the best sniper we've had in the team. We're here to kill the enemy. When we are on patrol, we all kill the enemy, including Slack. I'm not going to say anything to anyone about him taking off at night in a thunder storm to kill the enemy."

The other three team members nodded their agreement, but one of them muttered under his breath, "there's something really weird about him!"

Two days later the team went out on another long-range recon patrol. Slack was carrying the AK-47 as a back-up weapon. The other team members didn't seem to notice the drizzling rain, but the team leader did something different when they left from the team camp on their patrol. He had the team leave when it was fully dark.

CHAPTER THIRTY-TWO

It was mid-morning when Kat found her way to the Monterey Sheriff's department. She showed the receptionist her credentials, and asked if they had a murder squad.

"We have a Homicide Squad. Probably the same thing, under a different name," the receptionist said.

"I'd like to speak to the officer in charge of the Homicide Squad. Tell him I'd like to talk with him about the Staff Sergeant Charles Fowler murder," she told her.

In a few minutes a rather tall, slender man in his thirties came from an office with the receptionist following him.

He stuck out his hand in a friendly way and said, "My name is detective Dick Wilson. The receptionist tells me you want to talk with someone on the Homicide Squad about an open case we have."

Kat shook his hand and told him, "I'm Kat McNally, Detective Wilson. I'm a private detective investigating a murder that occurred in San Francisco county. There might be a possibility that your murder and mine are related in some fashion. I'd like to go over your murder case and I'll share what I have on the case in San Francisco."

Detective Wilson told her to follow him back to his office. He turned and started back down the long hallway, while over his shoulder he said, "we've hit a brick wall with our case. The military aren't being very forthcoming with background information on the victim. Anything you might know should be a help to us."

The detective's office was small. There were the normal I've been there and done that plaques and photos on the walls around the office.

Kat wanted to get information and give little back, after all, it wasn't up to her to do the police departments investigation for them. On the other hand, Kat was an expert at picking up the small things that were mentioned in passing and building on them. She figured this detective would consider himself and expert also.

Kat opened up the discussion with, "since I'm the one interested in whether the murder I'm working on, and the case you are at a brick wall on, I would like to hear about your case first."

Detective Wilson couldn't believe he had been beaten to the punch. He planned on getting her information and giving her little back. If he broke his case, and also solved the San Francisco case he could likely build that into a run for county sheriff that was coming up in the fall. If he gave her what little they did know about the drill sergeant's murder, she would then give him much better information on the San Francisco murder. He was going to run with that.

He started with the trash truck driver and the call to the sheriff's office. The military I.D had given him a line to his work as a drill instructor for new recruits at Fort Ord. He was told by the military the drill sergeants platoon completed the basic training course the day before he was found stuck in the back of a dump truck at the county dump. The toxicology report told them he had a very high blood alcohol content. Fowler's throat was slit from ear to ear and the tip of his index finger on the left hand had been cut off. We checked the truck's stops for that morning and found only one bar on that route. The Full Clip bar was a military hangout. The bartender remembered Staff Sergeant Fowler as being the last man out of the bar the night he was murdered. He had been celebrating with another Staff Sergeant named Bill. The bartender didn't know his last name. We contacted the M.P. office on Fort Ord to find out how many Staff Sergeants on the base were named Bill or William. The round figure they gave us after a two week wait, was that there were a lot of them. The round figure they gave us for the number of troops that were on the base was fifty thousand. That's all we got from them. "What was the bartender's name?" Kat asked.

"Sam Cameron." The detective answered.

"That's all you've got?"

"I told you we were stopped at a brick wall!" Detective Wilson said, his voice full of exasperation. "Now give me what you have that might tie the two murders together.

"Unfortunately, I'm in the same boat as you are. Very little evidence at the crime scene. The victim was a young maid at a private mansion. Her throat had been cut so deeply that the spinal cord was the only thing that was holding her head on her body. There were no witnesses."

"You've got less than I do. How did you find out about the murder down here?"

"It was such a gruesome murder, I went to the public library and did a search for recent murders with victims throats cut in the state of California. Your case was the only close match." Kat told him. It was sort of the truth, she was going to do just that until she found the envelope with the name on it from the draft board. He didn't need to know that. It would just confuse him more with an added murder for him to solve.

Detective Wilson stood up at that point and told her, "it doesn't look like we have much information to share. Give me your business card.

If we find anything that might tie the two murders together, I'll make sure you are notified."

They shook hands in the office and Kat left the detective's office alone. She didn't feel bad about not giving up her information. She knew cops hated to deal with private investigators on any basis.

"The end of his index finger on his left hand had been severed," that one piece of information was worth the drive down from San Francisco.

She found her way back to the main gate of Fort Ord where the corporal M.P. guard was still on duty. She stopped at the gate house where he was sitting on tall stool, trying to keep out of the sun. He must have recognized her, since he stood up and waved her through. Instead on driving forward to the low bar blocking the entrance, she pulled her car over to the gate house and rolled down her window.

"It looks like I'm going to be around Fort Ord for a while. I'm an ex-Staff Sergeant in the M.P.'s. Usually the NCO's have a local watering hole to let off steam and to tell war stories. Where's the local hangout?"

The guard smiled broadly and told her, "the one that most of the Non-Commissioned Officers from the fort spend their off time at is the Full Clip bar." He continued by telling her how to find the Full Clip, and told her good luck.

It was mid-afternoon when she pulled away from the entrance to Fort Ord. It was too time: too early to go to a bar for her, too early for a late-night bartender to be at work, and too late for lunch. She went back to the motel and made a three-day extension of reservation. It was hard telling what would click for her when she started talking with the bartender.

She went to her room and made a call to her Taekwondo school, and asked the owner to take her Friday private class. She was out of town and wouldn't be able to get back in time to take the class. The Taekwondo master agreed quickly.

Kat thought she might end up the night, by still being awake until the next morning. She stretched out on the sofa in her room and took a nap.

With her evening meal completed, it was time to head for the Full Clip bar. It was a stand-alone brink building with an alley on one side and a parking lot on the other. The lot was only partially full when Kat parked and went in the bar. The interior was dark, like most bars of the type, and was large enough to have a dance floor and a small bandstand. A pool table took up one corner of the large table and chairs area and long bar leading from one side of the building to the other. There was a narrow hallway that ran to the back of the building on each side of the bar. On one side was the men's room and business office. The other side was where the women's restroom was located. The walls had various military pieces of equipment from the wars in the past, and insignias for all the outfits based at Fort Ord scattered around the interior.

There were two waitresses that Kat could see working the bar, and one bartender taking care of the those that set at the bar. She went to the end of the bar where the bartender was standing watch over the bar.

A Juke box was playing, 'Twist and Shout,' by the Isley brothers, loud enough to rattle the framed posters hung all over the walls.

She yelled over the song to the bartender, "My names Kat McNally, I'm doing a private investigation of the murder of Staff Sergeant Fowler that happened near here. Can you tell me what was happening that evening? Who was Fowler with or was there a fight? Anything like that?"

The bartender looked at her like she was an ugly frog or something and said, "the cops have already grilled me on that night. I don't want to talk about it anymore."

"I can do something that the cops can't do after our interview!" Kat said over the Juke box playing, 'Wild Thing,'.

That got the bartender's attention. Which was what Kat intended it to do.

"What do yah mean, you can do something for me that the cops can't?"

"I can pay you for your information. Fifty dollars for what you told them or a hundred for something special that you might have left out when they talked with you," offered Kat.

"Like what do you want to know?" The bartender asked her.

"Start somewhere and end somewhere. I'll take a bottle of beer and we can talk between your bartending for the people at the bar and the waitresses," she told him loudly.

The bartender brought back a long neck bottle of beer with ice water still dripping off it and a glass to pour it in, if she wanted.

He served several men that were setting down the bar in their fatigues and drew a few beers for one of the waitresses.

He shuffled down the bar and stood leaning against the corner of the back wall and the flip top that allowed access behind the bar.

"There were a lot of people in here that night. More than usual," he said. "It was a combination of things that made it crowded. There were non-coms from two companies of recruits that had graduated that day celebrating the end of their platoons training. They normally hit the Full Clip after a graduation. It was raining that night like cat's

258

and dog's, and there was lighting and thunder that made the sky look like it was blowing up. Sergeant Fowler came in and started drinking. He was hitting the booze pretty hard that night. Harder than I remembered him doing before. He had a drinking buddy from another company of recruits that had just graduated join him shortly after Fowler arrived. They came in most every Saturday night. With the Juke box playing loudly, I heard nothing of their conversation. From the physical appearance of Fowler and the way that his drinking buddy was reacting, I'd guess that something major was upsetting Fowler."

"What is the name of his drinking buddy?" Kat asked him.

The bartender held up his hand, as if telling her he had to leave for a moment, and walked over to where one of the waitresses was standing, at the waitress area of the bar. He placed the drinks that she needed on her tray, and walked back to Kat.

"I told the cops his name was Bill, but I didn't know his last name. I didn't think it was important, since he was sort of with Fowler, and he left earlier than Fowler did. For that matter, Fowler was the last person to leave the bar. That was around two o'clock in the morning. Like I said earlier; they were in deep discussion, like drinking buddies will do, and there was no anger between them, that I could tell."

"Tell me about his drinking buddy. I need his full name, and if you know it, his unit information," said Kat.

"He is a Staff Sergeant, like Fowler, but in a different training company. His name is Bill, as I said. I don't know his last name, and I don't want to get him in trouble with his commanding officer or anything. I don't know his outfit either, but I can tell you something better that has happened since the murder, and the police don't know."

That brought a tingle at the back on Kat's neck. Maybe this guy was going to give her something important to go on!

"Okay, Bill's got him a new girlfriend! The bartender looked at her like he had just divulged a state secret. They come in here every Saturday night to have a few drinks, and dance to the music if we have a band or to the Juke, if we don't. I'd bet a dollar they'll be here this Saturday night, and you might talk with him then, if you want."

"Anything else you can think of that you didn't tell the police, and would like to let me know about," she asked as she took a swig off her long neck.

"That's it. You want another beer?"

"No. But here's your money. She paid for her beer, and slipped a hundred-dollar bill under it."

"I'll see you Saturday night. Don't tell Bill that I am coming by, or that we had a talk. I just want to talk like we have. I don't want to scare him off."

"No sweat. I'll be working behind the bar, and will point him out to yah."

"I forgot one thing. What trash pickup does the bar use?"

"Monterey Trash and Waste Removal."

"Do you remember the name of the driver that does your route?"

"No. I don't remember ever being told his name, but the owner told me about him coming into the office really angry about the smell of our trash dumpster he was about to explode. Seems like he thought we had put garbage in the trash dumpster. That's against the rules around here."

"I'll see you Saturday evening."

CHAPTER THIRTY-THREE

K at drove into Monterey to have a seafood diner at a restaurant on the water and tried to relax from the long day. A couple of glasses of good white wine took the edge off. She returned to her motel room outside Fort Ord and had another long night of trying to sleep. She sat up in bed in a start and wondered what terrible dream she was having that made her sweat while she was sleeping. Her sheets and pillow were damp.

The sun was bright and shining through the motel window right into her eyes. She took a quick shower, dressed in a clean pair of Levi jeans and a summery t-shirt with her cowboy boots. She planned on going to the office of the trash company, and talking to the young driver of the trash truck that had Fowler's body stuck in it.

She checked the yellow pages book for the Monterey area and found the phone number and address. She called the number and a young woman told her directions on how to find their location. She wanted some morning coffee and a good breakfast that would last hopefully for the entire day if necessary. She hit the donut shop and pick up a cup of coffee to go and a bag of bear claw pastries. All she had to do was to keep getting coffee and she would spend the day eating the pastries wherever she might be. What a great idea.

The Monterey Trash and Waste Removal company had a neat row of large trash trucks that were being washed one by one through a large open truck wash. She told the front desk clerk that she wanted to talk to the driver of the truck that had the body in it. After she had discussed why she wanted to talk with the driver, the clerk brought the owner of the company out to meet her to decide if they would release the name of the driver to her.

He told her the young man was one of the men cleaning a truck, before the day's runs.

"I'll have to check with him and make sure it is okay with him to talk with you since you're not a police officer," the owner said.

"I'll wait here."

The owner came back with a young man in tow. He was tall and lanky with a cowboy hat tilted slightly on his head. He wore blue jeans and western boots with a large western buckle on the front of his belt.

"This is Rick Hopper. He's the man you want to talk with about the body being in the trash."

The owner left for his office, and the young man asked her if she wanted to go outside to talk to make sure it wouldn't bother the front desk clerk.

Kat told him, "that'll be fine with me."

There was a small wooden pick-nick table with bench seats on the other side of the building. A large dark blue umbrella gave shade to the table and seats.

"How can I help you Miss McNally?"

"Let's use first names, if that's alright? My name's Kat. I would like for you to tell me about finding the body in the trash from the very beginning. Try to remember for me each step you took and what was said to you by others," she told Rick.

"I was half-way into my route when I stopped at the enclosure at the Full Clip where the trash bin was located. Everything went as usual until I lifted the bin and shook it a few times to get all the trash from the bin into the compactor on the back of my truck. The compactor was having some trouble at one point and I got out of the cab of the truck to manually operate it. Sometimes hard or long things keep the compactor from working and I jack it back and forth a few times and it pushes on through the hang-up and starts working again from the cab.

This time when the compactor started working again, a God-awful smell hit me, like a baseball bat hitting a home run. I figured the clean-up man had dumped some drunks puke in the trash again. They had done it before, and they were warned there would be an additional fee charged to their monthly bill. It was a real problem for the drivers, when the bars did that. We have to clean it all up from inside the compactor to keep our trucks don't smell like rotten meat all the time.

I went into office of the Full Clip and talked to owner. He told me he would find out who had put the puke in the trash and reprimand him. He was upset that I was going to tell my boss about it and that he should apply the clean-up fee to the Full Clip.

I ended my run and weighed in at the entrance to the dump. We are billed by the county by weight. I drove over to the daily dump area, and started releasing all the trash. When the compactor was empty I check the inside, that's when I saw the body all tangled up with the push bar at the head of the compactor. I ran over to the weigh station and told the clerk there about the body in the compactor, he called the county sheriff.

"Did the county sheriff talk with you about the body or ask where you thought it might have come from?" Kat asked.

"I told him the same thing I just told you."

"Why were you so certain the smell started when you dumped the trash from the bar's dumpster? Couldn't it have been placed in a bin earlier in you route?" Asked Kat.

"No, mam. It's hard for me tell you what the smell was like. It was a smell that I'd never smelled before. There's no mistake about it, if you smell uncooked meat that is decaying rapidly in the open air. It'll knock your socks off, mam," the young trash truck driver told her.

The putrid smell begins quickly after death. How often do you run the route that includes the bar?"

"Bars make a lot of trash. We do this route every other day. The longest it could have been in the bin would have been two days. The day and night before I ran the route when the body was discovered were a nightmare of waves of cascading rain, lighting so heavy it made Monterey look like daylight at night and made the black rolling clouds look like a hurricane was ripping up the coast. I've never been in the Army mam, but one of the other driver's told me the morning that I made that run the thunder the night before was like the roaring of a battery of Howitzer cannons firing in rapid fire. He should know, he was with a Howitzer company during the Korean War."

Kat ended the questioning abruptly when she realized the young man was simply the guy that found the body and nothing else. She didn't feel like she had wasted her time, after all it was a thing to do and a check off her list of things to do.

She drove to the beach and caught some rays, while she prepared her thoughts about questioning Staff Sergeant Fowler's drinking buddy on Saturday night.

CHAPTER THIRTY-FOUR

It had started raining steadily the day after the Lurp team had been inserted by helicopter two days from a small village that was in the high mountains, near the Laos border. The communication security people had picked up enemy radio traffic coming from the village a few days earlier. The team was to recon the area and take out any officers if it was a large base, or to call in airstrikes if there were no villagers left at the village.

Slack was pulling slack as usual. His Dark Persona was keeping him alert in the rain, but not taking over like it would during a bad thunder and lightning storm. It made his senses ultra- sensitive. Each off-color jungle leaf or vein was examined quickly and discarded as not a threat. The trail was being checked and cleared by the team leader, as he moved cautiously forward.

The team leader signaled for the team to stop in place. The village they were to recon was down in a ravine that had a mountain stream cascading from a point well above the village into a small pond that the villagers had built out of bamboo packed in mud and rocks from the ravine floor. The damn had a low spot in the middle of it that allowed excess water to over and continue down a small steam that passed through the village.

The team leader signal for the team to spread out along the hill top and take up hides that allowed them to check the village out. The rain was heavy enough to keep visual recon to a minimum with the fog that was hanging over the ravine, making it almost impossible to see the enemy that might be in the village. They made this a cold camp with no smoking.

The rain subsided in the early morning of the next day, but there was a gray overcast still hanging over the ravine. Slack and his spotter had taken the time to set up a hide that was advantageous to his sniper assignment. When the gray dawn turned into a sunny morning it was obvious to all the team they had moved into an area that was filled with the enemy and they were all N.V.A. The team leader worked his way slowly from one hide to the next telling each man what his plan of action was going to be.

When he reached Slack and his spotter he told them, "we're smack in the middle of what looks like an enemy battalion, and those people moving bundles on bikes are on the Ho Chi Minh Trail. We need to call in air and get the hell out of here.

"What about the officers?" Asked Slack.

269

"Take them out, if you have the chance. I'm going to take the rest of the team back to a place where we have cover in an area away from the air strike zone."

"I'll take out any officers I can before the air strike starts, then we'll get the hell back to the rest of team," he told the team leader.

"Call out Texas when you're moving back to us. We don't get into a friendly fire situation," answered the team leader.

"Roger that!" Slack told him.

The team leader went back up the line of hides and had the other team members moving toward the east ridge of the ravine when the spotter tapped Slack on the shoulder.

"Standing on the porch of that stilt hut in the middle of the village! That's a coronel standing on that elevated porch with his aids, all of them officers. I count six. Do you have them?" Asked Slack's spotter.

"Got 'em," whispered Slack. The spotter knew Slack was ready. Slack's body relaxed, his breathing slowed down, and there was a sharp crack from the M-14. The general flew back against a bamboo wall of the hut; into a heap on the porch deck. The spotter watched through his spotting scope as crack after crack sounded next to him. The bodies of the other five officers flew in five different directions off the high deck of the hut.

The two men rushed to pick up all the brass from the fired bullets and took off for the ridge to the east where the rest of the Lurp team was located. They had barely started to move through the jungle when there was a loud roar of a Navy jet flying down the center of the ravine from the south. It dropped its load of bombs on the village and the Ho Chi Minh Trail. Right after the jet pulled up over the top of the north ridge of the ravine two Douglas Skyraiders came across the ravine and dropped their loads of napalm over it. The blast from the bombs threw the two men off their feet. When they were able to stand again, they headed in the direction the rest of the team had taken.

Slack and his spotter worked their way to the rest of the team that were stringing out for quick regress to the exfil site were the chopper would pick them up. A burst of enemy fire came from the side of the trail they were moving down. The RTO was hit and was down. The rest of the team returned fire on what sounded like a small ambush of N.V.A soldiers. They were using old bolt action weapons and were over run by the remaining team members in a quick flank attack that the team leader had signaled from his point position on the trail.

One of two men on the other flank tossed a grenade into the middle of the enemy soldiers. Slack felt a shearing burn on the top of his right shoulder. It wasn't bad enough to keep him from engaging an enemy soldier. He hit the soldier in a running crunch, like a football player that was hitting an opponent lineman. Slack's M-14 went flying, as he fell on top of the enemy soldier. He rolled off the enemy

271

soldier and grabbed his killing knife from its case on the left strap of his ruck sack. The enemy soldier was trying to crawl away, kicking and screaming as loud as he could. He managed to get to his hands and knees and tried to scurry off. Slack jumped on top of the enemy's back, and thrust his killing knife into the right side of the soldier's neck. Blood flew everywhere as slack jerked the killing knife back toward him, and severed the enemy's spine. He continued the slice of the knife with all his strength to the other side of the enemy's neck by shifting his hold on the killing knife to his left hand. He stopped the driving cut after he had cut the man's esophagus through. Slack's Dark Persona was in rapture!

The ambush site went silent for a minute.

The team leader yelled, "sound off!"

Three men answered his call.

"Let's get the fuck out of here. RTO is down. Take turns carrying him back to the exfil site. Back up RTO, get the radio and call for pick up. Do it now! Anyone else wounded?" The team leader yelled as the three men closed in on the trail where the first RTO was lying in some huge old ferns at the side of the trail where the ambush had first started.

Slack was bleeding from the wound he had received when the grenade went off but didn't bother to say anything about it. He broke open a sulfonamide powder packet and pulled his jungle fatigue top off his shoulder and sprinkled the white powder on the bloody furrow at the top of his shoulder. He slapped a bandage on it and pulled his fatigue jacket back on to hold it in place. He could hear the backup radio telephone backup man calling for exfil at the pre-arranged site about a mile from the village.

The chopper came in with a gun ship flying cover. There had been heavy contact with the enemy in the area. The exfil went according to plan.

The chopper co-pilot called in for a medic to meet them at the team's camp when they landed, and a pick up for the body of the RTO. They would tag and bag the body and send it down to Danang for transfer back to the states.

The medic cleaned the wound on Slack's shoulder and put more of the white powder on it. He smoothed some cyanoacrylate, better known as Quick Glue, over the top of the wound to keep it clean and keep it from bleeding. He told Slack the glue would take the place of any stitches that he may have had at an aid station. The medic took his information to report the wound for a purple heart decoration. Slack told him he thought it was a friendly fire situation. The medic told him that didn't matter, as long as he was in combat at the time of the wound.

The team leader caught Slack cleaning his equipment at the team's ready area, under a tent that had its flaps tied up to allow the breeze off the mountains to act as a not so good air conditioner. He told Slack that he had just made his patrol and after-action report to the commanding office. He told Slack that the newest man on the team always cleaned out a dead team mate's personal stuff before it was set back for shipment to the relatives, to avoid them getting anything that might upset them, including any pieces or body parts that might be in the soldier's foot locker.

Slack wondered what would happen if he was killed and the jar in his foot locker with the fingertips of his Dark Persona's was found. Probably, nothing, he thought. After all, it was common to see soldiers with ears hung on their dog tag chains.

When he was finished cleaning his equipment: his knife, pistol, M-14 and AK-47 he went to the tent a few yards away, where they all slept and started to check out the stuff that was around the dead RTO's rack. The RTO had picked up a wood shipping crate with two dividing shelves in it. He was using it for pictures of his girl back home, and a clock on the top shelve; actually the side of the upright rectangular box. There was an old M1911 colt .45 caliber pistol lying on the second shelf that had a full magazine with one bullet in the tube. He stuck it in his jungle fatigue pants pocket. Why let some re-echelon troop have it for a souvenir? He checked under the RTO's pillow where a lot of men kept a pistol, just for an emergency. He must have planned on using the M1911 A-1 for that, there wasn't a pistol under his pillow.

He opened up the foot locker at the end of the dead RTO's bed. There was the usual military clothing in it and at the bottom of a neat stack of rolled underwear, which most Lurp members went without; to keep from getting a severe case of crotch rot. The foot locker was neat with all the clothing folded and stacked in an orderly fashion. Slack started to close the lid to the footlocker when he noticed a manila envelope taped to the inside of the footlocker lid. He carefully removed the tape so he wouldn't tear any papers that might be in the large, yellow envelope.

He opened the envelope and pulled out a small amount of letter sized papers. He looked through them quickly. They were all orders for his travel and assignment to Vietnam and a copy of his promotion orders with a decoration citation for a bronze star. There were several other Vietnamese award citations and at the bottom there was a certified copy of his birth certificate. He was the same age as Slack. He started to put all the papers back in the envelope, however his Dark Persona stopped him. He folded the birth certifcate to fit in his fatigue pants pocket on the other side from the M1911 A-1 .45 caliber pistol.

CHAPTER THIRTY-FIVE

McNally was setting on the beach in a pair of shorts and a T-shirt thinking about what she could accomplish during the rest of her day. She was going to the Full Clip bar later in the evening to see if the friend of Staff Sergeant Fowler brought his girlfriend to drink and dance the night away. She started her stretch routine that she used before beginning her classes with novice Taekwondo students. She was certain, for some reason, that she was going to need to be in her best shape before this case was concluded. When she finished she felt like she had run a fast five miles. She was covered in beach sand so she picked up the towel she had taken from her motel room and dusted the sand off as best as she could. Her car was parked at the edge of the beach where a short boardwalk from the beach up the dunes to the parking area was located.

She started her car, and thought as she drove out of the little beach parking lot that she should go by the guard shack at the entrance to Fort Ord. Maybe the guard she asked about a bar that non-coms frequented was on duty. He knew, right off the bat, the name of the Full Clip bar. Maybe he knew the full name of Fowler's friend. She did a U-turn on the narrow black-top beach road, and headed to the highway that led to the fort.

There was a short line of cars waiting to be checked into the military post fort when Kat made it there. The same guard was on duty at the guard shack and recognized her as she took her turn being checked for entrance to the fort.

"Nice to see you, mam. What's your business at the fort today?" The guard asked her.

"I need a name. I thought you might be able to help me. You came up with the right hang-out for non-coms yesterday. There was a staff sergeant Charles Fowler that was murdered not long ago, and I'm trying to find his killer. I was told by the bartender that Fowler had a drinking buddy that was also a staff sergeant with the first name of Bill. I thought you might remember his full name since you check men in and out of the fort all the time."

"I remember staff sergeant Fowler, too bad about him getting killed that way. His buddy and him were regulars on Friday nights. His friend's name is staff sergeant Bill Jenkins. He's still using weekend passes. All the cadre have them available.

"Thanks so much corporal," she told him and did another U-turn to leave the fort's check in area.

She went directly to the motel to shower and get the sand off. All the while a little crack of light was opening for her on the case, she thought, as she parked her car in front of her motel room.

Kat dressed in the jeans, blouse and boots she had on before she went to the beach, after she had a long shower and washed her hair. She made sure her pistol was fully loaded and tucked it under her blouse, in front for a change. She left the tails on the blouse outside her jeans. She wasn't sure why she put the .357 Magnum there, nevertheless it seemed right for the night. It was still too early to head over to the Full Clip bar: she went to the café for a spicy dinner.

The sun was dropping over the edge of the Pacific Ocean when she pulled her car into the parking lot at the side of the Full Clip bar. She locked her car door, and positioned her .357 Magnum to a more comfortable spot for a right-hand draw. She could her faint music coming from the open front door of the bar. There was a bouncer standing just inside the front door; he could have been an off-duty police officer. Kat noticed a .38 caliber police special at his right side in a leather, inside the waistline, holster. She showed her California driver's license and started to walk inside when all hell broke loose!

Wood splinters started flying from all around the doorsill; the police officer was hit in the left shoulder. She saw a black four door sedan racing by with the windows down and flashes from inside the car

278

pointed in the front door's direction. She heard a loud bang and felt the recoil from her Smith and Wesson: she didn't know she had drawn it. She went to her knees and continued firing at the speeding car, while she acted as a shield for the police officer. She emptied her .357 Magnum at the driver's window that wasn't down. She saw bullet holes striking the glass, and all at once it exploded into a thousand pieces. She grabbed the .38 police special from the downed police officer's hand and continued firing. The fire from the car had stopped for a moment. She fired again at the drivers shattered window trying for a hit on the driver. The racing car flew across the curb; across a sidewalk, and smashed into a palm tree near the side of the street. The engine began to smoke: she heard a distant siren screaming its way toward the bar.

The bartender, Sam Cameron, started to drag the downed police officer into the protection of the interior of the bar. Kat checked the .38 police special for bullets: there were three left. She slammed the gate closed on the gun's cylinder and ran in a zig zagging path toward the wrecked car. The sound of the siren was growing louder by the time she reached the smoldering car. She dropped to a crouch; turned with the hammer on the pistol cocked, ready to fire. What she heard was the pounding of combat boots on the pavement. Fatigue dressed soldiers were storming out of the Full Clip bar and running toward the fire fight. The soldiers started opening doors. She had the driver's side door open with the police special point through the shattered window. The inside of the car was filled with smoke. One of the soldiers called out that the man in the back seat was dead. The driver had a head shot and was obviously dead: the back of his head was missing. He must have been looking out the window at Kat when one of her rounds hit him in his forehead.

Kat stepped back from the group of soldiers and said in a loud voice, "leave 'em where they are, guys! The police will want to document everything including the positions of the shooters."

The soldiers left the bodies as they were and came to stand near Kat. They were concerned for her safety and made a small ring around her facing outward. One older man in civilian clothes told the rest, "there's no need to protect this lady, she took the car and two shooters down and didn't blink an eye. She can be in my squad any day."

That started it. There were strong pats on Kat's back, and everyone wanted to shake her hand. One even told her, "when the cops and the ambulance for the wounded bouncer are finished with you come back to the Full Clip, your drinks are on the me!"

One police car skidded to a stop right by the crowd of soldiers. The policeman scrambled from his driver's seat and stood behind the car with his service revolver held over the roof. He asked some of the soldiers standing around who was involved in the shooting.

The older man dressed in civilian clothes told him, "the lady here, he pointed to Kat, was standing at the door of the bar when the I.D.

checker took one in the shoulder from the speeding car there at the tree. She returned fire, with a heavy-duty pistol from the sound of it, and shielded the downed man at the door. She continued fire and the car crashed into that palm tree. She took out the shooter; the driver, and protected the downed man at the entrance all at the same time. She's one hell of a woman, in my estimation!"

Kat was surrounded by police officers, all asking different questions at the same time, when the circle abruptly parted. Homicide detective Dick Wilson walk through the gap in the circle and confronted her.

"What in the hell went on here and why were you involved in it, McNally?"

"Mellow out detective Wilson. Let's go to your car an I'll tell you the entire story," said Kat in her best tough woman voice.

Wilson turned on his heel without saying another word to walk back to his unmarked car with the emergency lights flashing through the grill.

Kat knew that Wilson was doing a power thing: making her walk behind him would tell the other police officer's he was the cop in charge. She waited until he was standing by the driver's side door of his vehicle, then she walked over to the emergency ambulance where the wounded bouncer was being treated before transported to a local hospital. Wilson watched her as she walked up to the medical tech that was treating the bouncer, and asked if she could talk with the wounded man for a moment. She explained that she was the one that was standing with him when the firefight broke out.

"He's stable now. Make it quick and try not to upset him. He was about to go into shock when I got to him," the medical tech told her.

She stepped into the back of the ambulance and found the wounded man looking at her from the collapsible gurney he was reclining on.

"Man-O-Man! You sure did the job on that drive-by. You have some type of training?" He asked.

"Army. You're going to be okay they tell me. Why were those men spraying lead all over the entrance to the bar? Some kind of gang thing or was it about you?" Kat asked the bouncer.

"I don't know. I'm an off-duty police officer picking up some extra money to pay the bills. As far as I know this has never happened in Monterey. Might be about someone in the bar or it might have been about you. What's your bag?"

"I'm a private investigator, working on a case. I hadn't thought about that possibility," said Kat. She didn't mention what popped into her head at that moment. The two guys in the car on the bridge!

She left the wounded man, went over to detective Wilson's car and sat in the shotgun seat. Wilson was still standing outside, acting like he was observing the scene of the drive-by shooting. After a few moments he opened the car door and sat behind the wheel.

"You sure took your time getting in the car when it was your suggestion in the first place. This was a nice, quiet town before you came here. Why were those men trying to kill you?"

"It could have been anyone at the bar, or the bar itself. It could have been a drive-by shooting looking for a place to happen. Did you ever think of that? No need in pointing fingers at me."

"The cop in me tells me you are connected to it, in some fashion. There was a wreck on the Bixby Canyon bridge the other day. Two men were killed when their car went over the guardrail and plunged down to the bottom of the canyon. We received I.D.'s on them yesterday from state and federal agencies. They were both known soldiers of the San Francisco Mafia. Were you involved in that?"

She didn't answer his question. But said, "I'm here looking for the killer of a maid in San Francisco. I'm not here to have a shoot-out with the local hoods. The sergeant over there has all of my statement about the drive-by and how I was involved. He has my contact information. You should be wondering why a soldier from Fort Ord was butchered at the bar that was just shot up, and what connection that could have with this drive-by shooting at the same bar! If you are finished, I have better things to be doing, beside sitting in an unmarked cop car, listening to your bull shit innuendos about some Mafia goons that were killed in an auto accident."

She pulled the door handle and stepped out of the car. There was no way she was going to involve herself in the deaths of two Mafia soldiers. She wondered why they were trying to kill her. They had no cause to be after her. She thought quickly of the two men in the drive-by and came up with the possibility of them being Mafia, as well. She stopped by the shot-up entrance and re-loaded her pistol. She had a brief thought about someone that might have a reason to pay for a killing and then tossed that idea to the side. She went into the Full Clip bar hoping that the man she wanted to talk with hadn't been there when the shooting started and then left to protect his new girlfriend.

When she talked with the bartender he told her Bill hadn't come in yet. Kat went to the end of the bar to sit down. One of the waitresses brought over a beer that she told Kat was free. Kat started her watch for Fowler's friend. She nursed the beer through the next hour before she decided Bill wasn't going to come to the bar with all the shooting that had occurred earlier. She needed to be alert if she stayed. She was going to make it one more hour and waved the bartender over.

"Give me a club soda with a twist of lime, Sam. I don't want to get high, incase Bill and his girlfriend show up."

"Gotcha. One club and lime coming up."

Kat looked over the setting area of the bar, searching for what, she wasn't sure. The crowd size had increased during the last hour even with the police presents still around. She had to hope they wouldn't run Bill off.

The Juke was playing some old rock and roll songs and couples were starting to dance to the music on the dance floor when the bartender, Sam, brought her club soda with lime to her and spoke in a voice she could barely hear over the loud music and crowd noise.

"That's Bill and his girlfriend standing at the door, looking into the bar. I guess they are worried about coming in, after the gunfight out on the street, he said quietly.

Kat was turned toward the crowd around the dance floor. She moved her eyes toward the entrance and saw an average looking man and woman, the man in civilian clothes, obviously discussing whether they should enter the bar. Her heart rate raised slightly, in anticipation of what she might learn from Bill when she talked with him.

The couple turned to leave bar, the woman shaking her head negatively, pulling on Bill's arm with authority. Kat jumped from her bar stool, and ran down a narrow isle that gave the waitress room to serve customers near the dance floor. The lights on the police cars were still lighting the area around the wrecked car where a tow truck was pulling it to its back. The two bodies had been removed; the driver's side door was smashed so badly it stood ajar.

Kat scanned the shooting scene quickly looking for Bill and his girlfriend. She spotted Bill closing the left front door of an older sedan in the bar parking lot. She ran that way, but at the corner of the building a police officer stepped in front of her and asked where she was going in such a hurry.

"I am a private detective, officer. I need to talk with the two people that are about to drive away. Let me catch them before they leave the parking lot."

"I saw you talking with the detective in his car earlier. I don't know if you are cleared to leave the area. Come with me while I check with the detective."

The police officer grabbed her arm in a tight hold, and started to power walk her toward the unmarked car and detective Wilson. Kat pulled out her badge and flashed it at the officer. He glanced at the badge then let her arm go.

He asked hurriedly, "do you need assistance?"

McNally was running at top speed toward the car about to exit the parking lot and didn't hear the last part of the police officer's question. Bill's car turned onto Buttercup Blvd. headed south. She ran for her car parked near the entrance to the parking lot. She unlocked her car; started it, and was moving down Buttercup Blvd., after the dead man's friend in record time. She was able to see Bill's tail lights in the beginning darkness, while keeping a respectable distance; not wanting to alarm the couple in the car ahead of her.

Red tail lights turned to bright red brake lights a block ahead of Kat. A right-hand turn signal started ahead of the car's headlights turning to the right onto Military Ave. It started to the west toward the more commercial area of Monterey. Bill's car continued west on Military Ave. with McNally not far behind until he reached the intersection of Fremont Blvd. where he turned back north. Kat had to slam on her brakes at a stop sign intersection when a car pulled out in front of her. She narrowly missed the rear of that car and was lucky enough to see Bill's brake lights go on after his left turn signal started. He was turning into a parking lot filled with cars.

When Kat drove up to the parking lot off Fremont Blvd. There was a large brightly lighted sign at the front of a free-standing building that indicated it was the Gold Mine Grill. At the side of its name a blinking light was flashing Dance Hall in bright orange letters.

McNally parked next to the car Bill had driven to the bar and looked the area over. There were two men leaning against the exterior wall by the entrance talking and smoking cigarettes. She noticed they were wearing jeans and western shirts. She figured she would fit right in with the people in the bar if it was kicker bar. She was still wearing

287

her jeans and western boots, and she loved cowboy bars. There was a row of motorcycles parked at the front of the building. When she saw them she figured it was a biker-kicker bar. They were sometimes rough and tumble; she touched the back on her shirt and felt the reassuring grip of her .357 Magnum.

She walked inside the front door and stood to the side letting her eyes get used to the low lights in the bar. The large room was smoke filled and crowded. There was a bar with stools at the back of a open room and a dance floor and band area at the right rear corner next to the end of the bar. The Juke was playing, 'Skip a Rope,' by Henson Cargile, and the dance floor was crowded with couples scooting around the dance floor doing the Texas Two Step.

Bill and his girlfriend were seated at a table against the fall wall that had good access to the dance floor. The waitress was taking their drink order when Kat started to walked through the tables that had no lanes set up for the waitresses to do their work easier. It was a maze, like the photographs of green foliage mazes at the backs of English castles.

McNally made it to Bill's table, and had her identification wallet in her hand. The girlfriend spotted her coming. She must have told to look behind him, Bill had his back to Kat. She stopped at the last minute and looked directly at Bill.

"Bill, my name is Kat McNally. I'm a private investigator working on a murder case that is very similar to the murder of your friend staff sergeant Fowler."

She handed her I.D. to Bill to examine continuing to speak to him at the same time. "I know you were with him at the Full Clip bar the night he was killed. I want to ask you a few quick questions about that night."

Bill handed the wallet back, saying, "Can't you see I'm on a date with my girlfriend. We want to enjoy the evening together. Now if you would please go, we will continue our night out."

"I can't do that Bill. The few questions could very well save someone's life. Why haven't you offered to talk to the police about his murder?"

"Let me talk with my girlfriend for a moment. Walk away, I'll wave you over if we want to share a few minutes with you."

Kat walked over to the dance floor and watch the couples dancing, while Bill and his girlfriend had their heads together at their table.

A rough looking man dress like a biker walked up to Kat and asked her to dance with him. She told him she was waiting for someone and wouldn't want to start a dance with him and leave in the middle of it. He didn't like being told no. He reached to grabbed her arm, like he was going to pull her on to the dance floor whether she wanted to dance with him or not. Kat reached between them with her other hand and hit his wrist a knuckle blow with that sent the biker to his knees, all the time holding his wrist with his other hand. The couples around them stopped dancing and drinking to watch the show going on between the biker and Kat.

"You broke my wrist you little bitch, you broke it!" Screamed the biker.

"You had it coming, and don't call me a bitch!"

Several of his friends came over to help their friend. "Take the little bitch down for me, guys!" Yelled the guy with the broken wrist.

Two of his friends turned on Kat while another was helping the biker that was down to his feet.

Kat looked at first one and then the other guy coming at her. She held out one hand and told them their friend had grabbed her and tried to take her to the dance floor.

"I don't dance with men I don't know and particularly those that try to manhandle me."

"I'm going to break your wrist just like you did my buddy, bitch," said the bigger of the two men closing the space between them.

"There's that word again. I came here to chew gum or kick ass and I'm all out of gum," she stepped into the bigger biker guy and rammed the heel of her hand as hard as she could under his chin. His head flew back, and he hit the floor out cold. Kat swirled around and faced the second biker. "You want some of me or are you satisfied with your two friends down on the floor?"

The last biker started shaking his head in the negative and backed up like he was going to check on the second guy that was down on the dance floor. Kat watched him as he bent over his friend. Someone threw a glass of water on the unconscious biker to wake him.

The bouncer walked over and told the bikers that he had seen the entire thing. He didn't call it a fight: Kat was never hit.

"You boys pick up your friends and take them outside. I don't want to see your bikes outside again tonight, take 'im home!" The bouncer told them.

The bouncer turned to Kat and told her to sit down until he could make sure the bikers had left the parking lot.

Kat looked back at the table where Bill and his girlfriend were setting. Both Bill and his girlfriend waved to her, wanting her to come back to their table. She drew a chair back and sat down.

"I'd like to buy you drink McNally. I'm glad I was here to see you put those guys down. It's obvious you've been well trained," with emphasis on put down those guys.

"Sixth degree black belt in Taekwondo, and three years as an army M.P and C.I.D. They may be waiting for me outside so I'd like a club soda with a slice of lime for now, and thanks."

"My girlfriend is Ginger, I'm Bill, as you know. What do you want to know about the night that Charlie was murdered?"

"What's your last name, to begin with?"

"Jenkins."

"Tell me about that night at the Full Clip. Anything unusual about him that night?"

"We used to meet at the bar on Friday evenings to shoot the shit about that week's training of the recruits and other army stuff. You know, you were in the army. That night was special, we both usually put one on the night of graduation for the recruits. That night, I remember, Charlie was worked up about one special recruit in his platoon. There's always some recruit that's completely inept about anything and everything that he is told to do. There was one particularly bad one in his recruit platoon. He started calling him, "Fuck-up."

CHAPTER THIRTY-SIX

Slack's long-range recon patrol team was one man short when they left for a special assignment. There had been no replacement of the radio telephone operator that was killed a month before. The back-up RTO had taken his place. The team left the base in the middle of the night, like Slack had started doing right after the rainy season started. The team leader decided moving out at dark thirty was a good idea.

The team was to travel southwest from Dok-To toward the Vietnam, Cambodia border in Kon Tum province to check out heavy enemy activity picked up there by the Army Security Agency in one of their Cessna O-1E Bird Dog aircraft earlier that week. The enemy force was thought to be the 174th Regiment PAVN, People's Army of Vietnam, commanded by general Tran Tra Van.

If the team determined it was the 174th, they were to back off and call in airstrikes. Slack was to take out general Tran Tra Van, before the airstrikes were called into hill 875 where the signals intelligence located the heaviest radio traffic.

The closer the team came to hill 875 and the Cambodian border, the more enemy patrols and booby traps they were encountering. The team kept their intervals, but stayed off the trails and paths that were cut or worn into the surrounding jungle. After four days of hard jungle movement the team leader called the team together and showed the rest of the team where they were on his map of the area. The main camp of the 174th regiment was close by: only two klicks, kilometers, away.

The team leader and the back-up radio man went ahead to verify exactly where the main base camp was located and if it was the 174th PAVN. They returned when the light was fading in the jungle. The team leader had called in the coordinates of the main camp and verified it was the 174th regiment. They had located the headquarters base with its PAVN flag and the unit flag flying in front of a series of bamboo huts with thatch roofs. Heavy artillery and air-controllers had been informed that the main base was located at the base of hill 875.

The team leader stayed with the remainder of the team, while Slack and the radio man left when it was dark to work their way down the side of the hill they were on, and over to the next hill, until they could see the light from a central fire at the main base camp. The sun had started to make the dark sky the light gray of morning, when the backup RTO spotter for Slack touched his shoulder and nodded his head. Slack used his rucksack as a rest for his M-14 sniper rifle and began fine tuning the scope for windage and distance. He and the spotter estimated the distance to the fire at a little more than a half-mile. Once that was done, the spotter settled down next to Slack with his spotting scope, and waited for the time when the soldiers at the camp started to move about.

The sun had made the early morning mist disappear when a group of officers gathered near the fire in front of the largest hut. The spotter tapped Slack on the shoulder twice. The general had come out of the larger hut and the spotter had matched his photo to the man standing in front of the junior officers. There was a crack from the M-14 and the head of the general blew up. The spotter kept his scope on the other officers. One by one the junior officers fell dead from the perfectly placed shots that Slack was making. The spotter counted six officers down including the general when Slack started picking up the empty rifle bullet casings. The two men hurried back to the high hill where the team leaderf and the second team member were waiting for them.

Nothing was said when Slack and his spotter returned. The team leader had his RTO on frequency for the heavy artillery. He said softly into radio telephone handpiece the code word for the artillery to begin firing. The 155mm artillery fired its first round from fourteen miles away. The team leader change frequencies to the air controller flying overhead and said, "target ready."

The team leader pointed his hand to the northeast and started through the jungle headed back to their base camp about four days away. The going was tough, they were still keeping off any trail they saw along the way. The morning of the fifth day they could see the base ten clicks away on the top of a hill. The team hit the trail they had used a few times to leave and return to the base from their incursions into to enemy country. The team leader was on point, then the RTO, then the back-up RTO and at the drag was Slack, the position he always took.

Slack saw quick flashes in front of him: then horrific, shattering explosions of lightning striking at his feet. He was blown off his feet; into the air where he did a back flip with his arms and legs flailing in the air, his body hit the ground like a huge rock falling from a high cliff.

CHAPTER THIRTY-SEVEN

The agreed upon date and time had finally arrived. Mrs. Robinson was floating off the ground with anticipation mixed with vodka and cocaine. The two weeks had gone by slowly for her; patience was not one of her attributes. It could be said she was chomping at the bit, by the time she slipped behind the steering wheel of her car. The G Shop was a short drive to Chinatown and another short walk down Grant Street to the lesbian bar. The young femme was going to take the place of the young maid, and fill the needs of her sex addiction when she didn't have what she wanted; when she wanted it.

She was checked at the entrance and was physically shaking by the time she reached the same barstool she had sat on a few weeks earlier. She ordered a vodka on the rocks and started to search through the darkened interior for her young woman. By the time her drink came she hadn't spotted the one she was looking for. A quick wave of worry came over her, mixed with it came anger. She tossed back her drink and waited for the bartender to notice she needed another drink. She had a slowly growing tension in her body, as the wait for her future protégé grew longer. She watched the entrance to the bar checking out each lesbian that was checked by the butch bouncer.

Forty-five minutes had passed, and Mrs. Robinson was getting plastered. At the same time smoldering in anger that the young lesbian bitch had stood her up. She had so many plans for her. She was so full of disbelieve and anger that she didn't hear the young butch say softly in her ear, "if you're not meeting someone, I'd like to spend so time with you. I like it when a woman can show anger."

The second time the butch said it, Mrs. Robinson heard the soft, deceptive, destructive, and ultimately dangerous siren's song that made her in one instant forget about her protégé that went missing. The only thing she seemed to be able to think about was that the woman standing next to her was cut from the same cloth as she. This butch would require no induction to Mrs. Robinson being the Dominatrix. She could sense that the butch that was lightly touching her left breast under her blouse, was an experienced Dominatrix as well.

"Why don't we leave here and go to my apartment where we can enjoy each other without interruption?" The butch asked her.

"I'd like that very much. I want to take you to the mansion I live in. I have a pleasure room there where we can take full advantage of all my things, without thinking of anything else than pleasuring one another."

"That sounds awesome! I'll follow you to your mansion in my car. That way we won't have to come back here."

They left the bar arm in arm.

Mrs. Robinson took her newly found friend down the hallway to her bedroom, but stopped in front of the hidden door and unlocked it. The butch had brought a travel bag with her from her car.

"We must go down one flight in the elevator to reach my totally sound proof, hidden pleasure room."

The younger woman nodded in understanding and waited for the sliding door to open to reveal the wrought iron gate to the small elevator. They both entered at the same time: the butch carried her travel bag with her. Mrs. Robinson closed the gate and pushed the button to take the wrought iron cage down to what she called her pleasure room.

The younger Dominatrix stepped from the other side of the wrought wire cage into a large open room that was crowded with everything a Dominatrix could wish for. All the normal gadgets were along the walls except on one side where there was a large heavy looking metal door. The rest of the room was filled with what looked like ancient torture devices. The one she recognized was a Rack that was positioned at an angle to the floor where a submissive was tied or shackled to the devise and wheels on either side were turned until the pry's appendages were dislocated or pulled from the body. There was a Pillory that pinned the arms, legs or head in any combination to hold a submissive in place while they were being tortured in a myriad of ways. She noticed a set of thumb screws on a horizontal bench. There were several other ancient torture devices that she wasn't familiar with. It was truly a pleasure room for those who loved pain and torture to the point of orgasm, or unconsciousness prior to death.

She watched as Mrs. Robinson dressed in a Dominatrix outfit made of black leather. She hurriedly undressed, and expectantly waited for the first punishment that would be used. Mrs. Robinson started with simple control play. She made the other woman lick her boots while she used her leather whip on her player's butt and back. That was fun for the both of them. Mrs. Robinson wasn't ready for a climax. She made the butch get down on all fours, and rode her around the room and between all the torture equipment. Then tied her player in the rack, and stretched her out until she screamed to be released. Mrs. Robinson left her like that while she prepared a large curved dildo and pushed it into her vagina. She was wet already and the dildo slipped in to its handle. Mrs. Robinson pushed the switch to make it vibrate inside the butch's vagina while she rubbed the butch's clitoris. In just a few short minutes the butch screamed out in ecstasy and fainted.

When the younger woman had recovered sufficiently, they each did a rail of cocaine and made love on the king size water bed that was part of the furniture in the large pleasure room. They enjoyed a five-hundred-dollar bottle of French wine from a built-in wine cellar in the wall of the pleasure room. The butch asked about what was behind the large metal door. It looked like a bank vault door to her. Mrs. Robinson unlocked the heavy door, and eased it slightly ajar, so the butch could see the interior. It was sub-freezing cold, like a meat locker, and the submissive could see stacked along the sides of the huge freezer various sizes of things in shadowed relief. Mrs. Robinson stood at the outside of the heavy door, and pushed with all her strength to get it to swing closed again. She left the key to door in the lock. There was no key lock on the interior of the huge door.

They went back into the room. The butch asked Mrs. Robinson what was stacked in the freezer. She replied that it was storage for various types of meat from ranches around the area. She told her the meat in the groceries was often as not, poor quality and over frozen, which ruined the taste of it. She kept her own supply of fresh frozen meat from ranches that only sold the best of meat. Satisfied with that the butch opened her travel bag. Mrs. Robinson watched in sheer pleasure as the butch took her personal Dominatrix outfit from her travel bad and dress in it. They started with the same power and control play that they had done earlier with the butch as the Dominatrix giving the commands and using the whip. When they were both whipped into a sexual frenzy, the butch took her to the rack and started the same sequence for her as she had done for the

301

butch. Mrs. Robinson was at the peak of sexual pleasure when she collapsed into an unconscious state. The butch tried to wake her; she would not respond. She was still breathing very shallow, rapid breaths.

After a few minutes of trying cold water and even slapping her face, there was still no response from Mrs. Robinson, she decided to move her to the freezer. If she was going to die, the butch didn't want to be held responsible or be sent to jail for the rest of her life. She would keep her cool until she awakened from being unconscious. She had heard of reports that people that were in a deep state of unconsciousness came out of it, even weeks later and were okay if they were cold.

She positioned the limp body of Mrs. Robinson near the huge metal door inside the dark, cold room and started to swung the heavy door closed. Light that was cast into the opening seemed to focus on something along the opposite side of the cold freezer. The butch walked past the limp body of Mrs. Robinson to see what was there. She stopped in apoplectic shock: it was the most macabre, evil sight she could ever imagine. There were men and women's bodies stacked in naked, frozen positions of sex acts all the way around the walls of the cold freezer, with several rows between. It was the most horrific scene she had ever encountered. Stuffed animal heads killed by a big game hunter flashed before her eyes, hung in death on the walls of his den.

She ran out of the freezer and pushed the huge door closed behind her. She didn't hear the locking bolt slide into place: all she could think about was getting the hell out of the now revolting hidden sex room.

The butch quickly dressed in her street clothes and grabbed her travel bag up to the main floor of the mansion by climbing up the metal supports of the small elevator. She ran across the large living room, leaving the hidden elevator door open. She left the front door unlocked thinking that she would return that afternoon to make sure the crazy woman was alright. She ran out of the mansion and drove off in her car, intending to go to her apartment to take a shower and rest after the rough and tumble day if she could. She thought about calling the police, but decided she didn't want to get involved in what had been taking place at the mansion.

The butch was deep in thought, remembering the horror she felt and the total disgust that made her skin crawl. She had been with sex addicts, but never one that was as unbalanced as that crazy bitch.

She didn't see the red traffic light and went speeding into the intersection where another speeding car raced into the intersection on his green light and t-boned her car. The butch died instantly.

CHAPTER THIRTY-EIGHT

Without definite proof that the recruit had been the killer of staff sergeant Flower, the military would do nothing about it. Kat had to get proof that the recruit was the killer and connect him to the maids killing as well. Then the military would act. If she couldn't prove the two murders were committed by the same person, she would have to wait until he was discharged from the military and then stop him in a civilian court or she had to stop him, anyway she could.

She left Monterey for her apartment outside of San Francisco. The drive was uneventful, but the first thing she saw when she entered her apartment was the damn blinking light on her phone recorder. She put her travel bag on the sofa and went out to her mailbox. The phone would have to wait. Her box was full. The postman had pushed her newspapers into the box instead of placing them on the paper holder under the box. There was a phone bill, an electric bill that she kept, but everything else, including the newspapers, she threw in the trash can next to the apartment mailboxes.

The red blinking light continued blinking until Kat had put her dirty clothes in her laundry basket and checked the amounts of the electric bill and the telephone bill. Then she walked over to her desk and stood there, with her hands on her hips, glairing back at the red blinking light. She picked up a pen and notepad, pushed the play button on the recorder, and started to listen to the calls that turned out to be all calls from the same person. Someone had lost their dog. She made a note to call her back. Maybe she could find the dog while she was still working the murder case. After all, she still needed to pay the two bills.

She called the number that the lady had left on the recorder. A woman answered the phone and Kat told her she was returning her call about the lost dog.

The woman was silent for a moment and then said, "I made those calls over a week ago. The dog returned on its own, no thanks to you!"

The phone was hung up in Kat's ear. You win some, loose some, call some a draw. This dog case, Kat figured was a win. The owner was, for sure, a bitch.

Kat went down to the apartment parking lot, planning on going over to Mrs. Robinson's to tell her what she had learned since last talking with her. She didn't look forward to the meeting, after the last one was such a pain in the ass. She pulled out of the lot and started toward the bay bridge when she spotted a vehicle pulling out of her apartment parking lot with two men in it. After all that had happened since she went to Monterey, she was overly suspicious of cars with two men in it that started to follow her. She continued watching in her rearview mirror, hoping they would turn off or drop back. They continued on her tail while Kat checked her .357 Magnum. A trip to Las Vegas wasn't in the future for her. The way her luck was running, she'd lose everything she had, including the clothes she was wearing.

There wasn't any way to ditch them while she was crossing the bridge; the lanes were narrow and packed with cars going into the city. The car she was watching in her mirror stayed one car back all the way to the west end of the bay bridge. She was driving in the inside lane when she saw her chance in traffic. She swerved into the middle lane of traffic. The car she cut off blowing his horn at her move. The far-right lane was a turn lane off the bridge to highway eight. It went down to a stop light that controlled the traffic coming off the bridge and onto fourth street going north or south under the bay bridge, onto highway two-eighty running in a loop south. She could hear the honking of horns as the car following her tried to make the same moves. there wasn't enough distance for them to make their way through traffic, and follow her onto fourth street.

Kat watched her rearview mirror for a couple of minutes waiting for the sedan to show behind her. When she knew she had lost the car that was following her; she smiled to herself, and increased her speed heading for the west intersection of two-eighty with highway eight again, that went north and south down the middle of the peninsula.

She exited onto highway eight north; and drove back toward the center of San Francisco where she exited onto Fell street, and went west to Golden Gate Park. She turned off before she reached the park to make her way through local streets to the Robinson mansion.

Kat started to turn into the long, paved driveway, when her heart skipped a beat, and she did a double take out of her side window. Two blocks down the tree shaded street a black sedan was parked on the left side of the street; the mansion could be seen through the giant oak trees. She glanced at the parking area in front for the mansion. It was empty. She checked the private parking area at the side of the mansion, Mrs. Robinson's car was in its normal parking spot. She wanted to drive down the street to confront the two men in the sedan. She could take care of that after confronting Mrs. Robinson. She reminded herself that she was at the mansion to discuss what she had uncovered about the young maid's murder.

She set in her car when she had parked; taking out her Smith & Wesson .357 she thumbed the loading gate open and added the sixth shell where the hammer normally rested. Kat wanted to make sure when she left the mansion she could do the Girl Scouts moto for the two men in the sedan, in case they tried to kill her. DO A GOOD TURN DAILY.

Kat pushed the doorbell button. She heard the chime ring inside the living room. She waited a few minutes and tried the doorbell once again. She looked around the covered front porch wondering if Mrs. Robinson was at home and simply too drunk or too high to answer the door or by chance was not at home at the time. Her glance around the porch and stopped with an abrupt halt. What she saw was something that she would never be able to forget during her life. It was a military footlocker. A big wooden box that soldiers used at the end of their bunks to keep clean uniforms and personal items in an orderly fashion. She forgot for a moment about Mrs. Robinson not answering the doorbell; she walked over to the large wood box to check it out. Mrs. Robinson's name and address were on a shipping label on the lid. What she saw next made her stop and close her eyes, the soldier's name was still on the lid, next to the shipping label. On a three-inch strip of white paint, the soldiers name was still readable.

The first thing that came to her was that footlockers weren't shipped from overseas assignments until after the soldier was already back in the states. There was another reason for shipping the footlocker back to the address on his military record as the place of residence. That happened when the soldier was dead. She needed to know which was right for the footlocker on the Robinson Mansion porch. How she would find out was an entirely different matter...

Kat walked over to a large mail box that was setting on a stand made of the same stone that covered the foundation base of the mansion. She opened the mail box. It looked like her box when she came back

308

from Monterrey. It was to the overflowing point. Mrs. Robinson wasn't checking her mail box or she wasn't home and hadn't been for a long time. Maybe she had taken one of her international trips. She didn't have to tell her if she did. She left the footlocker and mail box like they were and went back to her car. She placed her .357 Magnum on her seat at her right thigh and pulled out of the driveway and headed down the street where the sedan was parked. She parked head on with the sedan with the two men in it and ran to the side of the car where the driver was seated, leaving her car door open. The driver didn't have time to roll his window up, not that it would have helped the two men. Kat shoved her .357 Magnum in the driver's face and told them to toss their weapons out of the car.

"You so called Mafia soldiers go back to your Capo and tell him he has made a bad contract. He has sent six men to kill me. Four of them are dead. You tell him I'll come after him next."

The man riding in the right seat reached to the inside of his door, and pulled a nasty looking four shot pocket pistol from the door pocket and pointed it at Kat.

She shot the man in the knee that was next to the driver and said, "you're getting off easy."

She returned to her car and backed up so the sedan could drive away. The sedan with the two men in it did a U-turn in the street, and roared away from Kat's car. The car continued to race down the street blowing through stop signs and swerving around traffic like they were at the Indy 500. Kat continued down the street for a few more blocks and turned toward the bay bridge that would take her to Emeryville and her apartment. She needed to think about what she had or hadn't found at the mansion and what about the Mafia soldiers in the car. They had to know where she was going or they couldn't have beat her to the mansion. What she started thinking really bothered her. Mrs. Robinson was the person that could have set the Mafia on her.

She stopped on the way to her apartment and picked up a hamburger and fries for lunch that she missed and the dinner that she was about to eat. She popped a top on a PBR, a Pabst Blue Ribbon Beer from her fridge. She spread everything out on her small kitchen table and took a long swallow of her beer out of the can. She smacked her lips, sat the can down, took a bite of the juicy looking hamburger. She poured a dab of catsup on the hamburger wrapping paper and dipped the tip of a fry in it. She was in casual heaven.

The morning came bright and clear. Kat dressed for a run along the bay. She had missed running for the past few weeks. The Smith and Wesson .357 Magnum was too bulky to take running. She kept a Walther PPK .380 caliber in a drawer by her bed just for that reason. It was less weight, slender and a semi-automatic. She loaded it with an eight-round clip, and one in the tube. It rested comfortably at the small of her back under her t-shirt that she left hanging out.

During her run, Kat pored over the things that had happened and what she had unearthed from her stay in Monterey. The two men that had followed her were more than a problem for her; particularly when they started trying to kill her, the whereabouts of Mrs. Robinson, and the footlocker on the mansion's porch. By the time she had finished her morning run, she had planned what to do about two of the three things that needed answers.

CHAPTER THIRTY-NINE

S lack was being discharged from Letterman Army Hospital and the United States Army on the same day. He had been promoted to sergeant, and awarded an oak leaf cluster for the wounds he received on the way back to his base after all the other men in the Lurp team were killed. The radio operator was wounded when the mortar shell booby trap had exploded on the trail going back to the team's base at Dok To. The radio man died later of his wounds he received from the booby trap. He looked at himself in the wall mirror in the lobby of the hospital. He was wearing his uniform with his decoration ribbons pinned to his dress coat. The cycle like scar running from the corner of his nose to the front of his ear, in a loop sort of way, on the right side of his face seemed to balance out the patch that he wore over his left eye. It had taken him a while to become use to vision out of one eye only. The scar and eye wound were from the booby trap that killed all the other team members. He had scars from minor wounds over the left side of his body that were covered with his uniform. All of them, but one, he had suffered when the mortar shell booby trap had blown up.

He was angry that the army had shipped his footlocker to the mansion, instead of the storage locker that he had rented. His military papers had the storage locker as his address. The elderly man that owned them was being paid to place anything that arrived at his facility for him: he would place in his rented space. It was all paid for monthly from one of his personal accounts. He was told the army had used the address from the papers he filled out when he signed up for the draft when he was eighteen years old. That address was for the mansion in San Francisco. What was the old saying that army personnel used all the time? Oh yah, it was, "situation normal, all fucked up!"

There was a short line of taxies in front of the hospital. He took the one in front, and had the driver take him to the nearest men's store. He walked out of the store in casual civilian dress that felt really good, even though they were brand new. He caught another taxi to the airport and rented a car for a few days, with his California driver's license and credit card until he had time to go buy a new car.

He drove past the mansion several times to make sure there were no parked cars in the front and none in the private parking at the side of it. There was one in the private parking lot. He figured it belonged to the mansion. He saw his footlocker off to the side of the large front entry door on his second pass. When his recon of the mansion satisfied him that no one was home, he parked in the front visitor's lot. He waited in the car for a few minutes to see if anyone came from the mansion. When no one came he went up the steps, and walked directly to the locker. He did the combination on the lock and opened the lid. The smell of Vietnam hit him. He dug down to the bottom of the footlocker looking for a set of civilian clothes, and feeling for a manila envelope he had placed under them. He found it in the same position that he had placed it. He was quick about closing the footlocker and taking the envelope with him to the car. He drove to the driver's license office that he had used when he turned sixteen. He took the birth certificate of the deceased lurp soldier with him when he parked the rental car at the license office. He frowned when he opened the entry door. There was a long line curving around the lobby. He went to stand in the line that was always there. He figured he should be able to do the line easily, after doing the lines in the army.

A young woman behind the counter called his number finally.

"How can I help you, sir?"

Slack wasn't use to people staring at his face. He turned his face away slightly and told the young woman he needed a new California driver's license.

"No problem," the young woman said, "I'll need to see your old one and one other form of identification."

"I don't have my last one. It was lost while I was in Vietnam. I do have my birth certificate."

The young woman was hesitant for a moment. "You don't have any other form of I.D."

"No mam, I've been in Vietnam for the past year,and all my records are still being processed through the army since I was hospitalized with my wounds." They took my military I.D. when I was medically discharged. I need the new driver's license to act as my I.D. until all that paperwork comes through the government bureaucracy. I can't do anything without my California driver's license until then."

The young woman looked exacerbated for a moment and then said, "if I can't trust a man that has served his country, who can I trust. I need to take you over to the testing area and make sure you know the signs and your vision is okay. Then I'll take your information from your birth certificate with what you have filled in on your new request form. The camera is over by the sign that says, recognition exam. I'll need a frontal photo also," he passed all the visual tests with no problem.

He took a number and went back to the waiting area while the young woman made his new driver's license. His number was called in a few minutes. The young woman had his birth certificate and his new driver's license with the car storage building as his permanent address. He walked out smiling to himself. What a bunch of dopes.

Slack rolled his new name over his tongue a few times when he was in the rental car. He was no longer Slack; he was still a psychotic killer that was controlled by lightning, thunder, and trained by the army. He was an expert with a knife, a long-range rifle, or machete, and had become an Anthropophagite, a man-eater, while he was in Vietnam.

Next on his list to accomplish was to get his new name on his bank accounts at one of his banks in San Francisco. He showed the bank assistant manager his new driver's license with a different name. He explained that while he was in Vietnam there were people in San Francisco that had brought his name into a murder investigation and he changed his name to keep from dealing with all the bad, ugly publicity.

The assistant manager became very agitated at his request. He probably wouldn't have a job in the morning if he refused to let him change his name on his accounts. The bank might lose two multi-million accounts. He called a clerk into his office and explained what he wanted her to do. It took a few minutes for the records to have his new name placed on them.

He asked the clerk to give a book of counter checks to the stock holder to use while he was waiting for his revised checks to come to the bank. He didn't have a permanent address yet.

He left the bank without a smile or thank you to the clerk or the assistant manager. He was going to change banks as soon as he could. If the two employees of the bank were that easy to run over, he didn't want his money with the bank. He'd keep the stock.

It was beyond belief how easy it was to corrupt their banking rules, if you maintained a lot of money in their bank.

He didn't want anything to tie him to the car that he left at the long-term storage building in Modesto. He stopped at a filling station and looked up the new car dealers in the area yellow pages. He found a Ford dealer not far from the filling station and drove directly to it. He started looking over the cars in the lot like he didn't know what he wanted to buy. It didn't take long for a salesman to show up.

"In the mood to buy a new car today?" The sales man asked him.

"I'm not sure. I like the regular sized cars, I had one before I went to Vietnam but I'm use to driving bigger vehicles now. Do you have anything that is four-wheel drive?"

The salesman beamed with delight when he heard four-wheel drive. The dealership had recently received a shipment from the Ford plant in Wayne, Michigan. It was the only plant in the country that made the Bronco. The salesman walked him to the back of the dealership where there were twelve brand new Bronco's lined up to get detailed after the long trip from Michigan. They walked along the line, as the salesman in his dealer jargon, told him about the four-wheel drive Broncos.

A root beer colored one caught his eye. "Can I take that one for a trial drive?"

"I'll need to get the keys. They're in the office." The salesman wrote a number down that was on the windshield and left him to look over the SUV.

When the salesman returned with the key's he said, "I'll have to ride along with you. It's the dealerships policy."

The salesman rattled through all the things the Bronco came with; the V-8 engine, on the fly transfer case to go into four-wheel drive, the front wheels could be locked after the transfer case was put into gear, the top could be removed, there was no power steering, but a kit was available to put it on once the Bronco was purchased.

When they finished the test drive, the salesman asked him if he would like to go into the dealership and discuss purchasing it.

The discussion of purchase price was always like a well-practiced dance. After a while, and the intervening of the sales manager which always happened, was to make the potential buyer feel like he was special and getting the best deal.

At the end of all the push and shove stuff, the salesman thought he had the buyer settled in on a price. It was a good price for the dealership.

"I will pay cash, so I want a much larger discount. I want the car cleaned and ready for me drive it away before you close tonight. I am driving a rental car now. I want your dealership to take it back to the rental agency. I want drive away with my new car without the hassle of hiring someone to take my rental back there."

They went through the haggling again, but in the end the manager gave him the price he wanted.

The manager said, "give the salesman your information and we'll work on the sale at that price."

The salesman started with his name. The name on his new driver's license. My bank is the San Francisco National bank. I have the account number and routing number written down for you."

He stayed at the dealership until the bank had confirmed that he had an account and there was enough money in it to pay for the car. He wrote a counter check for the Bronco and left the dealership to continue checking things off the list he had made while he laid in bed at Letterman Army hospital.

CHAPTER FORTY

McNally was parked on the street where the sedan had been parked when she found the footlocker on the porch of the Robinson mansion. She parked there earlier that morning in the hopes of catching Mrs. Robinson at home, or catching someone taking the footlocker from the porch.

Mrs. Robinson's car was still in its parking space. She couldn't see the footlocker but presumed that it was still on the porch. The morning changed to early afternoon. Kat opened the brown paper bag that contained her lunch. She had packed a ham and cheese sandwich on Rye bread with Gulden's Spicy Brown Mustard, plus tomato and lettuce. A stop at a ma and pa store for an iced drink and a bag of potato chips on the way to the stake-out was plenty for the day time stake-out. She needed to talk with Mrs. Robinson and figured she would come out of the mansion at some point, or she would go ring the doorbell before she left for the night. There was a lot of crap that she needed to straighten out with her.

The sun was dropping in the west and shadows were being cast from the trees along the street where Kat was parked. She was getting tired of setting in one place; her butt was trying to go to sleep. She changed from one hip to the other in an effort to slow the tingle down. A car pulled into the visitors parking lot in front of the mansion and took her mind off her butt. She scooted down in her seat and picked her binoculars from the seat next to her.

Kat watched for a moment, waiting for someone to get out of the car. She looked through the driver's window and could see a man setting there. He seemed to be looking around the front and side of the mansion. There was something dark covering the edge of his left eye. She moved her binoculars around the side and back of the car and stopped to look at the license plate. It was a rental car's plate.

The driver's side door opened, and an average height, slender young man stood behind it looking around the mansion and the street fronting it. He stopped his search for anything unusual and stopped his visual search when he saw Kat sitting behind the wheel of her car. She dropped her binoculars and hoped his visual search around the mansion moved away from her and her car.

She had a good look at the young man while he stood behind the door of his car. He was almost skinny, probably a bit under six feet with a black eye patch over his left eye. There was a long curving scar from the ala of his nose to the front of his ear on the right side of his face. His dress was casual but something was wrong about the clothes. She figured it out quickly. The clothes, all of his clothes, looked brand new, from his shoes to the shirt he wore.

He stood behind the door for a while, like he was ready to get back in, and drive away in a hurry, if he felt threatened. When he did close the car door he walked to the steps going up to the porch and looked around. He didn't ring the doorbell, as Kat had thought he would. He disappeared toward the footlocker behind the tall shrubs that were recently cut to form by the gardener Kat had talked with right after the maid was murdered.

Kat drove her car into the visitor parking lot and parked behind the rental car. She sat in the driver's seat until the young man stood from behind the shrubs. His right hand was behind his back. Kat opened the door and stood behind it.

She asked, "you looking for Mrs. Robinson?" Something about the young man made her reach to her back to grip of the Walther .380 that she had tucked there.

The young man with the eye patch shook his head as he said, "frankly no!"

"You interested in the footlocker on the porch?"

"It belonged to a friend of mine. He was killed and I knew his footlocker would be sent to this address."

"How would you know where it would be sent, if he was killed?"

"I don't know why I'm answering all these questions. Who are you and what business is it of yours, what I do and or when I do it?" He asked in an aggressive fashion.

For some reason she felt like she should tell him she was coming up to the porch with her identification. "I'm a private detective working for Mrs. Robinson. I'll show you my I.D. if you want?"

"I'll wait right here," he said.

Kat left her car door open and walked around it. She reached in her back pocket for her credential folder as she went up the porch stairs. She stopped an arm's length away from him and held out her shield wallet. Her feet wear in the attack position.

He took it and looked at it, all the while keeping his vision on her, over the top of her wallet.

"Why does Mrs. Robinson need a private detective?"

"You don't need to know that. What I need to know is what you're doing with her son's footlocker."

"That's none of your business!" He replied.

"You can stay here with me, until the police show up. It looks to me like you're planning on stealing the footlocker, or at best, stealing something inside of it."

"He was my best friend in Vietnam! Come closer and let me show you that I'm not going to steal anything."

He went over to the footlocker and waited for Kat to come closer to see what he was going to do. He squatted down to began moving the combination dial back and forth several times, then pulled on the lock to open it. He reached inside the foot locker, shuffling clothes around until he felt what he knew was there.

"Be careful what you bring out of the footlocker!" Kat warned.

He very slowly brought out a plastic bag with some metal pieces in it. He came up with a story for the bag and what was in it: some of it true, some of it a lie.

"Slack, his nickname, was my buddy. He gave me a Chinese pistol he had taken off an NVA officer. It was a great souvenir. He told me to kept it to remember him by. He was afraid of being forgotten if he was killed. It was okay for us to send back stuff like that when we rotated to the states, but you had to take anything like a weapon apart when you shipped your footlocker back. The plastic bag is what M16 ammunition came in. Two magazines to a bag. There's a message printed on the bag telling NVA soldiers, that might find them, to defect. I gave him an M1911 A-1 .45 caliber Colt. A handgun my father had during world war two. I put his in my footlocker and he put mine in his footlocker. While I was in the hospital, I learned he had been killed in action, right after I was wounded and sent back to the states for treatment. I was just released from Letterman hospital, and discharged from the Army. The first thing I wanted to do was to come to his home and asked whoever had the footlocker to give me the M1911 that was in his footlocker. It means a lot to me, and I don't want him to think I forgot him."

"Let me see your driver's license," she asked.

She believed some of what the young man told her, but there were parts that didn't ring true. She wanted to be able to find the guy, if things he told her turned out to be false. The neck tingle thing was doing her alarm for some reason.

"This license is brand new," she said.

"I had to get a new one, my old one was lost in Vietnam," he told her.

"Is this your present address?"

"It was my address when I was drafted into the army. I don't have a permanent place yet. I was just released from the hospital a few days ago."

"Why didn't you wait until you have a new permanent address to get a driver's license?"

"You have to be kidding me. Without a driver's license, you can't do a damn thing in California!"

"Did you try the doorbell. You should tell his mother about her son and the footlocker."

"I had the feeling that he and his family were not close. I just wanted to get my gun out of the footlocker and get the hell out of here."

"I'll ring the doorbell and you'll wait until someone comes to the door. There's no way you should take the gun and not say a word to the deceased man's family. I think his mother is the only one alive now."

Kat rang the doorbell and both of them waited. She rang it again, when no one answered the first ring. No one came to the door.

"Take your gun. There doesn't seem to be anyone home. I still recommend that you come back and tell her about her son."

The slender young man started to salute from habit; stopped it midway into it and went to his rental car and drove away, leaving Kat confused, and uneasy about the entire thing that had just transpired.

There were just too many loose ends and unfinished thoughts that the young man with the eye patch left hanging.

Kat went back to her car, wondering about Mrs. Robinson and if what the man with the eye patch told her was the truth. If it was true, then she thought the murder investigation on her part was complete. Why did she not believe that? She had a feeling there was a connection between the soldier she was looking for and this guy she had just talked to. Maybe there was more to it than met the eye. She was going to check him out with Letterman hospital. They would be able to tell her if he was discharged a few days ago. She gripped her steering wheel tightly while she mulled everything over and drove to Letterman hospital.

CHAPTER FORTY-ONE

The almost skinny young man went back to the Ford dealers and watched them finish cleaning his new Bronco. The temporary California plate was already in place and his temporary title was handed to him by the salesman that gave him ownership of the Bronco. He gave the keys to the rental car to the salesman and drove off the lot in his new Bronco. He had one more place to go before heading out of San Francisco.

He used the Bay bridge to get across the bay, and drove straight to Modesto. He made it to the long-term auto parking garage just before the office was closing. He walked quickly into the office, hoping to get his question answered.

He wanted the clerk to feel his rush. "A friend of mine has been killed in Vietnam. His family asked me to check on his car that he parked here in long term parking. Can you help me find out what the status of his car is at this time?"

"I'm so sorry to hear about your loss. Normally we need some type of identification to give out that information. Considering the circumstances, I think we can bend that rule for you and his family. What was his name?"

He told her the name, and waited for her to leave the counter.

"Do you know what make the stored car is?"

"Sure, it's all he ever talked about in Vietnam. A Ford Mustang!"

"I'll be right back, I need to go into the file room to get his storage record."

The clerk hurried back with a business card waving in her right hand. "I'm afraid that vehicle has been sent to a salvage yard near here for the delinquent payments that were owed to the owner of our storage facility. This is their business card. You may be in time to stop a re-sale. It wasn't taken over there long ago."

He snatched the card from the clerk's hand and went out to his new car to drove toward the highway going south to Hayward. He pulled into a parking lot of a grocery store, and took the time to put his M1911 Colt .45 together. He wiped the well-oiled pistol, and rammed in a magazine full of .45 caliber bullets. He jacked the slide back feeling that tingle that always came to him when he was preparing to drift into his Dark Persona.

He caught the I-5 south from Modesto trying to calm his Dark Persona. He kept telling himself there was no way that he could now be connected to the Mustang or the bloody clothes under the front seat. He had his new identity secured. His stinking-thinking brought him to the private detective that questioned him on the mansion portico.

It had to be something other than the killing of the maid. That was a police thing! Maybe Mrs. Robinson had the P.I checking up on one of her many lover/Dominatrix/submissive men and women. Never mind the P.I. His Dark Persona knew every detail of his life. It would protect him, and continue to give him relief from his cataleptic fear of the lightning and thunder that accompanied the storms off the ocean.

Before he realized how fast he had been driving, he was at the turn off for the San Mateo-Hayward bridge that crossed the southern part of San Francisco bay. He crossed the bay without noticing the water at all. He was in the trace like state that held him between reality, and deep delusion that was his Dark Persona.

He needed to stop at one of the hunting supply stores for more gear, ammunition and a hunting rifle that was exactly like the one he used to kill so many in Vietnam. There was store that sold what he needed at the edge of the San Cruz mountains. He could see the mountains in the distance outlined by the reds and golds of the sitting sun. He slowed the Bronco down to make the left hand turn onto a dirt road where the supply store was located.

He stuck the pistol at the small of his back an felt his Dark Persona start to awaken. The old man that was the owner of the store greeted him when he walked up to the counter. An old golden retriever was stretched out on a rug next to his owner. The dog raised her head off the floor and began a soft, subtle growl. The owner told her to stop the growling.

"I can't believe she doesn't remember you, but then you have changed. The last time I saw you was several years ago, if I remember right."

The Dark Persona fell over him like a cloak that was dropped out of the sky. The old man was right, it had been at least three years, but he remembered him, even with the grotesque mask that was his new face.

He handed the old man a list of things he needed and walked over to the hunting rifle display. The weapon that he wanted was in the middle of the gun rack with a light chain running through the trigger guard. He stopped the old man, and asked him to take the chain off, so he could look at the Remington model 70 rifle. It was exactly like the one he used in the Vietnam at the sniper school except there was no sling, and no high-powered scope attached to it. The old man watched him for a minute, recognizing a man that had handled that particular rifle regularly.

"I'll take the model 70. I'll need a good scope and a leather sling, also. I'm going to be doing some target practice to get zeroed in; better give me a full box of ammunition, along with everything else."

"I'm going to need a full box of ACP .45 caliber bullets for some pistol practice too."

"I'll throw in some targets for free," said the old man.

The old man had everything stacked on the short counter and started to add the cost together. He told the young man that he figured had been in the war, that he didn't have a machete for sale in the store, but put the one he used to cut down the weeds that grew around the exterior of the store, was in his bundle, again for free.

The man with the eye patch paid his bill and the old man offered to help carry everything out to his car. It took two trips to get everything in the back of the Bronco. The old man walked back to his store very pleased with the sale of all the merchandise. It would help him make ends meet until hunting season came around.

The machete had been recently sharpened. Dark Persona knew what to do with the machete. The old man recognized the man with the eye patch. The Dark Persona took over! He entered the front door of the small hunting supply store with the machete behind his back.

The old golden retriever came around the end of the short counter in a growling rush. She hit the man with the eye patch with a leap and knocked him back a couple of steps. The golden retriever was tearing at his pants leg. The machete came up from where the man's arm laid on the floor and in one wicked cut severed the golden retrievers head from its body. Its body kept making the moves to tear the man's leg off, but its head had been knocked a few feet away.

The old man was standing in shock with a pistol in his hand. He was too shocked to pull the trigger. The man with the patch crossed the few steps to the counter where the old man was and cut off the forearm that was holding the pistol. The back swing of the machete, that was being wielded by the man with the patch, hacked off the old man's head. It fell on the small counter with its eyes still showing fright. The blood from the headless body was pumping blood over the head and the small counter.

The man with the eye patch walked slowly out of the small hunting supply store with the same euphoria that the Dark Persona had learned to enjoy when he was killing the enemy in Vietnam.

He started to leave the dirt and gravel parking area but then thought of something he needed to do that wasn't necessary while he was in Vietnam. He left the car running with the driver's door open and walked back into the carnage that had been a quiet little hunting equipment and supply store. He went to the body that was still slumped against the counter and cut the end of his index finger off and tossed it into his mouth for a treat. He opened the cash drawer and took all the paper money from it. He didn't need the money: it would make his butchery appear to be a robbery gone bad.

CHAPTER FORTY-TWO

The Presidio at the northern tip of San Francisco was where Letterman hospital was located. It had been converted to a military post in 1850, after the gold rush had started. It was a located at the entrance to San Francisco bay. Kat made her way from the Robinson mansion to the entrance of the Presidio, and was flagged through the sometimes occupied, main gate to the installation. The hospital was built in the old Spanish style with red roofs and stucco exteriors.

Kat went to the information desk that was close to the main entrance and asked the clerk there if she could get information about a soldier that was a patient there.

The clerk asked her to wait for a minute and walked back to a glass enclosed office. A nurse captain walked with the clerk to the information desk and said, "I'm sorry, any information about our men and woman in the hospital for treatment is restricted to family only. Are you family member of the person you're requesting information about?"

"I'm an employee of the family."

"Unless you have a signed and notarized permission form, we can't answer your questions about any potential patient being treated here," the captain told Kat.

Kat told the nurse she would get the required document and return. She left the hospital disappointed. She thought her idea was a quick, simple way to connect the dots on whether she was dealing with two men or one. She drove to the nearby Chinatown and had Oriental for dinner with a large glass of rice wine. The wine smoothed over the disappointment for the time being. She changed into her running clothes when she reached her apartment and headed over to the running trail as the sun was setting with its red, orange and yellow streaks glowing in the in burgeoning softness of the evening shadows.

The run was cool since the sun was setting. She ran with a will. Still trying to figure out who this man with the patch was or wasn't. She kept at it until she realized she had reached the turnaround of the trail. She kept seeing the man dial in the combination of the lock on the footlocker. Would a soldier tell someone else how to unlock his personal footlocker? She didn't recall ever telling anyone the combination on her footlocker in Korea.

She continued on her run toward the end of the trail and to her car working those few moments that she had been near him; she was like a little terrier gnawing on a bone, until the bone was gone, or she got tired of gnawing on it. There had to be something that she could point a finger at, to take her doubt away. Was the man that took the M1911 Army Colt from the locker not who he said he was or was he who he said he was? She had to figure out who the wispy ghost was that kept moving in and out of her first big case.

Kat picked up her mail on her way to her apartment and tossed it on the tiny table next to the door, as she walked toward her bedroom, taking off her running clothes along the way. She threw her clothes in the clothes hamper, and turned the water on in the shower. She always felt better and could think more clearly right after a shower.

Kat put on her bathrobe and checked to see if there was a red blinking light coming from her desk. She went over to the desk by the door and sorted through the advertisements, throwing them away as she went. There were two bills, that she had paid a few days earlier. She kept glancing at the two envelopes, while she scanned the paper for any interesting news. She couldn't figure out why she was glancing at the bills that were already paid. She tossed them in the trash along with the newspaper and went to her bedroom. She was asleep quickly. It had been a long day, with no real progress. What was it that was bothering her?

She decided to stake out the mansion again. Maybe she would find Mrs. Robinson home. She sat under the trees where she had been the first day. This time she had several peanut butter and jelly sandwiches with a bag of fresh strawberries she purchased at a grocery store on the way to the mansion. She was looking around neighborhood when she started to focus on the address of the mansion that was embedded in a large stone cairn that also held its mail box.

She started her car and drove around the area. She was looking at the addresses on the other large homes and Mansions. She knew there was something that she should take from them, but was still uncertain what to make of her sudden interest in addresses. She returned to the shade trees and watching the mansion.

The short-tempered man standing on the mansion porch telling her he would wait for her to leave her car and come to the porch to show him her credentials, started to pop into her head. She kept trying to focus on him. She could see him after he checked her I.D and she asked him to show her some identification of his own. That was it! That was what had been bothering her for the last day and a half. It was the address, that caught her eye. She remembered saying something about it to him. The address was in Modesto. It was a simple address. She closed her eyes and tried to recall the exact address. 777 Paradise Rd. It was early in the morning when she left the mansion stake out and drove back across the bay bridge. She reached the city limits of Modesto an hour later. She pulled up in front of 777 Paradise Road. She wanted to kick herself in the butt!

She was setting in front of the long-term parking garage where the Ford Mustang had been stored.

It had been sometime since she was at the garage asking about the car that was the object of all the past due payment notices she found in the apartment. The guy with the eye patch was using the garage as his address on his driver's license. Even though that was circumstantial, it was enough for Kat.

Kat decided to go to the office and check if anyone had been inquiring about the Mustang, other than herself. The same clerk was setting in an easy chair in the small lobby area reading a newspaper. Kat asked her if anyone had asked about the Mustang after she had been there. The clerk put the paper down on a side table by a stack of magazines, and stepped behind the counter.

"You must be playing tag with the guy that was asking about the Mustang. He came rushing in here at closing time asking about that Mustang for the family of a deceased soldier," she told Kat.

"What did he look like?"

"You know, I don't normally pay much attention to people coming and going around here. It's a busy business, the storage of cars. The guy was something special. He was close to six feet tall, by the marker over there by the front door. He had a ball cap on, but it didn't have anything on the front of it. Just plain. I think he must have been in

Vietnam. He had a fairly fresh scar on his right check that went from the corner of his mouth to the front of his ear. He was wearing a black patch that had an elastic strap around his head," she told Kat. "Which eye was covered?"

"It was the left one. He seemed in a hurry and he was sort of gruff. He grabbed the paper that I had written the address for the salvage company on and went hurrying out the door, like his pants were on fire."

"Why do you think the scar was recent?" Asked Kat.

"You know. It was kind of puckered looking and was still that red color against his white skin. That was something else, his skin looked like he had been out of the sun for a long time. He was really white! You know what I mean?"

"You bet. Like he just got out of the hospital," said Kat.

"That's right. Just out of the hospital," the girl answered.

"One last question. Did you notice what kind of car he was driving?"

"It wasn't a car, so to speak, it looked like a new SUV. I do remember the color. It reminded me of my favorite flavor of lollipop, root beer," the clerk told Kat.

Kat turned to leave the office thinking that the young woman clerk was a fountain of information and very observant when she noticed a bold print headline on the local newspaper that was laying on the side table. She picked the paper up and read the entire headline.

"CRAZED KILLER ON THE LOOSE IN SAN MATEO COUNTY."

The article didn't give many details only that the owner of a hunting supply store and his golden retriever were found with their throats slashed late in the night before last. She threw the paper back on the side table and asked the young woman at the counter if she knew how to get to the hunting supply store in San Mateo county.

"No, I don't, but my boyfriend will know. He goes hunting all the time in the Santa Cruz Mountains. The store is at the base of the mountains on the east side. He works at the construction company down the road a piece," she said.

"Okay," she thought. I need to keep on his trail. She was torn between physically getting sick or going over to the salvage company to see if he had gone there to see if he could get the Mustang back that had the blood soiled clothes under the seat.

She walked into the oily smelling office of the salvage company, and saw the same stupid creep at the counter.

"I have one question for you and then I promised I'll never come back here again."

"Shut you're trap, bitch! Get out of here or I'll call the cops!"

"No need to call the cops," she flashed her shield and told him, "I am the cops!"

The greasy guy stood silent for a moment, and then asked her what her damn question was.

"Has there been anyone in here after I left, wanting to know about the Mustang that I looked at?"

"Nah. Nobody's been in here about the Mustang. If that's all you got, then get out of here!"

"Shove it shit face," she turned to go, but the greasy guy jumped over the counter and came at her with his right hand ready to knock the crap out of her. She turned on him, and at the same time slapped a grip on his right forearm, shoving it up and away from her, leaving him wide open. She threw her knuckled right fist into his throat with all her weight behind it.

The greasy asshole dropped in his lunge toward her and hit the cement floor with a thud. He was curl in a fetal ball struggling for a breath. One of the salvage yard men came into the office, and asked what the hell was wrong with the counter clerk. Kat told him he ran into her fist and walked out of the office.

She didn't wait to hear the salvage yard man say, "it's about time you got your ass kicked, and by a little woman. Wait 'till the rest of the guys in the yard hear about this. You might have to find a new job, jerk."

Kat put the nasty salvage office clerk behind her as she headed south on I-5 to San Mateo county. It was the next county south of Stanislaus county that Modesto was in. A pickup truck passed her and took the next exit. There was a large decal on the back window of a rack of deer horns. Kat swerved to make the exit behind the pickup; thinking that it was going to the gas station. She followed it into the gas station and parked behind the pickup.

The driver of the pickup, a middle-aged man with a full beard was starting to fill his tank when Kat walked up to him and asked, "do you know the way to the hunting supply store in the Santa Cruz mountains?"

CHAPTER FORTY-THREE

The Dark Persona had faded enough for the man with the eye patch to drive along California highway nine that went through the mountains from north to south: he knew exactly where he was headed. He made sure he was staying inside the speed limits along the way. When he reached the small mountain town of Boulder Creek, he turned onto a narrow blacktop road marked number nine that took him deeper into the mountains and their solitude.

The mountain home that he had purchased when the Dark Persona first started to appear, was at the end of a fire patrol trail a few miles north of highway nine. He found solace there in all the larger wild animals he was able to kill. There, he began eating the raw flesh of the animals he killed. He wondered, as he neared the small cabin, if it would still be in the order that he had left it in just before killing his first human and experiencing the ecstasy and euphoric glow of contentment that it gave him.

He drove the new Bronco across a drainage ditch and maneuvered it through the trees until he reached the cabin. He turned the Bronco around and faced it toward the trail. He locked it and went up the steps to front porch. The lock on the door was still in place. He moved the dial, entering the combination, and pushed the door open.

The interior was as he left it. A smell of being closed up while he was in the army made him leave the door open. He went quickly to the back door and the windows around the two-room cabin to open them and get the air flowing again. He brought in the supplies he had purchased and went to the back of the cabin to push the electricity lever back between the two metal contacts in the metal box.

Later that evening he crouched in the dark of the cabin already thinking about his next conquest. The old maid hated taking care of him and would beat him; then lock him in his closet when a lightning and thunder storm came. He was deathly afraid of storms. He screamed and cried and clawed at the closet door. He was left there until the storms passed. Mrs. Robinson started to give him more attention when he was eight or nine years old. She didn't want him near her during a lightning and thunder storm. But there were times, when he was nearing ten years old that he filled in when she needed an especially erotic partner. She ended up lusting for him so much that she used him as her masturbation partner when he was in junior and high school. She was at her best being a Dominatrix with the child, turned young man, until he left the mansion for an apartment while he attended university. His first triumph was planned well, but it was the wrong person. Never mind that, he thought. He would find the old maid and kill her!

Thinking of killing, brought the Dark Persona to the edges of his reality. He was back in the United States. There were laws here and police to back them up; unlike Vietnam where everything went and he took advantage of that, killing whenever he liked, and whomever was available. He had discovered he could reach a climatic episode without the need of a lightning storm. It was still the best euphoria and the Dark Persona liked the hunt as much as the killing.

He started to relax into his cloak of the Dark Persona. The persona wanted to make plans on killing the people that he hated. A flash of warning from the Dark Persona made him grip the arms of his chair. That woman that stopped him on the mansion's porch. She could be a danger to the Dark Persona. It had felt the force that radiated from her. She must be sacrificed to the Dark Persona, to make him even more powerful. The Dark Persona wanted to take revenge on the people he hated during a storm; he must be ready for the next lightning storm. He wasn't the frightened, frail boy any more. He was getting stronger each time the Dark Persona sucked the life from its conquests.

He had inserted new batteries in the portable radio that he had left in the cabin for so long, and tuned it to the channel from San Francisco. He took the radio and sat down in the small closet in the tiny bedroom and waited to hear when a storm was coming. He hated the lightning and thunder, but his Dark Persona was strongest then.

When daylight brightened the interior of the cabin he took the radio with him to the other room and started preparing his new sniper's rifle. After he put the new scope on he went outside to sight it in. He was an expert at killing from long distances thanks to the army. He cleaned his M1911 Colt pistol and made sure his hunting knife and machete were sharp and clean. It took him a while to clean the Machete.

CHAPTER FORTY-FOUR

The sheriff for San Mateo county was in the center of a group of deputy sheriffs standing in the dirt and gravel parking lot in front of the hunting supply store when McNally parked her car. She stood outside the circle for a few moments before anyone in the circle acknowledged her. She showed the sheriff her credentials and asked if she could talk with him in private for a moment.

"Can't you see I'm busy. I have a murder investigation to run here."

"I have only one question for you, sheriff," she said.

"Okay. Make it quick. You can ask it from where you are. My men won't bite you!" He said with a smirk on his face.

Kat looked around the little circle and decided to burn the smart-ass sheriff's fingers. She looked around the circle of men and asked, "Was the murder victim missing the end joint of his index finger?"

The group of men looked at each other and they all focused on the sheriff. He pushed a deputy sheriff that was standing next to him out of the way to reach Kat. He reached for her arm to pull her away from the small group. Kat slapped his arm away and told him she could talk with him without being pushed around.

"What's your name?" He was obviously embarrassed by Kat's quick move to brush his arm aside.

She pulled her wallet out again, and gave him one of her cards. "My name is Kat McNally and I'm afraid you have more than a murder on your hands."

"What's that mean?"

"From your reaction and the reaction of your deputies, I know something that hasn't been released to anyone else: including the press," she said.

"How did you know about the missing tip of the victim's finger?" He asked.

"I'm investigating a murder that sounds like your murder. It happened in San Francisco a while ago. The thing is, you have a serial killer on your hands. This is the third murder that has all the same characteristics. There was a murder at Fort Ord that was done just like this one, and the one in San Francisco, down to the missing tip of the victim's index finger. Apparently, I'm the only one that has placed this killer with all three of the murders."

"If that's the case, I need to contact the people in charge at both places to coordinate our investigations. I'd like to keep in contact with you. Is the phone number on your card the best way to reach you?"

"That's right. I'd appreciate you keeping me posted on what your investigation reveals," said Kat.

The red light was blinking when Kat opened her apartment door a few hours later. It was a message from Ben Cooper, the weapons' expert in San Antonio. He was asking whether she had found more proof that George C. Robinson had been murdered. She didn't replay to his call immediately, but began wondering if Mrs. Robinson had ever returned to the mansion. The only way for her to find that out was to check at the mansion.

Kat left the following morning after rush hour, she headed for the mansion. She parked her car under the trees on the street after she had checked out the visitor parking lot. It was empty. She saw Leroy, the handyman-gardener shuttering the swimming pool house and wondered why. The footlocker was missing from the front porch when she went to ring the doorbell again. She rang the doorbell several times and waited. Nothing happened. She tried the door knob. It was unlocked. She opened the door slightly and called inside,

350

hoping Mrs. Robinson was in the house somewhere. She had to be at home, her car was still in the private parking area. Maybe Mrs. Robinson had fallen and hurt herself. That could happen with all the liquor and drugs she did.

Kat wasn't about to enter the mansion uninvited, knowing what rages Mrs. Robinson was capable of having. A confrontation about entering the mansion without her express permission would be atomic.

She remembered Leroy out at the pool. She walked around to the side of the house looking for him. He was on the back patio cutting some low limbs off one of the trees that surrounded it. She stood under the tree and asked if he could take a few minutes to help her. He came down from under the tree and said, "I'm cutting some low limps off the trees. There's going to be a big storm later today the radio said."

"I've been trying to contact Mrs. Robinson for several weeks, Leroy. The front door has been unlocked, but she doesn't answer the doorbell. Any idea where she might be?"

"I haven't seen her for a long time, Miss Kat. There was a big wood box that was sitting on the porch for a long time as well. I finally put it inside the pool house so no one would take it."

"I'm wondering where she might be. I want to see if she had fallen, and hurt herself or something like that. I would like you to go inside with me. "Will you do that for me?"

"I've been thinking about that as well. You lead and I'll follow."

The two of them searched the empty house looking for Mrs. Robinson. There were some dirty drink glasses in the kitchen sink. Kat notice that there were two different shades of lipstick on them. An empty container marked valium was laying on its side near a half empty bottle of vodka. They found nothing else in the mansion until they started to walk down the hall to Mrs. Robinson's bedroom.

A hidden door that was pushed back into an open space in the wall studs was still open. Kat thought of the hidden door in the hall by the maid's quarters. Did it lead to the same place the one near her bedroom did?

She tried to make the wrought wire cage come up, but it wouldn't budge from the room below. She could see the room below filled with various types of equipment. She needed to get down there and see what the room was all about, but first they needed to finish looking for her in her bedroom.

The bedroom was a mess! There were clothes thrown haphazardly around it. The king size bed was unmade, and looked like there had been a fight in it that ended down on the floor. They checked the bathroom, and huge walk in double closets. They found where Mrs. Robinson had been, not where she was.

"Leroy, let's get that extension ladder that you are using while you trimmed the trees. I want to go down to that room, and see if she is there," she said.

It took both of them to jockey the ladder through the metal supports for the cage, and extend it to the floor of the hidden room. Kat climbed the side of the wrought wire cage and stepped gingerly onto the long ladder. She tested it with her weight while Leroy was holding it in place. It was stable enough for her to continue down the ladder into the hidden room. Her heart was pumping extra hard when she reached the floor of the large room.

She stood by the ladder and looked around the room. She knew exactly what it was when she saw it. There was a bed the size of an aircraft carrier to one side of the room, it had been used and not made up. The walls were covered with ceiling to floor mirrors. The ceiling was one large mirror with large fans hanging down from it. There was a wardrobe filled with men's clothing, pants, shirts, suits and women's lingerie of every style, including several styles of leather corsets in multiple colors. There was a chest at the side of the wardrobe. She opened one of the draws and found sex toys galore. There were blindfolds, crops, handcuffs. On the walls were restraints with two and four cuffs that were made of metal, clothe and one with brown colored leather for both wrist and ankles. It was a Dominatrix dream!

Something about the leather cuffs on metal chains that were attached to the wall by heavy closed hooks, bothered her. Then she remembered the stains on the young maid's wrist, that no one seemed to know what caused them. Mrs. Robinson was using her, as a submissive. What a bitch.

She looked around the rest of the room, and saw the large metal door in the side wall. It took up a third of the wall. She picked up a hand towel that was next to a built-in shower, and went over to the door. She pulled on the lever. It opened the door with the towel. The door swung open effortlessly. She stood still in her shock, holding onto the huge door for support. She couldn't take what was inside the huge cold storage freezer. She stood there for a short time, and then took another look inside. There was no light inside the freezer, but at the door she found Mrs. Robinson. The first thing she notice were her finger nails. There were none. Just bloody finger tips from trying to open the big freezer door when there wasn't an interior door handle.

She was frozen solid, like a huge rock, laying there at the door. It would take a coroner to figure out if she froze to death or ran out of oxygen.

Kat saw the rows and stacks of naked human bodies that had been frozen in different sex positions. It was the most abhorrent, horrifying, revolting thing she had ever scene. What kind of sick, sex addicted mind could kill their pry and freeze them in sex positions, as trophies. She knew she had to maintain her sanity. After she regained control she heard Leroy calling down to her. It sounded like he was concerned about her not answering his calls to her.

She called back to him in the strongest voice she could muster, "Leroy, I've found Mrs. Robinson, she's dead. Please call the police, and have them come to the mansion. I'll wait down here for them."

CHAPTER FORTY-FIVE

There was a severe storm coming on shore that afternoon. At first the killer of the old man and killer of his golden retriever couldn't believe his luck. His battery powered radio that was tuned to a San Francisco news station had announced that a severe thunder storm was approaching the city. He gathered his gear and started his drive to San Francisco and the mansion. The Dark Persona was going to make his first truly revenge killing. The Dark Persona was starting to take over when he reached the fire trail and headed for the little town of Boulder Creek and then straight north to San Francisco.

The Dark Persona was astonished when it turned on the street where the mansion was located. The street was blocked off from both ends by police cars with their lights going full blast. There were police cars everywhere; parked on the street, parked in the visitor's lot, parked in the private lot, and parked all over the front and side lawns with multiple ambulances around the pool and back patio.

The policeman at the road block signaled for him to continue past the intersection. He was using his flashlight to direct traffic because of the dark storm clouds lurking over San Francisco. It was the storm he had been waiting for. The portable radio had called for heavy rain, possible hail and strong winds. It was going to be a perfect storm!

The uniformed police moving all around the mansion's exterior reminded the Dark Persona of NVA soldiers in Vietnam. If he couldn't kill Mrs. Robinson when the lightning and thunder started it would give him satisfaction to kill as many cops as he could while the storm lasted. He could hardly wait.

The hill at the back of the mansion was the perfect hide for a sniper. The Dark Persona went into an uncontrollable rage when he saw the parking area had ambulances filling the space. He had to find another place to kill from. He was berserk with anger, and needing a killing. He was gripping the steering wheel with dribble coming from his clenched teeth, and out the corner of his mouth. The rain was starting and it was heavy. That much was a good thing. He left the small parking lot area and drove around the area looking for the perfect spot to snipe from, and then he saw it. The television tower with a platform for workers just below the transmission equipment. That was perfect!

The police came to the mansion in a long screaming cavalcade. Two officers climbed down the long ladder to the Dominatrix room, and shinned their lights into the interior of the room size freezer. One of them started retching the moment he saw Mrs. Robinson. The other officer spoke into his Motorola handpiece.

"We're going to need the murder squad, and all the ambulances that are available."

From then on it was a morbid circus, with too many police, and not enough ambulances to take the frozen nude bodies from the cold storage unit.

Kat sat in a chair in the mansion's living room and told a police captain what she thought had been happening at the mansion. She reminded him of the bloody murder of the young maid. Then told him the bodies in the cold freezer were victims of sex abuse and torture. Mrs. Robinson didn't want any loose ends running around talking about her need to dominate her sex partners. She had even more erotic pleasure knowing that her victims were frozen in her freezer, and she could visit them when ever she pleased. It gave her great pleasure to know she had killed so many; and could be with them, and remember each one's contributions to satisfying her sex addiction.

A sudden bright lightning flash gave the Dark Persona, positioned flat on the workers platform on the super tall television transmission tower, a perfect view of the ants, that were men, moving around the exterior of Mrs. Robinson's mansion. He had jacked a round into the receiver of the Remington model 70 rifle and waited for another flash to start his killing spree. His sense of arousal was the highest it had ever been including the multiple kills at one time in Vietnam. Another lightning strike gave him his opportunity. He let out part of his breath, picked a target and took up the slack on the trigger. The rifle jumped in his arms and a police officer flew backwards, eight hundred yards away.

The dead police officer's partner thought he had tripped on something in the yard. He waited for him to get up. When he didn't he told him to quit screwing around and to get up out of the sloppy grass. He bent over, and turned his partner to his back. Part of his face was missing. He had been shot; there was no sound of a gunshot. He called for help.

The police didn't know where the shots were coming from. They didn't figure out that the shots were coming at the same time a lightning bolt and a consequent thunder clap happened. The men scattered, the ambulance personnel ran for cover in their trucks. It kept on until everyone was undercover, no one was moving, and the sniper had made a new record of ten kills.

Kat was watching the distant tower. She knew that long distance snipers were capable of killing from over a mile away. She picked up on the flash from the rifle each time there was a lightning bolt.

She ran through the heavy rain to her car and drove her car around the helter-skelter police cars parked everywhere. She ended up driving over the curb and driving over the manicured lawns of the mansion. She passed the small parking lot with the ambulances in it and drove back on a street headed toward the television tower. She raced at break neck speeds toward the tower, and was in time to see an SUV turn from the access road to the tower onto the street below.

Kat put her foot down to the floor on her car's gas pedal. She was gaining on the SUV racing down the street until her car started to hydroplane. She let off her gas pedal, but kept the SUV in view with rapidly happening lightning bolts everywhere. It was a Bronco, a new one, that she was following. Like the one the clerk at the long-term storage place told her about. The Bronco was headed for the Golden Gate bridge. Her windshield wipers were having a hard time keeping up with the down pouring rain. She started to turn on her lights and then thought better of it. Maybe the driver of the Bronco didn't know she was following it.

The Dark Persona was feeling the rapture of what it had accomplished. Ten kills from one hide. That had to be some kind of record. He was going to his favorite place in the area to celebrate his record. The lightning and thunder would keep the Dark Persona in control, but would make the euphoria continue as long as the lightning storm lasted.

Kat missed a turn that the Bronco took in the drenching rain. She backed up the street and waited to turn until she saw the Bronco's brake lights go on for a moment. She turned her steering wheel as far right as it would go and slid around into the street the Bronco was on. She forgot about the Golden Gate bridge. The Bronco was headed into Golden State park!

She stopped her car when the Bronco turned into a parking area where a Ramada appeared not far away. She touched her Smith and Wesson .357 Magnum short barrel to make sure it was still at the small of her back. The shooter was better armed: he had a rifle. She ran for cover under some trees and started to make her way forward.

The Dark Persona notice the car stopping a block away. A person ran from the car into a small grove of trees. He sat down on the cement seat under the ramada and jacked a round into his rifle. The rifle and scope would make the difference. He watched the front of the tree line for the unknown person to come towards him. He caught a flicker of movement, like someone running bent over in the rain. He waited for the sure shot.

Kat was moving forward, and at the same time, moving toward the parked Bronco. That was the closest cover that she could reach. She didn't know for sure where the killer was located.

The Dark Persona watched as the running person reached the Bronco. He put the scope on the rifle on the head of the individual looking around the corner of the Bronco. The Dark Persona rejoiced. It was that woman from the porch at the mansion. The private investigator. He was going to mark her off his list.

Kat dropped down to her hands and knees and crawl along the side of the Bronco toward the front of the SUV. She looked around the front of it and was knocked on her back by a hot searing pain going through her shoulder. She laid on her back with the rain pouring down in her face. She used all her will power to roll over and move up on her knees. She crawled under the Bronco hoping to get a clear shot at the killer. She was sure her pistol's range was good enough to hit him, but she wasn't sure she could hold it steady enough to hit him.

He jacked the bolt on the rifle back and forward. An empty casing flew to the ground. He knew he had hit her but he was not certain it was a kill shot. He started walking toward the Bronco to make sure she was dead. He wrapped the leather sling over his right shoulder and pulled out the M1911 A-1 Colt pistol. He kept the rifle pointed in the air, and moved slowly until he reached a better shooting position, in case she wasn't dead.

She saw him coming toward her. She scooted back under the SUV until she could lean again the door and outside mirror. She had one shot. If she didn't kill him, she was a dead duck.

Blinding light and a hot wave of air hit her. There was a huge explosive noise and the strong smell of sulfur. It knocked her over on her back. The sound that followed was deafening. Her ears were still ringing when she was able to stand again. Her shoulder was bleeding and starting to hurt badly. She sneaked a peek around the outside mirror and didn't see the killer at all. She couldn't believe her eyes. He had been walking toward her with his pistol in his hand and the rifle pointed in the air waiting for the kill shot.

She went around the back of the Bronco and looked for the killer. She saw a bulky looking object on the ground not far from where the killer had been. There was no movement, but smoke was raising in the rain from clothes on the killer's body. One of his boots was on the ground near the Bronco. She cautiously moved toward the man on the ground. His hair was smoking, the rifle he had over his shoulder was blown apart. It was in pieces all around the prone figure. There was no sign of the Colt M1911 pistol.

She rolled him over with her foot and looked down into the burned face of the psychotic killer. He had been hit by a bolt of lightning that struck the upturned barrel of his rifle. It turned him into a crispy critter. The eye patch over the left eye was burned; and its ashes were on the ground, the unwanted son of Mrs. Myra Jean Robinson, had been killed by a lightning stike.

Kat made it back to her car. She started driving to Letterman Army hospital, where they knew how to handle bullet wounds. It was only a few blocks away. She was having nausea, a rapid heart rate, and shallow breathing caused by the loss of blood from the shoulder wound. She needed to make it to the hospital before she died from shock.

Made in the USA
Middletown, DE
04 October 2022

11667603R00215